Also by Linda Green

The Marriage Mender
The Mummyfesto
And Then It Happened
Things I Wish I'd Known
10 Reasons NOT to Fall in Love
I Did a Bad Thing

while my eyes were closed

LINDA GREEN

Quercus

First published in Great Britain in 2016 by

Quercus Publishing Ltd
Carmelite House
50 Victoria Embankment
London EC4Y 0DZ

An Hachette UK company

A CIP catalogue record for this book is available
from the British Library

PB ISBN 978 1 78429 281 2
EBOOK ISBN 978 1 78429 280 5

12

Typeset by Jouve (UK), Milton Keynes

Printed and bound in Great Britain by Clays Ltd, St Ives plc

For Susan Stephenson, for holding my hand on the journey into motherhood and for bringing such love, light and joy to the world

'I watch a bird as it brings food to its chicks. How it looks after them, how it protects them. And then I say to myself, "You're a better mother than me" '

Hatidza Mehmedovic, mother of two sons murdered at Srebrenica

Your body realises you have lost your child before your brain does. The invisible umbilical cord between you snaps. Everything inside you goes loose and limp. Only then does your brain register what is happening. It kicks into action, trying to prove to your body that it is wrong. You do what it tells you, of course. You scramble in every direction. Pulling and pulling on your end of that cord. Hoping that if you pull hard enough, if you shout and kick and scream, if you can only get to the other end, you might somehow find your child still there.

When they are not. When it is clear that they have gone. That is when the guilt kicks in. You are their mother. You have a duty to look after them. And you have failed in that duty of care, therefore you are a failed mother. How can you be anything else when it happened on your watch? While your eyes were closed, for goodness' sake.

That is when you start to shut down inside. One by one, your vital organs cease to function. It is hard to know how you carry on breathing, how the blood pumps around your body, because you are certainly not doing it willingly.

You wish that somebody would be kind enough to put you out of your misery. Until you realise that this is the price you must pay – to suffer in the way that your child has. You deserve nothing less for letting them down so badly. And so you live your non-existent life. And every day when you wake up, if you have been lucky enough to get any sleep at all, the first word you say is sorry. They can't reply, of course. But you say it all the same. In the hope that somehow they will hear and forgive you. Even though you know you will never forgive yourself.

1

LISA

'You haven't seen me climb up to the big slide yet, have you, Mummy?' says Ella, who is lying on top of our bed in her grubby *Frozen* pyjamas.

I am not the sort of mum who beats herself up about missing 'firsts'. I missed Chloe's first steps (though Mum, bless her, described them to me afterwards with a commentary befitting the moon-landings), but I wasn't particularly bothered about this because trying to earn enough money to get our own place was more important to me than being able to tick off a list of milestones in some crappy baby book that your mother-in-law gave you. (I didn't have a mother-in-law at the time, on account of Chloe's father not having hung around long enough after I told him I was pregnant for me to even meet his mother, let alone marry her son, but if I had done, I reckon she would have given me one of those books.)

But today, for some reason, Ella's words sting a little. Perhaps it's the fact that since she first conquered the route up the rope climbing frame on Monday with Mum watching, Dad, Alex and even Otis have all seen her repeat the feat. Or maybe it's the fact that today is her last weekday of freedom. Ella starts school on Monday. And although she is excited about it now, I am well aware that when she realises she also has to go to school on Tuesday, Wednesday, Thursday and Friday, not just the first week but every week from now on, she will be furious at being denied the chance of spending her afternoons in the park, as she has this week.

'No, how about I come and see you do it today then?' I say. Ella beams at me, her dimples showing and two rows of tiny teeth bared in one of those smiles which children stop doing when they become self-conscious.

'I thought you had clients this afternoon,' says Alex, rubbing his eyes as he comes round.

'My three o'clock's cancelled, and Suzie's already offered to do my last one if I want to get away early. It'll give Mum a break too. She'll be shattered after the party.'

'What party?' asks Alex, who has never been able to get his head around our children's packed social calendar.

'Charlie's party,' says Ella before I can answer,

jumping up and down on the bed. 'He's going to be four but he's still not as old as me.'

We both smile. Charlie Wilson lives next door to us. He and Ella are almost a year apart but will be starting school together next week. And she is so not ever going to let him forget who is older.

'Where is it?' asks Alex.

'Jumping Beans,' I reply.

'Oh, shame you've got to work then. You'd have enjoyed that.' Alex turns to me with a wry smile, being well aware of my aversion to soft play centres in general and the one with the crappiest party food in town in particular.

'Yeah, never mind eh,' I reply. 'I'm sure there'll be plenty of others once she gets to school.'

Pretty much every other weekend, from what I can remember with Otis, who will thankfully soon be entering the more chilled-out going-bowling-with-a-few-mates party phase.

'Are you going to come and see me get my football medal then?' asks Otis, who has been lying quietly on the other side of Alex (we have got the four-to-a-bed thing off to a fine art).

'Yeah, as long as you behave and don't do a Luis Suarez on the last day.' I smile. Otis grins back. Having been blessed with his father's temperament, we all know this is highly unlikely.

'Are you coming too, Daddy?' he asks, climbing over onto Alex.

'No. Sorry, mate,' says Alex, ruffling Otis's hair, which has grown longer than it probably should have over the holidays. 'I'll drop you off at footie camp, but then I've got to go to a meeting in Manchester. You can show me your medal when I get home though, can't you?'

Otis nods. 'And Grandad,' he says. 'I'll take it to show Grandad too.' My dad has a bet on Otis playing for Leeds United and England by the time he's twenty-five. Otis is good but I'm not sure he's that good. Not that it matters. The important thing is that he prefers to spend his time running around outside kicking a football, instead of hunched in front of an Xbox or a tablet. How long that will last I don't know, but I'm going to make the most of it while it does.

'Right,' I say, stretching out under the duvet. 'We'd better get up and get sorted then. Last one down to breakfast has to clear up afterwards.'

Ella and Otis scramble up in a blur of limbs and hair and disappear from our room. Alex rolls over to me. 'When do you think that one will stop working?'

'I don't know. Hopefully not until they start having lie-ins.'

'And remind me when that is again,' he asks, tucking a strand of my hair back behind my ear. 'It's all a bit of a blur to me.'

I smile, remembering how Alex, having earned count-less brownie points for being such a brilliant stepfather to Chloe, then lost as many by being utterly hopeless with sleep deprivation when we had Otis and Ella.

'I think Chloe was about twelve.'

'Great, only another seven years to go until the end of the early mornings then.'

I dig him in the ribs before kissing him. His breath is warm. His lips taste of mornings. I pull him closer to me, wishing we could have a bit longer in bed. Sometimes I feel the need to introduce myself to him when we finally grab a few minutes together.

'Hey, don't start all that stuff,' he says.

'Why not? We are married, apparently.'

'Are we? When the hell did that happen? Did I actually wake up in time for the ceremony?'

I kiss him again to shut him up. 'Only just.'

'Anyway, I need a shower,' he continues. 'Sticky night. I smell like a pig.'

'No, you don't,' I reply (working in a gym qualifies me as something of an expert on this subject). 'And anyway,' I add, running my fingers down his back, 'even if you did, I could put up with it.'

'Shame someone will be barging in here in two minutes complaining that his sister has nicked the Coco Pops then, isn't it?'

I smile and give him one last kiss.

'They won't like it next week, you know,' I say. 'When it goes back to being boring, healthy stuff for the school term.'

'Well, if you set yourself up as the evil cereal dictator, you have to deal with dissent in the ranks.'

'Thanks for your support.'

'No problem. And just so you know when you have to referee the fallout, it was actually me who ate the Coco Pops.' Alex leaps out of bed so quickly that my foot misses his backside.

'I'll get you for that later,' I call out as he disappears into the en suite. I lie there for a second, breathing in the stillness, feeling the warmth of the early-morning sun, which is streaming through the new cream Ikea curtains just as Alex warned me it would. I can already hear the sound of bickering drifting up from down-stairs. Ella's voice, as usual, is the loudest.

I try to block it out as I wonder how Chloe is doing. Whether she's actually allowing herself to have a good time in France or if that is still too big a leap for her. I've only had a couple of brief texts so far. There was a time not so long ago when she'd have been texting me all the time. That was before, though. When we were still best friends.

There is a shout of 'Mummy' and associated commo-tion from downstairs. I swing my legs out of bed. The laminate floor is warm already. It's going to be another hot day. Though at least the gym is air-conditioned. I try to ignore the pile of laundry in the linen basket and the heap of clean clothes hanging over the balustrade on the landing still waiting to be ironed. I also try not to think about what Mum would say if she could see the mess which greets me in the kitchen. She offered to come and do some cleaning after Ella was born. I had to say no, even though I knew the house needed it. Because I also knew that if I said yes, she would still be our cleaner when Ella was sixteen.

By the time Alex arrives downstairs the cereal fight has been broken up and Otis has just finished counting out the last of the Coco Pops so he and Ella have exactly the same amount in their bowls.

'Mummy says you owe us a box of Coco Pops,' Otis says, clearly still riled by the perceived injustice.

'Grass,' Alex mouths to me before turning back to Otis. 'And you owe me about sixty quid for replacing the glass in Mrs Hunter's greenhouse, which you mistook for a football net, remember?'

'Oh yeah,' says Otis.

'Quits?' asks Alex.

'Quits.' Otis smiles, getting back to his Coco Pops.

I swear under my breath as I knock over the open pack of ground coffee at the exact moment I realise I've forgotten to get the bread out of the freezer for Otis's packed lunch.

Alex comes over, puts his hands on my hips and whispers, 'Chill out. Sit down and have your breakfast; I'll sort it.' I smile at him and for once don't argue. He knows I'm uptight about Chloe. He was the one who suggested the holiday, said it would do her good to get away. He was right of course, though it pains me to admit it. But he doesn't worry about her as much as I do. Nobody worries about her as much as I do.

I pour myself a bowl of muesli, take two slices of bread from the freezer and put them in the still-warm toaster on my way past, and sit down at the kitchen table.

'How many sleeps now, Mummy?' asks Ella.

'Three,' I reply. She gives a little squeal. I have never known any child be quite this excited about starting school. Chloe was nervous about it, Otis was entirely unbothered, but for Ella it appears to be on a par with Christmas.

'We ought to be videoing this,' says Alex, 'so we can play it back to you in ten years' time when you're saying "I hate school" and refusing to get up in the mornings.'

'Why would I hate school?' asks Ella.

'You won't,' I say in between mouthfuls of muesli. 'It's just that some teenagers can be a bit grumpy.'

'Like Chloe, you mean?' she says.

I glance up at Alex. Chloe has made an effort to be her old self in front of Ella and Otis. She made me promise not to tell them what had happened. She didn't even want Alex to know, although I couldn't agree to that. There are some things which can't be passed off as teenage moods. Anyway, I wasn't prepared to lie to him. It was the one thing I insisted on before I finally gave in and agreed to his marriage proposal. Always being honest with each other. Which was why he said he didn't think it was a good idea for me to be his personal trainer any more. Not unless I wanted to know what he really ate when he was on the road every day.

'Chloe's not grumpy,' says Alex, crouching down next to Ella, 'not compared to Daddy Bear when he discovers Goldilocks has eaten all his Coco Pops.' He goes to grab Ella's bowl. She squeals and collapses in fits of giggles as Alex tickles her. I smile, finish my muesli and wonder for the umpteenth time what I ever did to deserve him.

2

MURIEL

The house reeks of emptiness. It does so all the time but I notice it particularly in the mornings. Not that it was ever a noisy house. Not like some of those chaotic places you see in documentaries about people on benefits on the television. But there was always some low-level noise in the mornings. A workman-like hum as Malcolm and Matthew went about their morning ablutions and got ready for the day ahead.

I didn't really notice it at the time. It is one of those things you only miss when it has gone. There are rather a lot of those. Malcolm was generally considerate with the toilet seat, Matthew perhaps not so much. It is strange to think how it used to bother me. And now I am bothered by something I do not have to do. Do not have to remind someone of.

And socks. I am disturbed by the lack of socks in the house. It hardly seems right, does it? I mean most women are forever complaining about having to wash them (my mother even used to iron my father's socks) and find lost ones. But now, living in a house without socks doesn't seem right somehow. It is yin without yang. Everything is out of balance. There are plenty of houses with only female occupants of course. It is simply that this house was never meant to be one of them.

I reach over and turn on the radio. I am not particularly fond of Classic FM. I rather like John Suchet – although I could never understand what he was doing on ITV instead of the BBC – but I would prefer not to have to listen to the adverts. Still, it was one of the things I discovered after Malcolm left – that *not* having Classic FM on in the mornings reminded me more of his absence than having it on.

I think Matthew preferred it on too. Although maybe for the same reasons I did. I don't know because he never spoke about his father after he left. Matthew knew better than to bring such things up at the dinner table. Or anywhere else for that matter. And I, of course, know better than to discuss Matthew's departure too.

I hear Melody miaowing outside the door. She has never been allowed in the bedrooms. It troubles me that so many people do permit such things. Certainly she has been a huge comfort to me, and I understand the human soul's need for comfort, I truly do. But we should not accept another species into our most private room. That is how the lines start to become blurred. People have this ridiculous notion that we and animals are somehow on the same level. I blame Disney films. I blame them for a lot of things. All of this over-sentimentality and the vulgar Americanisms which have crept into our language. I saw the P. L. Travers film at the cinema. They had it on for elevenses at the Picture House in Hebden Bridge. *Saving Mr Banks*, I think they called it. Though personally I think it was Mr Disney who needed saving. Poor Miss Travers was rather lazily portrayed, I thought. I mean it's all too easy, isn't it? The middle-aged, middle-class Englishwoman as an odd and emotionally cold spinster, out of step with the modern world. Maybe if we'd listened more to the likes of her then the world would be in a rather better state today.

I prop myself up with the pillows. I've never believed in jumping straight out of bed. You need a little time to acclimatise, to see the world from a vertical position before you actually set foot in it. I listen to the news, or rather I am aware that the news is on. The words themselves wash over me. You get to an age where you have heard it all before. Each item only a variation on well-worn themes, and it doesn't really matter that the names are different, or even some of the details. Because nothing changes. Whatever sort of fuss is kicked up about these things, the old order will be maintained.

And one day these young people, young people like Matthew, will accept it as I do, rather than thinking they can somehow change the way things are.

I tune back in for the weather. It is going to be another hot day. Too hot by far for what is the tail end of summer. I miss the seasons we used to have. Four distinct ones with clear demarcations between them. Not two. Summer and winter. Both of them being far too long. One shouldn't complain. That is what people always say. The lady in the baker's does, at least. Not that I subscribe to that view. These over-long over-hot summers are not good for people. They become suffocating. People find it difficult to breathe. At least one of the benefits of living in a Victorian house is that the high ceilings give the air more room to circulate. And the thickness of the walls keeps the temperature down to a bearable level. It is one of the reasons I never liked staying in Jennifer's house. It was like a pressure cooker in weather like this. I don't know how she and Peter could stand it. Why she went for a newbuild I'll never know. There again I'll never know why she went for Peter either. Odd to think that a sister of mine should have such questionable taste. I suppose that's the one good thing to have come out of all of this. They've given up asking me to stay. You can only ask someone so many times, you see. And at least now I don't have to feel embarrassed about declining. Everyone deals with these things in their own way. That is what Jennifer says.

Melody miaows again. I let Matthew name her. Even when he was young I could trust him to do things like that. He was always such a sensible child. He chose it because she used to walk along the keys when he was practising the piano. I suppose the name overstates Melody's musical capabilities somewhat but it does have such a lovely, lyrical tone. It would have been a nice name for a girl. I often used to think that. Melody or Meredith. You don't hear those names nowadays. They say that all names come round again in time but I have not heard those two. I have several Olivias who come to me for piano lessons, which is nice as it was my mother's name. And at least two Graces – though I have noticed that those who are called Grace rarely possess the quality themselves. No Melodies or Merediths though. Or Muriels, come to that. I think my name is one which has been consigned to history, never to be brought out again. There was a film about a girl of the same name some years ago. Awful thing it was. Australian. A rather uncouth young woman playing the supposed bride-to-be. I remember sitting through the whole thing and not laughing once while those around me appeared to find it hilarious. I do not go the cinema very often. Perhaps that is why.

Melody miaows for a third time. That is my cue to get up. I put on my slippers, pull my dressing gown over my nightdress and walk over to the sash window. I draw back the curtains and twist the blinds just enough so that I can see the world but it can't see me. I look beyond the rows of terraced houses to the line of trees in the distance. Matthew used to love living so close to the park. It made up for not having a proper garden. Only a paved yard at the back and a small, neat front rose garden, not the sort a child could play out in.

The park provided open space for him to let off steam. Not that he used to charge around it like so many children do nowadays. But he could play on the grass. We would sit and make daisy chains. Little boys would sit still and do such things in those days. He would wear the crown of daisies on his head for the rest of the day, telling anyone who asked that he was the prince of the fairies. Never the king. Always the prince.

I sigh and turn away. Sometimes it is too painful to remember him like that. When these empty-nesters complain about missing their offspring once they have gone to university, I don't think it is the eighteen-year-olds they miss. It is the children they once were.

3

LISA

As soon as I pull into Mum's road I become sixteen again. You would have thought after twenty years I would have broken free of the place. Not so. I hear Alex saying, 'You can take the girl out of Mixenden . . .' He never gets any further than that because I always give him a clout. It's not that I'm embarrassed about where I grew up. Not really. Simply that I like to think I've moved on. I'm not known as the 'chippy girl' in Warley for a start. We don't even have a chippy in Warley. Although I smile as I remember Mum saying, 'Well, what on earth are you going to do for your tea on Friday night?' when I told her we were moving there.

Still, there's something reassuringly familiar about my old road. The cluster of precariously angled Sky dishes, the broken cooker dumped in the front garden of number 12 that's been there for as long as I can remember, the kids hanging about on the corner, mouthing off at each other and taking the piss out of whichever one of them hasn't got the right trainers on.

I swerve to avoid a pile of glass in the road and pull up outside Mum's house. Ella is at the front door before I have even turned off the car engine. She jumps up and down and waves something in the air from the doorstep. Mum is standing behind her, wiping her hands on her apron. She looks knackered. It's easy to forget how much of a handful Ella is and that Mum isn't as young as she used to be. Added to which she isn't good in the heat; the tan is out of a bottle.

'Mummy,' shouts Ella, running out onto the pavement to throw her arms around me. There are tell-tale smears of chocolate on her face.

I shake my head and smile down at her. 'Hello, chocolate-chops.'

'We had choc ices at Charlie's party. They're like Magnums but they forgot to put sticks in them.'

'Lucky you.'

'Grandma says I'm a lucky girl because I've had ice cream every day this week.'

I give Mum the same look she used to give me when she caught me wearing her shoes as a teenager.

Mum shrugs. 'Well, a few ice creams never did you any harm. I mean look at the size of you. Proper skinny-minny you are.'

I resist the urge to point out that being a gym instructor and running ten miles a week may have something to do with it.

'Well, thanks for taking her,' I say. 'I think you deserve a rest this afternoon.'

'Bathroom won't clean itself.'

'You should get Tony to do it when he comes home.'

'Fat chance of that happening.'

'And whose fault is that?'

Mum makes a face at me. She is well aware of my views about why my younger brother is such a lazy arse.

'Any road, I've got to be at chippy at four to give your dad a hand with Friday-evening rush.'

'People won't want chips on a day like this. They'll be having barbies in the back garden.'

'Not our regulars, they won't. Besides, they reckon the weather's going to break. Might even be a thunderstorm. It needs it, mind. Too muggy for my liking.'

Ella is tugging at my hand, clearly desperate to get to the park.

'Right, missy,' I say, looking down at her. 'What do we need to say to Grandma?'

'Can I have my party bag?'

I roll my eyes. Mum laughs. 'Oh bless her, she's right. I nearly forgot. And her balloon, she'll be wanting that.'

Mum goes back inside and emerges a few moments later with a party bag with pirates on it and a red balloon on a piece of ribbon. Ella rushes up and takes them from her.

'My balloon from Charlie's party,' she says proudly. 'And there are bubbles and loom bands and sweeties too.'

'Fantastic,' I say, seeing the sea of tat on the kitchen table swelling in my head. 'Now, what else do you have to say to Grandma?'

She looks at me blankly for a moment before the penny finally drops and she turns to Mum. 'Thank you,' she says, giving her a big hug and one of her best sloppy kisses. Mum's eyes glisten.

'Bye bye, sweetheart. You be good for Mummy now.'

'I'm going to show Mummy how to climb up to big slide.'

'Well just you be careful,' says Mum. 'Nearly gave me a heart attack first time she did it with me.'

Ella grabs back hold of my hand and pulls me to the car.

'Thanks again,' I call over my shoulder as I take the balloon and party bag from Ella, strap her into her seat and walk around to the driver's side. Across the road a group of teenage lads are mucking about with a shopping trolley. Bashing it against someone's wall. If Dad was here they wouldn't dare. Not that he's a hard nut or anything, certainly not any more. But he's lived here all his life and knows too many people to be messed with. I look at them again and remember another of Dad's favourite sayings. You don't shit on your own doorstep.

'Oi, sling your hooks,' I call out to them. They look over, scowl at me, then slink off with the trolley. I smile to myself. I still get a little kick out of it sometimes. Being Vince Benson's daughter.

'Right, let's go,' I say, getting into the car and fastening my seat belt.

'What did you say to the big boys?' Ella asks.

'I told them to go away.'

'Were they being naughty?'

'Yes.'

'Where will they go now?'

'I don't know. But at least they won't be bothering people in Grandma's street.'

I glance at Ella in the rear-view mirror. She nods, apparently satisfied with that, and picks up her *Frozen* sticker book from the back seat.

The car park is packed. I wonder whether to wait for a space or try to find one outside. I pull over when I see a woman struggling towards her car with a toddler, a baby in a sling and a massive changing bag. Quite why people take that much stuff with them when they are simply going to the park, I don't understand. I'd never been one for designer changing bags, opting instead to stuff a spare nappy, wipes and a little gym towel which doubled as a changing mat into my bag. I'd always got by fine like that, although no doubt I would have failed those 'Are you a super-mum?' questionnaires in the baby magazines.

The woman mouths 'Sorry' to me as she begins loading both offspring and baggage into her car. I smile and back up a bit so she doesn't feel I'm hassling her.

'Can we go to the park now?' asks Ella.

'In a minute. We just need to let this lady get sorted and then we can have her space.'

'Have they been to the park already?'

'Yep, looks like it.'

'Did that boy climb up to big slide?'

'I doubt it. He only looks about three.'

'How old was Otis when he could climb up to big slide?'

'I don't know. Four or five, I expect. I don't think he did it till he started school.'

I glance in the rear view mirror. Ella is sitting there with such an incredibly smug look on her face that I have to try hard not to laugh.

The woman finally pulls away and we squeeze into the space she has left. I hold the car door as Ella scrambles out, balloon in hand.

'You don't need to take that with you.'

'Charlie gave it to me.'

'I know. But you're going on the climbing frame now and you can't take it with you.'

'You can hold it for me when I'm climbing.'

'Why don't you just leave it in the car?'

'Because I don't want anyone to steal it.'

I sigh. My car was broken into a few months ago when I left the satnav on the dashboard. Ella woke every night for the next week and asked a million questions about it. Clearly, she still hasn't forgotten.

'OK,' I say, deciding it will be quicker to go with it than to get into another protracted conversation about why the naughty boys did it. 'But I'll carry it for you so you don't lose it.'

She nods. I take the balloon from her and grab her hand to stop her careering across the car park, noticing as I do so that her nails are dirty and need cutting.

'This is where Grandma parks,' Ella says as she steps onto the gravel. 'Near the ice cream van.'

'Well you've had quite enough ice cream this week, remember. Do you want to go to the butterfly house before we go to the playground?'

Ella gives me a look. She is not a butterfly-house kind of girl. She wants to be where her brother would be. Even when he is not here.

'OK,' I say, as we reach the grass. 'You can run now.'

I let go of her hand and she tears off towards the playground, her lime-green Crocs kicking up dust on the parched, worn grass. The playground is heaving but she makes straight for the climbing frame, undeterred by the number of children already on it. She glances back once, to check I am watching, before beginning to climb. By the time I reach the base of the frame she is already halfway up. Her face is determined, her hands straining to reach each new level. There is no way she will ask for help, though. She passes a bigger girl dressed entirely in pink, whose father is coaxing her up, showing her where to put her feet as she picks her way daintily up the frame. I see Ella open her mouth and say something. It is impossible to hear it above the noise of the playground but I am pretty good at lip-reading. 'I can do it all by myself.' I know I should feel embarrassed, maybe even say something. I'm sure the other girl's dad didn't appreciate the boast. But what I actually feel is a surge of pride. No one is going to tell my kick-ass daughter that there are things she can't do. Not now. Not ever.

There is a whoop as Ella gets to the top. I look up at her grinning face, shielding my eyes from the sun and wishing I hadn't left my shades in the car. I raise my fist in celebration of her triumph. A second later she has disappeared inside the tube slide. I hear her yelling 'Geronimo' from inside the slide as she comes down. She has picked it up from Otis, who got into *Doctor Who* when Matt Smith used to say it all the time. A moment later she explodes out of the end of the slide and straight into my arms.

'Hey. Well done you,' I say, ruffling her hair.

'I'm going to do it again,' she says. And with that she is off. Straight back up the climbing frame. I glance at my watch. Quarter to three. We have about half an hour before we need to leave for Otis's presentation. He will have to put up with Ella going on about this all the way home in the car. And I will probably get it in the neck for saying Otis was older than her when he learned to do it. The toddler in the buggy next to me wakes up and starts crying. His mum thrusts a packet of Haribo sweets into his hand, takes a drag on her cigarette then puts her hand, still holding the lighted cigarette, back on the buggy handle. I am tempted to ask her how she thinks her toddler feels about having smoke forced down his lungs but decide against it. Mainly because I can imagine what Alex would say if I start some scrap in the playground. It was me who once told Alex he was a 'fucking idiot' for going to the gym and standing outside having a fag afterwards. Apparently he'd gone home and smoked five cigarettes straight off that night because I'd riled him so much. It worked though. He'd stopped by the time he asked me out the following Christmas.

When Ella slides down the next time, I manage to shout 'One more go' as she whizzes past me on her way back up again. She always wants to play hide-and-seek before we leave, and I don't want to be late for Otis. I watch her on the final climb. She knows exactly where to put each hand and foot now, expertly manoeuvring past several children older than herself on her way to the top. I sometimes wish I could transplant just an ounce of Ella's confidence into Chloe – like parents ask one of their kids to donate an organ to a brother or sister who desperately needs one. Not that Chloe would agree. You can't address a problem until you acknowledge you have one.

Ella arrives back at the foot of the slide. Her cheeks are almost as red as her balloon but she appears barely out of breath.

'Can you time me?' she says. 'I want to see how fast I can do it.'

'Next time we come,' I say.

'Ohhhhh, I want to do it now.'

'Don't you want a game of hide-and-seek before we go?'

'I do, I do,' she squeals. 'You hide first because you're no good at it and I'll find you easily.'

'Thank you,' I say, poking my tongue out at her. 'And where are you going to count?' She looks around and points at a large oak tree near the bottom entrance to the park.

'OK, go on then. But make sure you count to one hundred, otherwise I'll have no chance.'

She grins and runs off towards the tree. I realise that I am still holding her balloon. I may as well give up now and just stand here but I know that she will be cross with me if I do that. I hurry over to a large tree not too far from hers and stand behind it, trying lamely to hide the balloon. I hear her shouting, 'Coming, ready or not.'

I press myself closer against the trunk, feeling the roughness of the bark against my bare arms and calves. I hear footsteps running towards me. Small footsteps. And a moment later 'Found you' is shouted at a ridiculous level of decibels. I turn to look at her. She appears torn between being chuffed at finding me so quickly and disappointed in her mother's total failure to find a decent place to hide.

'Easy-peasy,' she says, hands on hips. 'I saw my balloon.'

'Yes, well it is rather a giveaway.'

'You won't find me.'

'Come on then, missy,' I say. 'One hide and then we need to be off to get your brother.'

'Make sure you count to one hundred.'

'I will do.'

'And shut your eyes.'

'Yes.'

'Now, Mummy. Before I go. Please.'

I shake my head and do as I am told. 'One, two, three . . .' I begin out loud. There is a little squeal followed by the sound of footsteps running away. I am only on twenty when I hear her scream. I know it is her scream straight away. You always know, it is one of those mother things. I open my eyes and quickly scan the park. And then I see her, lying in a heap on the little footpath which crosses the park barely fifty yards away. She is crying. Proper hurting crying.

I get to her quickly – one of the perks of my job. Ella holds up her hands to me. She's managed to graze both of them, her left one quite badly. It's bleeding a bit. Her face is crumpled, and snot is beginning to trickle from her nose.

I help her to her feet. 'Come on, let's have a look at you,' I say.

'My hands hurt,' she wails.

'I know. All this grass and you manage to find a bit of concrete to fall on.'

I realise I haven't even got a tissue on me, let alone a wipe or a plaster. I think of the woman with the designer changing bag. I bet she'd have had a fully stocked first-aid kit in there.

'Never mind, you'll live,' I say, brushing a bit of dirt off with the hand which isn't holding the balloon. 'It's just a graze. We'll get you cleaned up properly when we get home.'

Ella looks at me doubtfully. 'I hurt my knees too,' she says, sniffing loudly.

I pull up the bottoms of her cropped leggings to inspect the damage. 'Yep, they're still there, but you'll have a couple of nice bruises tomorrow to impress Otis with.'

She manages a watery smile and wipes her nose with her hand before rubbing it on her dress.

'Come on. Let's go and get Otis.'

'But I haven't had my hide yet.'

'I thought you were too hurt?'

'I'm going to be a brave girl.'

I smile at her. Mum has probably said that to her when she's fallen over before. I glance at my watch. 'OK, super-quick though.'

'You go back to the tree to count.'

'Can't I just do it here?'

Ella shakes her head. There is no point in arguing with her, it will simply take longer. I turn to walk back to the tree.

'And don't forget to close your eyes,' she calls after me.

Before I can say anything in reply my mobile rings. I scrabble to pull it from my pocket and look at the screen. It's a client who's been trying to get in touch with me about increasing his number of sessions. I take the call and carry on walking over to the tree, struggling to hear what he's saying above the noise. It takes for ever because he has to keep consulting his diary to see what dates and times he can do. I think we manage to arrange two extra sessions for the following week, but I know I'll have to text him later to confirm it.

I reach the tree and put the phone back in my pocket and return to my counting position, my arms folded on the trunk, my forehead resting against them. And I do shut my eyes, mainly because my life will not be worth living if she catches me with them open. I wonder what number I should be on by now. Once, when I started to look for Ella too early, she was furious when I found her.

'You didn't do it properly. I'd only got to eighty when you started looking.'

It will stand her in good stead at school, her ability to count to one hundred. Her ability to speak her mind, however, will probably land her in a whole load of trouble.

A slight breeze ripples through the leaves above me. I realise Ella will probably be wondering where I am by now. I will have done it wrong again.

I open my eyes, blinking a couple of times as the light floods back in. I look around the park. There is no sign of her. She takes great pride in her ability to hide in tiny places. It is one of the rare occasions when being small means you can get one over the big people.

I wander over to a nearby tree and check behind it. Not that I think for a moment she will be there but it is all part of the game. I check the other usual suspects: behind the rubbish bins, the hedge on the far side of the playground, the various benches dotted around the park. And once I've drawn the expected blank I stop and scour the park, hoping I might see a flash of green and white stripe from her dress. It is like looking at one of her *Where's Wally?* books. When you know what you are looking for, it somehow becomes even harder to spot it among the sea of things you definitely aren't looking for. I sigh. I should have given her the balloon to hold on to. It is only as I think this that I realise I am no longer holding a ribbon. Stupidly, I look up to where the balloon should be, as if it might magically be suspended in the air above me. Not surprisingly, it isn't.

Fuck. I look up at the sky, shielding my eyes with my hand, and slowly turn through 360 degrees in case I can see the balloon anywhere, but I can't. That's the trouble with helium. In the old days you could let go of a balloon and find it five minutes later, stuck in some hedge; nowadays it will be orbiting the planet by the time you realise. I'm not even sure when I let go of it. It could have been when I took the call on my mobile, or maybe even before that when Ella fell over. I think she would have noticed if it had gone then, mind. Although perhaps she was in too much of a state to notice anything.

I groan out loud. Ella is going to have a complete meltdown about this. Alex once drove all the way back to Bridlington because we'd lost Bobby Chicken, and she thought she might have left him in the toilets on the front and refused to sleep without him. But Bobby Chicken was nowhere to be found when Alex got there and Ella cried herself to sleep for the next few nights.

I'll have to promise to buy her another balloon and it will end up being one of those three-quid Disney character ones the small bald bloke in town sells. And I'm not even sure I've got that much money in the car, and I know I haven't got my bank card so the likelihood is she's going to be howling all the way to football camp and probably all the way home.

I glance at my watch and realise I need to forget about the balloon and concentrate on finding Ella if I'm to have any chance of getting to Otis's presentation on time.

I go back to the tree where I was counting and try to remember every place she has ever hidden before. I go to each of them in turn: the war memorial, the tyre swing which is separate from the rest of the playground, the ice-cream sign, every hedge, every tree. Still nothing. I hurry over to the playground. The stickiness of the heat is starting to get to everyone. Children are looking hot and bothered; tempers are fraying; grandparents sitting on benches are beginning to wilt. I go to every piece of equipment in turn, check under the slide, behind the see-saw, in every one of those strange spinning circle things. I go back to the climbing frame and squint into the sun as I look at every child on it. It suddenly occurs to me that she could be hiding inside the metal tube of the slide. I peer up it from the bottom. It is hard to make anything out. I call up to a bigger boy who is standing at the top, about to go down.

'Is there a little girl hiding in there? About four, in a green and white striped dress?' He looks then shakes his head.

'Thanks,' I call back.

I sigh and shake my head, glancing again at my watch. This is getting ridiculous now. She is going to make us late for Otis.

'OK, Ella, I give up,' I shout. 'You win. Please come out now. We need to go.'

A few children look over at me. I feel a bit stupid, standing there calling out to an invisible child. I wait a few minutes, but when she doesn't emerge I move away and start a circuit of the park, calling the same thing over and over again as I run past all the places I have already looked.

'Come on out, Ella, right this minute. We're going to be late for Otis.' My tone changes as the minutes tick by.

I look again at my watch as I run past the playground a second time. We need to go. We need to leave right away.

'Ella, now!' I shout. 'Come here now.'

An elderly man, probably here with his grandchildren, calls out to me: 'Have you lost someone, lovey?'

'No,' I say. 'Not lost. She's just playing hide-and-seek. She won't come out.'

'Ice cream,' he says. 'That'll do it. Tell her you've got an ice cream for her.'

Maybe he's right. Maybe she's so bloody stubborn that I am going to have to resort to bribery. I don't do bribery, though. Certainly not with ice cream. Once you go down that path there is no way back.

'Ella, I'm going,' I call. 'We have to leave now.'

My vest top is sticking to my back. This is so ridiculous. Otis will be really upset. I look at my watch again.

We won't get there in time for the presentation but I still need to pick him up in twenty minutes. I dial Mum's number. I can't think of anything else to do.

'Hello, love,' she says. 'Is Otis going to pop in with his medal on the way back?'

'Mum, I'm really sorry. Can you go and pick him up for me, please?'

'What do you mean? Where are you?'

'I'm still at the park. I can't find Ella.'

'You've lost her?'

'No, I haven't lost her. We're playing hide-and-seek and she won't come out from wherever she is. You know what she's like.'

Mum starts laughing. 'Little monkey. As stubborn as her own mother, that one.'

'Would you mind going? If I find her in the next few minutes I'll give you a call, but I don't want Otis doing his nut. And tell him I'm sorry I missed his presentation. I'll make it up to him.'

'Course I'll get him, love. I'll take him to chippy with me after, shall I?'

'Yeah, I'll see you there. Thanks, Mum.'

I stuff the phone back into my pocket, cross that I am having to put other people out because of Ella's behaviour.

'Ella, come on. It's not funny,' I shout. 'Come out now.'

It is only as I look again behind the hedge that it occurs to me that she might not be being stubborn at all. She could be hurt. She's already fallen over once today. What if she's slipped and fallen down somewhere and I can't see her?

I look around me. I can't think of anywhere she could actually have fallen into though. There are no ponds or ditches that I can think of. Maybe I'm being ridiculous. Or maybe I'm missing something really obvious. I get out my mobile and call Alex. The phone rings several times before he answers.

'Sorry Lis, I'm about to go into this meeting. Can it wait till later?'

'I don't know. We're playing hide-and-seek at the park and I can't find Ella.'

Alex starts laughing. The same deep throaty laugh which I usually find attractive but right now irritates the hell out of me.

'Piss off. It's not funny.'

'Oh, I don't know. Being outwitted by a four-year-old is pretty amusing, if you ask me.'

'Alex, I'm being serious. I've been looking for ages. I've had to ask Mum to go and pick Otis up because I'm not going to make it in time.'

'You know what she's like. She'll be squeezed into some tiny space laughing her socks off at you.'

'Yeah, but I've been all over. I've shouted that she's won, that I've given up and she still hasn't come out.'

'She probably hasn't heard you. Or she's pretending she hasn't.'

'I don't know. I'm worried she's fallen over and hurt herself or got stuck somewhere.'

'She'll be fine. She'll be loving this. She'll go on about it for weeks when you find her.'

'I hope you're right.'

'Of course I am. Otis has probably told her what the world record for hide-and-seek is and she's trying to beat it.'

'I guess I'll go and have another look.'

'OK, and I promise I won't remind you about this call ever. Well, not more than once a day, at any rate.'

'Very funny.'

'Now go and smoke her out and let me get on with the meeting.'

'OK.'

'Love you. '

'Yeah. Call me when you're leaving.' I put the phone back in my pocket, feeling a bit sheepish. Remembering the time I rang Alex at work because I had taken Otis out for a walk in his new buggy, had put the brake on and couldn't work out how the hell to take it off again. This will be like that. He will never let me forget it. Only this time I'll have the kids ribbing me about it too.

I take a deep breath and look about me, sure that I am missing something blindingly obvious. My eyes settle on the butterfly house at the top of the park. That's where she'll have gone. She'll have thought she was being clever. Finding somewhere new she's never hidden before.

I start running. Weaving my way in and out of the people meandering along the path. When I get there I find an elderly man standing outside with an apron on. It is a pound to go in. I hadn't realised. Ella didn't have any money on her. She couldn't have got in. Not unless she'd slipped in with another group without him noticing.

'Have you seen a little girl on her own?' I ask. 'She's four, fair, shoulder-length hair, wearing a green and white striped dress.'

He shook his head. 'Can't say I have, love. It's been a busy afternoon, mind.'

'Can I just go in to check?' I ask. 'I'm really sorry, but I haven't got any money on me.'

'Course you can, love.'

I push through the plastic curtain. It's like stepping off a plane into a tropical climate. There is a path leading through the tangle of plants, which push up towards the glass ceiling. I hurry along the wooden pathway, apologising as I go to those who I push past. The path is roped off all the way along. Ella won't have ducked under the rope. She would have been too worried about getting into trouble. Besides, even if she had done, I'm sure she wouldn't have been able to stand the heat for long. I squeeze past the last group of people and out the other end.

'No luck?' asks the old man.

'No,' I say. 'I'll go back into the park. I'm sure I'll find her.'

I run back towards the playground. Stopping and checking all the equipment before I start calling again.

'Ella,' I shout. 'I've given up. You need to come out. Straight away.'

Nothing. I am aware of a couple of people looking at me. Probably thinking what a bad parent I am for having such a disobedient child.

'We're playing hide-and-seek,' I say to the woman next to me, by way of explanation. 'Only it seems she's better at hiding than I am at seeking.'

She nods, looking me up and down. I am suddenly aware that I am dripping with sweat from the butterfly house.

'I've just been to look in there,' I say, pointing back at it.

'How old is she?' asks the woman, who is wearing cut-off jeans and a T-shirt.

'Four,' I say. 'Nearly five. She's got a green and white striped dress on and leggings.'

She shakes her head. 'No, I haven't seen her, and we've been here a good fifteen minutes or so.'

I have a crunching sensation in my stomach. I wipe the moisture from my top lip.

'Never mind,' I say. 'I'm sure I'll find her soon.'

'What's her name?' she asks.

'Ella.'

'I'll get my son to help you look,' she says. Before I can stop her she has called over a tall skinny boy who looks about the same age as Otis.

'Lady wants you to find a little girl in a green and white striped dress,' she says. 'Her name's Ella. She's playing hide-and-seek, only her mum can't find her.'

The boy looks at me with what appears to be a hint of pity on his face.

'There's an ice cream in it for you, Dan,' his mum says.

'I'll get her,' he says and races off across the park calling out her name as he goes.

Somehow it makes it worse. The fact that someone else is now looking for Ella. Like she is actually properly lost or something. Every time I shout, I hear Dan's voice echoing her name back to me. I retrace my steps. Maybe she's changed her hiding place, but I don't understand why she hasn't come out by now. She must have heard me calling. Unless she has hurt herself. Maybe even fallen and knocked herself out or something.

Before I know it, other people are joining in the hunt. They don't even ask me; they just do it. I see Dan's mum talking to other parents in the playground, like she's organising some sort of search party. She's only trying to help, I know that. But it is too much. I don't want all this. I just want to find her without a fuss.

Soon the park is echoing to the sound of her name.

And that is the moment I know, know for sure, that something has happened to her. There is no way she'd stay hidden if she could hear other people calling for her. She'd want to come out and find out what was going on.

I wipe my eyes and am surprised to find my fingers are wet. Someone puts their arm around me. A middle-aged woman who smells of sun cream.

'Don't worry, love. We'll find her.'

I shake my head and turn away. I want to tell her to piss off, that it is none of her business. I know that would be rude, though. And right now I can't afford to be rude.

My mobile rings. It is Mum. I don't want to answer but I know I have to.

'Hi,' I say, doing my best to sound normal.

'Where was she, then?' asks Mum.

'I . . . I haven't found her yet.'

There is a silence on the other end of the phone.

'Why not?' she asks.

'I don't know. I let go of her balloon. Maybe she saw and tried to follow it. Other people are helping me look for her.'

'I'll send your dad down,' Mum says, her voice wobbling.

'No, there's no need for that, really.'

'Well he's coming anyway.'

'Don't worry Otis, will you? Just make it sound like a game.'

'OK, love,' she says. The line goes dead. I clutch the

phone to me, aware my hand is shaking. I try to move but my legs refuse to work. From somewhere deep inside me I feel something rushing to the surface. I try to stop it but I can't. It erupts from my mouth with a force that physically shakes me.

'Ella!'

Once the scream has left my lips I feel oddly detached from it. But I know it was mine. It roared over the top of all the other shouts. For a moment there is silence in the park. As if people are paying their respects. And then a whole chorus of 'Ella' begins again with renewed urgency. As if the infantry have been spurred into action by the anguished cries of their wounded sergeant major.

I pick up the phone again and call Alex. It goes straight to voicemail. He's obviously turned it off for his meeting. He still thinks this is funny. He has no idea that it isn't the slightest bit amusing any more.

I open my mouth to leave a message. Nothing comes out. I take a deep breath. Steel myself to form some kind of coherent sentence.

'Please call me as soon as you're free,' I say, struggling to keep my voice even. 'Ella's not here. She's disappeared. No one can find her.'

I end the call, my words still echoing back to me. It is not a game any more. All around me complete strangers are calling my daughter's name and she isn't coming out. She isn't answering. I don't know why not, but I do know that wherever she is I need to find her. I look down at the phone still in my hand. My finger hovers over the number for a moment. I have never done this in my life, and part of me doesn't want to. Part of me still thinks she will come running out from behind a bush any second and I will hug her and hold her and read her the riot act for giving me such a fright. But another part of me knows that I have no choice. I dial 999 and when a woman answers I ask for the police.

4

MURIEL

It is a while before I reach a point where I can get a clear view of Matthew's special place. It is hard when there are so many children in the park. So much noise and clamour. Warm fleshy bodies getting in the way. But when I do see it, I am relieved to find I can still see him sitting in the shade. He always burned so easily; the sensitive ones do. He sits quietly, humming to himself. Engrossed in his world of make-believe. I watch as he threads his chain of daisies together, using his left thumbnail to make the slits in the stem. I always allowed him to keep that one nail just long enough to enable him to do that. The others were all trimmed down hard to the skin. He threads each stem through easily, as if it is a huge chasm, not a tiny slit, then attaches it to the one before. Looking and measuring in his head. He knew, you see. Knew the exact length it needed to be simply by looking. And when he was ready, and only then, he would make the final adjustment before placing it on top of his smooth, fair hair. Sometimes he sat there for a long while afterwards, surveying all that was before him. On other occasions he would rise almost straight away and walk around the tree three times in an anti-clockwise direction. How he managed to keep the daisy chain on I will never know. His hair was so silky even the shampoo seemed to slip off when I washed it. But the chain always stayed in place. And when he had finished his circles he would pause, deep in thought, and look up at the tree as if for inspiration. What it said to him I never knew, but he would nod as if it had spoken wisely. And, content, he would look about again. Sometimes he would see me watching him and a smile would spread across his face. He would start to come towards me but I would shake my head and he would stop, understanding. I wanted him to stay in his special place. I did not want him to ever step outside that circle. He was protected there and, as much as I wanted to feel his touch, yearned for it even, I knew the most important thing was that he was safe. Away from other people. Away from a world which did not understand him or his gentle ways.

The girl's cry pierces the stillness around me. I am cross with her at first for interrupting my thoughts. Girls scream at the slightest thing, it always seems to me. But then I turn and see the crumpled heap lying on the path twenty yards or so from me. A dear little face, though snivelling now as she looks up, her hands shaking.

I look around for the mother. Quite why she is not by her side, I don't know. But then I see her running towards the child across the grass, dressed in Lycra shorts and a vest top which is too tight to be decent. Her thighs are muscly, far too muscly for a woman, her shoulders and arms taut and sinewy. It is clearly something bordering on a sin to be feminine nowadays, to have soft lines and graceful limbs. To wear clothes which float instead of cling. I look down at my own floral skirt, falling gently to my shins from my waist. Delicate shades of lilac and blue. The softness of cotton against my skin. These women have no idea what a natural fabric feels like. They have lost their link with nature.

The woman squats down by the child, who is now holding her hands out to her. She makes no attempt to soothe or comfort, merely inspects the damage and brushes some dirt off the child's palm before glancing at her watch.

Goodness, no one has the time these days. Not even to comfort their own child. She doesn't have a bag either. Imagine that, a woman out in the park without a bag. I am about to offer her a tissue from my handbag, but I fear she will spit on it to clean the child and I will not be a party to that.

She will have to take the child straight home to see to her wounds, but I am wrong about that as well. She turns and walks away. A moment later her phone rings and she answers it. They have time to talk on their phones but not to look after their own children. It's a disgrace, an absolute travesty. I hurry over to the child and bend to touch her gently on the shoulder.

'Let's take a look at you, my dear,' I say. The girl turns sharply. For a second she stares, a slight frown on her brow, and then her face breaks into a smile.

'Hello, piano lady,' she says.

It is my turn to frown. I don't recognise the girl and I have a good memory for my students' faces. Besides, she is young and I don't normally take them before six. Not unless they have a particular aptitude and the ability to sit still without fidgeting.

'Hello. How do I know you?'

'Me and Daddy come to your house to pick my brother up from piano. And I stroke your cat. The black one.'

'Ahh, I see. Let me take a look at your poor hands.'

She holds them up to me. I see straight away that there is dirt in the broken skin. I turn them over. Her knuckles are grazed and bleeding too. And her nails are filthy. Ridiculously long and filthy.

'I think I'd better take you to get cleaned up right away,' I say.

'At your house?'

'Well yes. That would seem to be the only option.'

'Can I see your cat?'

'She will no doubt come to see you when we get home. She always makes a fuss of guests.'

I put my hand on her shoulder and try to usher her in front of me.

'Is Mummy coming too?' she asks, looking in the direction of the Lycra-clad figure still walking away in the distance. I glance down. The pale skin has an almost iridescent quality. The blue eyes pool underneath rows of soft, long lashes. The fine, fair hair frames the face perfectly. Only the crown of daisies has somehow slipped from the silky hair.

'No, but she'll know where you are,' I say, guiding her quickly down the path towards the exit at the far side of the park, the one which most people do not use.

'Can I hide at your house and pop out and surprise Mummy when she comes to get me?'

'Let's get you seen to first, shall we?'

'How will Mummy know where to find me? She's never been to your house.'

'Mummies know everything, don't you know that yet?'

The child smiles and nods and starts to chatter as we walk. It is not altogether intelligible chatter but she has a pleasant enough sing-song voice. I would take her hand but I am worried that would hurt her. However, she trots obediently beside me.

When we get to the gap in the wall and I take hold of

her forearm ready to cross the empty road outside, she looks up at me.

'Will Mummy be looking for me now?' she says. 'She starts looking when she gets to one hundred.'

'We need to get your hands seen to straight away. You wouldn't want the dirt getting in, would you?'

She looks down at her hands doubtfully. 'And then will Mummy come and find me?'

'One thing at a time, eh? One thing at a time.'

We walk across the road and on past the first row of Victorian terraced houses. She is talking about the brother, who is a pupil of mine. Saying he is not doing piano lessons in the school holidays, which is why she hasn't seen my cat for a while.

'What's his name, my dear, this brother of yours?'

'Otis,' she replies. I know the boy. A slim lad of nine or ten with shoulder-length rather scruffy brown hair, which is constantly getting into his eyes.

'Ah yes. Otis.'

'He's at football camp, but Daddy says he has to go back to piano lessons when he goes back to school. I am going to big school too. I am going to be in Miss Roberts' class. She is a nice lady but I don't know if she has got a cat.'

The boy never struck me as being particularly keen. You can usually tell the ones who are there under duress. They arrive with a sullen look on their faces and clearly don't put in the practice. Otis is such a boy, which is a shame as he has a good ear for music. But if he only comes because his father insists then it will not be for much longer now. There's a point where the relationship shifts. Where a child is no longer driven by the desire to please a parent and where even the bribes they offer stop working. I know it all too well. And Otis is approaching that age. Usually I wait for the parent to tell me, but sometimes, if the child is not particularly agreeable, I will instigate the conversation myself.

'Here we are then,' I say as we reach the three-storey house at the end of the terrace. The weeds next door need doing again. I have been nipping across once a week since it has been empty in order to tidy them up. It's no wonder Judith can't sell the property when she doesn't even send someone to do the garden. She is not paying me to do it, of course. It is simply that I can't abide the mess. And I live in hope that whoever buys it will be a little more concerned about the appearance of their front garden than she ever was.

The child hesitates at the front gate. For the first time she looks back over her shoulder towards the park.

'Come along, dear. The sooner we get you cleaned up the sooner you can carry on with your game.' I push open the gate and she follows me up the path, waiting silently at the front door. I jiggle the key in the lock and turn it. Melody rushes to the front door and rubs against my ankles as I step inside. The child comes in after me and squats down to stroke Melody, who sniffs her before rubbing around her too.

What's your cat's name?' she asks.

'Melody.'

'That's a nice name.'

'Right, shoes off, please,' I say, pointing to the ugly lime-green lumps of plastic on her feet. She takes them off and leaves them on the tiled floor.

'Goodness, you're not very well trained, are you?' I say, picking them up and placing them on the shoe rack. 'Now, straight upstairs to the bathroom so we can get you cleaned up.'

'I've never been upstairs in your house,' she says.

'No, I suppose not.'

'Has Otis ever been upstairs?'

'No, my students are only allowed in the piano room.'

'And to the little toilet under the stairs. He went in there once when he needed a wee.'

'Well yes, there too.'

She glances back to see if Melody is following us and squeals in delight when the cat brushes against her legs as she dashes up the stairs. It is a light, musical squeal. One which succeeds in squeezing a smile onto my face.

'Right,' I say, as we get to the bathroom and I push open the wooden door and pull on the light. 'You sit yourself down on the stool and I'll get everything sorted.' I help her up onto the stool and she sits obediently, swinging her legs and looking around her as I run the hot water.

'Is green your favourite colour?' she asks. 'Green's my favourite colour. I don't like pink. Lots of things for girls are pink, but Otis says pink stinks.'

'Does he now?' I reply, putting the plug in when the water reaches the required temperature and watching as the level rises slowly up the sides of the Victorian basin.

'I don't like your bath green though; the green I like is this one,' she says, pointing to the brighter stripes on her dress. 'It's got a big pink flower on it too. Grandma bought it for me, but Mummy says it doesn't matter about a bit of pink and I've got to wear it.'

I test the water with my hand. It is hot but bearable. I reach up and open the cabinet, which is where the first-aid items are kept. I take the bottle of Dettol from the top shelf and carefully measure two capfuls into the basin of water and swish it around.

'What's that? It stinks,' says the child, screwing up her nose.

'It's Dettol. For your hands. Doesn't your mother use Dettol?'

She shakes her head. 'Is it going to sting? I don't like stingy things.'

'Only a tiny bit, but it will get the germs out of your hands.'

She wrinkles her nose again and looks down at her

hands, examining them closely. 'I can't see germs. Where are they?'

'You can't see them, but it doesn't mean they aren't there. Let's get your hands in the basin and we'll get rid of them for you.'

The child lets me take her hands and immerse them in the water. She winces only slightly but does screw up her nose again. 'I don't like smell.'

'The smell will be gone soon. Now, I'm going to dab them for you with some wet cotton wool. Make sure we get everything out.'

I take each hand out in turn and wipe over the grazed pink skin. My eyes keep returning to the child's nails. When we are done I dry her hands gently on the towel and take the nail scissors from the bathroom cabinet.

'What are you doing?' she asks.

'We're going to get your nails cut. They're filthy.'

'Have they got germs too?'

'Looking at the state of them they've probably got carrots growing under them.'

'I don't like carrots.'

'All the more reason to cut them, then.'

She stays relatively still while I trim each nail in turn and use one of the scissor points to ease the dirt from underneath.

'That tickles,' she says. When we are finished I take an emery board from the cabinet.

'What's that?' I am beginning to think her mother doesn't know how to care for herself, let alone a child.

'An emery board, to file your nails nice and smooth.'

She looks at it with fascination and feels the edge of the first nail I file.

'Nice and smooth,' she says.

When I am finished I place her hands back in the basin of Dettol.

'Are there still more germs?'

'Better to be safe than sorry,' I tell her. I dry her hands again. They look much better now. They look like Matthew's hands. She has long fingers for her age, like he did. I wonder if she has ever played the piano.

'There,' I say.

'Are we done now?'

'Nearly.'

I take the Germolene from the cabinet. I wish they still did the little tins of it. I have never got on with the tubes.

'What's that?'

'Germolene for your hands.'

'Why are you putting germs back on them?'

'I'm not. It's to protect them from germs.'

'I don't like smell.' I sigh and shake my head. I find it hard to think of a better smell. It is warmth and comfort and safety. A smell of mothers.

'Have you never smelt Germolene before?'

She shakes her head. I wonder what else she hasn't smelt. What she hasn't tasted. What love she hasn't felt.

'Is Mummy coming to find me now?' she asks.

'Aren't you hungry? I was going to make buttered crumpets.'

'I've never had trumpets.'

'Crumpets. They're flour and yeast cakes. The butter melts into the holes in the bread.'

'Are they yummy?'

I smile at her. 'Well, I think so. Why don't you try one?'

'And then will Mummy come?'

'Let's get you fed and watered first, shall we?'

'Can I come and hide here again? It's a very good hiding place.'

'Of course you can. We can have lots of fun and games here.'

I help her down from the stool. Melody is standing guard outside the bathroom. The child bends to stroke her.

'Please don't touch her,' I say. 'We don't want to get cat hairs on your hands or Germolene on her fur, do we?'

'No. She might not like the smell.'

The child stops on the landing and points to the framed photos on the occasional table.

'Who's that?'

'It's Matthew. My son.'

'Where is he?'

'He's grown up now. He doesn't live here any more.'

'My big sister lives at uniworsity but she comes to stay with us in holidays.'

I suspect she is going to ask why Matthew isn't here in the holidays and decide to get my own question in first.

'She must be a lot older than you then, your sister?'

'She's all growed-up but she's my half-sister, which means my daddy isn't her daddy but we share a mummy.'

'I see,' I say. I expected no better, to be honest. The child's mother certainly didn't look old enough to have a child at university. She looks younger than I was when I had Matthew.

'Well, let's get you that crumpet I promised.' I smile at her and bend down to move a strand of hair out of the child's eyes. Her fringe is in dreadful need of a cut.

'What's your name?' she asks.

I hesitate before replying. I do not want the child to call me by my first name. It would be far too familiar. 'Miss Norgate,' I say. What's yours?'

'Ella,' she says. 'Ella Jane. I was named after a singer lady. She is a big black lady, but me and Mummy and Daddy aren't big and black.'

'Ella Fitzgerald?'

'Yes,' she says excitedly. 'Do you know her? Did you teach her piano?'

I laugh. 'No, dear, though I wish I had. She had quite a voice.'

'Otis is named after a black singer man.'

'Redding?'

'Yes. Do you know him too?'

'I know his music. Who chose your names?'

'Mummy. Her name is Lisa Marie and she was the king's daughter, but he is dead now and that is why we've got a queen and Grandad calls me his little princess.'

I smile again and decide now is not the time to try to address the Elvis confusion.

'If you come downstairs with me, I'll find some Ella Fitzgerald songs for you to listen to while I make the crumpets.'

She follows me down the stairs, along the hall lined with photos of Matthew and into the lounge.

'Why don't you have carpets?' she says.

'They're difficult to keep clean, especially with a cat.'

'We haven't got a cat. We used to have a dog called Pumbaa but it died. Mummy has a Dyson to clean carpets. I like watching bits whoosh up.'

'Good. Now sit yourself down on the sofa and I'll find the songs for you.'

I go to the music cabinet. The CDs are arranged alphabetically. At least now Malcolm has gone, nobody puts them back in the wrong place any more. He never understood the importance of having things in order. I really don't know how he coped as a lecturer. Still, it was none of my business, I suppose.

I take the CD from the case, wipe it with the cloth which I keep on the top, and place it in the machine. The room fills with big-band sounds. With a deep, rich voice. The sound of another country. Another era.

Another culture. I look at the child. She smiles back at me rather vacantly. It is ridiculous really, naming a child after someone they have never heard of, someone they have no connection with at all. A family name is different. That is your heritage. Part of your DNA. But this is someone simply indulging their musical taste and clearly not thinking of the child.

'I'll call you when the crumpets are ready,' I say.

As I head to the kitchen I glance at the grandfather clock in the hall. I hadn't realised how long it has been. The mother will have missed her by now. Will be searching for her. Panicking even. Something twists inside me but I will not let it take hold. This is a mother who clearly doesn't know how to look after a child properly. She doesn't even keep her nails clean and short, for goodness' sake. Or possess Dettol. A different sensation rises inside me. I let it grow this time. Bubble up under my skin until it feels as if it is starting to blister. How dare she neglect the child. Some people don't deserve to be mothers. They really don't.

I switch the kettle on and warm the pot as soon as it boils, as my mother taught me to, before turning the grill on and placing two crumpets on the tray. I don't hold with toasters for crumpets. It is not the right type of heat. I wait until the first side is golden brown then turn them over with my tongs. When the other side is done I pop them onto the bread board and spread with butter before putting them onto plates, watching as the butter drips into the holes. I empty the tea-pot, scoop in the tea leaves and give it a good stir before replacing the lid and popping the cosy back on. Some people say it is a lot of trouble to go to when you are on your own but I don't see why you should let your standards slip because there is no one around to notice. I go to the fridge and take out the carton of milk. I am glad I stuck with the full-cream now that I have a young visitor in the house again. Children should always have full-cream. Though I don't suppose she gets it at home. It will be the milk the mother wants for her diet, no doubt. Nobody thinks of the children these days.

Ella Fitzgerald's voice is still coming from the lounge. I pop my head around the kitchen door and see the child standing in the hall looking at the photographs of Matthew. Melody is rubbing around her legs. The child turns when she hears me approaching.

'Who are all these boys?' she asks.

'Matthew. Just at different ages.'

'But his hair is darker in those ones,' she says, pointing at the more recent photos.

'That's right. Often fair hair gets a bit darker as you get older. Yours probably will too.'

She shakes her head. 'No. My hair is always going to be like this. Grandma said so.'

I decide not to take issue with this in case it upsets her. 'Come through to the kitchen now then. Your crumpet is ready.'

'Does Otis ever have crumpets when he comes?' she asks as she follows me through.

'No. None of my pupils do. I don't want greasy fingers on the piano, you see.'

'I'll tell Otis later,' she says. 'Tell him that I've had crumpets and he hasn't.'

I do not like the bragging tone in her voice. It happens with siblings, I am well aware of that. But it does make them appear ill-mannered compared to only children. Matthew never boasted or bragged. Not once.

'Well, you will sit down nicely to eat it,' I say. 'And whatever you may be used to at home, we have no talking with your mouth full here.'

She gives me an uncertain look as I pour my tea but sits at the table and starts to eat her crumpet. As it happens, I need not have worried about her speaking with her mouth full. She is too intent on eating to speak. Clearly the poor child was hungry as well.

She picks up the glass of milk and glugs a good half of it before putting it down and wiping the milk from the corners of her mouth with her hand. She has much to learn but I decide not to bombard her with everything at one sitting.

'I like crumpets,' she says as I take a sip of tea. 'But your milk tastes funny.'

'It's proper milk, with none of the goodness taken out.'

'Is it from different cows?'

'No, same cows. But it's the right milk for growing children.'

'Why does my mummy get the wrong milk?'

'I don't know,' I say. 'You will have to ask her that.'

The sound of a siren pierces the stillness of the kitchen. I know instantly that it is the mother. That she has called the police. The stupid, stupid woman. If she had been paying attention, if she hadn't been so busy with her silly phone, if she had taken care of her child properly in the first place, none of this would have happened.

'Excuse me,' I say as I stand up.

'Where are you going?'

'Just to use the bathroom.'

'Is Mummy on her way?'

'You finish your milk like a good girl.'

I leave the kitchen swiftly and go upstairs, where I look out of the landing window. I can see the flashing lights of a police car further up the road. It is impossible to see more because of the trees. They are looking for her now. I could put a stop to this so easily. Could take her back right away. Explain that she was hurt, that her hands needed taking care of. That it was all simply a misunderstanding.

I could give the mother her child back, but who is to say what she would do to her next? I will not let the child go back to be neglected like that. You hear about these cases on the news. How the social workers gave the family the benefit of the doubt because they missed all the signs. But I have not missed them. I know what the right thing to do is. The child needs protecting from her own family. Some people don't deserve children. They really don't.

I turn and take a final glance back at the park. The flashing lights will be disturbing Matthew. He does not like noise and fuss. He will understand though. I will explain it to him. How I had to keep the child safe. How I owed it to him to do that.

I go back downstairs to the kitchen.

'Is Mummy here yet?'

'No.'

'Is she looking for me in the park?' the child asks.

'Not right now, no. She's gone home. The police are at the park. It isn't safe.'

'Why?'

'Some big boys have been naughty.'

'Are they the big boys who broke into Mummy's car?'

'I don't know. But Mummy knows you're safe here.'

She looks at me, her eyes heavy, a frown on her face.

'I want Mummy.'

'She's asked me to look after you. Just till it's safe to go back.'

'But I want to go back now. I want to finish hide-and-seek.'

Her bottom lip is trembling. I know I need to act fast.

'Let's finish it here then. Were you hiding or seeking?'

'Hiding,' she says. 'I'm very good at hiding.'

'Show me then. Show me how good you are.'

'Can you count to one hundred?'

I nod. She gets up from the kitchen chair. She should go and wash her hands first really, but I decide to let it go just this once.

'You have to close your eyes,' she says. 'Till you get to one hundred. Or else it's cheating.'

I put my hands over my face and start counting.

'One, two, three . . .' There is a little squeal and then soft footsteps running away.

MATTHEW

Tuesday, 21 January 2014

Dad's left. So that's a good start to the year. Turns out he's been screwing someone else, another lecturer at college. He tried to have a talk to me before he went, all man-to-man like. He sat me down and said something about people growing apart and finding they need someone new for a new phase of their lives. Like it's OK to shag around as long as you're approaching retirement and can use that as some kind of excuse. I mean it's pathetic. He's pathetic. And then he has the cheek to ask me to look after Mum. So I just turned to him and said, 'I thought that was supposed to be your job?' He didn't say much after that, just mumbled something about not wanting this to spoil our relationship (as if we have a relationship to spoil). I don't really know what other people do with their dads; all I know is that I can't remember doing much 'stuff' with him, apart from the odd bit of birdwatching at the reservoir when I was a kid. He's this blurred figure in the background in most of my memories. It's not just that he wasn't around a lot of the time, but that he never actually did anything with me when he was. I don't think he knew what dads were supposed to do. Or maybe he considered himself too intellectual to get down on his hands and knees and play with me. Anyway, not that it matters. He's gone now. He said he'll email me his new address when he got something permanent sorted out. I don't know whether he will or not but to be honest I'm not that bothered. I'm not sure I'd want to see him anyway. I don't know what we'd do or even what we'd talk about. I think the only shared interest we have is birds, and that's like an interest from when I was ten, not from now. He couldn't tell you anything about me: what music I'm into, what my favourite book is or my favourite film. Not one single thing. So I don't really see what the point would be in going to see him.

I told Sparrow about it. She never even knew her dad so it must have been a bit weird for her. It was good to talk to her though. It's always good to talk to her. She asked me if I hated him. I said hate was too strong a word. I just thought he was a sad bastard. Pathetic, really. Like Boris Johnson but not even funny.

I'd almost feel sorry for him if it wasn't for what he's done to Mum.

She's not good, which is hardly surprising in the circumstances. The trouble is she hasn't even talked about it properly since. We had one conversation which went something like: 'Has he told you yet?' 'Yeah.' 'We don't need to speak about this to anyone.' 'OK.' 'In fact, I'd rather we didn't speak about it at all.' I shrugged cos she doesn't like me saying, 'Whatever.' And that was it. He must have come back to take all his stuff while I was at school cos when I got home his office had been emptied, and I don't know what Mum had done but it was like she'd cleaned the whole house so there was not one trace left of him. He has been photoshopped out of existence. I don't think she's told anyone at work either. She's probably too embarrassed. I bet she hasn't told anyone else at all. We'll probably still get Christmas cards addressed to both of them for years to come, and Mum will just cross out his name inside or something.

It's not good, I know that. Sparrow says Mum's in denial, which I guess she is, but not even Sparrow understands how weird she actually is. Sometimes I wish Mum would scream or cry or chuck a bottle at the wall – anything really to demonstrate how much she is hurting. But she doesn't; she just does that pursing-her-lips thing and leaves the room or starts rearranging ornaments or something. It's seriously weird. Mind you, if I didn't have Sparrow to talk to then maybe I wouldn't be any better. It's not like I've got any other friends at school, not ones I can talk to like her, anyway. Mum's asked a few times if there are any other boys from the sixth form I'd like to invite round. I told her we don't do stuff like that at my age; we just hang out at school. She doesn't ask about girls, of course. We never speak about girls. It's not something she's ever said to me; it's just an unspoken rule. *There will be no mention of girls in this house.* That's why I've never even mentioned Sparrow to her. I don't want to anyway, it would spoil things. When you love someone that much, part of you doesn't want anyone else to know about it because it would take a bit of the magic away. People at school just think we're best mates. Two nerdy geeks who hang out together because they haven't got any other friends. Although that's not true. Sparrow has other friends even if I haven't. I sometimes wonder what I'd do without her. I can't remember what life was like before I met her. I know I went to The Grange and that, and I remember what my uniform looked like, but I can't remember how I felt about anything. Not really. It's like I wasn't properly alive until I met her. And I certainly can't imagine existing without her now. I wouldn't see the point. Anyway, I don't have to worry about that. Not unless we both completely screw our A levels up, and according to our predicted grades that is not going to happen. To be honest I can't wait to get sixth form out of the way now. I just want to skip to the bit where we have both got our places at Leeds. That'll be amazing cos when we're at uni I can be with her all the time. Properly with her, not only during lessons. We can hang out together all the time and I won't have to worry about Mum seeing us or asking me where I've been and all that crap. It will just be me and Sparrow. We might even get a place together in our second year. I mean it would make sense and that. I wouldn't even need to tell Mum. I'll simply say I'm sharing with a friend. She hasn't got to know who it is. And then when we're done with uni we can maybe do a gap year and go round the world together or something. I wouldn't really care where we went, to be honest. As long as I was with her, that's the only thing which would matter. The only thing which will ever matter.

5

LISA

Everybody stops searching when they hear the police siren as if it's some sort of traditional party game where it's the cue to freeze. Maybe they think they might get told off for not searching correctly. Like the way people stop helping someone who's collapsed as soon as a paramedic arrives. The professionals are here now. They will tell us what to do. We will leave it to them.

I don't want to leave it to them, though. I want to carry on looking. It should be my job to find her. I'm the bloody mother.

The police car pulls into the car park and a few moments later two coppers emerge and walk towards the playground. The shorter one, a woman, walks a step or two in front of the man. They probably sent a woman because they thought I'd be in a state. I'm not in a state.

Not really. I just need to find Ella. As they get nearer I see them stop and talk to a woman who points at me. Suddenly everyone in the whole fucking park knows who I am. Half an hour ago no one gave me a second look. Now I'm some kind of celebrity. 'That's her,' they'll be saying. 'That's the one who's lost her kid.'

The copper smiles slightly as she approaches.

'Lisa Dale?' she asks. I nod. Her smile drops and my jaw tightens. For a second I think she is going to give me bad news. That they have found Ella dead in the road somewhere. That people have stopped searching because they have been told not to bother because it's too late.

'I'm PC Reynolds and this is PC McElroy. I understand you've lost your daughter.'

She says it like there is something wrong with me, that this is just me being stupid, like it's all some little misunderstanding.

'She's been taken,' I say. It surprises me as I say it. I hadn't even realised I thought that until now.

'I understand that you're worried and we're here to help, but we need to take this step by step, so we can build up a picture of what happened.'

'I know what happened, and someone's got her. She would have come out by now if she was hiding. And she wouldn't have left the park without me – she knows not to do that. She's never done this before. Someone's taken her. I know they have.'

My voice is surprisingly steady as I speak. I see them

looking at me, trying to work me out. Maybe wondering why I sound so calm when my daughter is missing. I am not calm inside, mind. Inside I feel like I'm having some kind of intense cardiovascular workout without actually moving my body an inch.

'Right,' says PC Reynolds. 'Well rest assured we're taking your call very seriously. We have three police community support officers who will be here in a moment and numerous other officers are on their way. Let me just go over some of the details you gave us. When did you last see your daughter?'

'About ten past three. We were playing hide-and-seek. She's very good at it. That's why I spent a long time looking for her before I called. I felt a bit stupid, to be honest. I didn't want to waste your time.'

'And can you describe your daughter for me?'

'She's four, five next month. Slim . . . well, skinny really. She's got dark blonde hair with a fringe. Kind of shoulder length.'

'What was she wearing?'

'A green and white striped T-shirt dress with a big pink flower on it. And green leggings and Crocs. I told you all this when I phoned.'

'I know, but we need to double-check all the details. Are there any other distinguishing features?'

'No. Not really. She had grazes on both hands, mind.'

PC Reynolds looks up at me.

'She fell over just there,' I say, pointing to the path.

'Did anyone else see her fall over?'

'I don't know. My eyes were closed. I told you, we were playing hide-and-seek.'

She is writing all this down in her notebook. I wonder if she thinks I am a bad mother. Maybe not. She doesn't look old enough to be a mother herself. Although that's a bit rich coming from me.

'OK. Can you take me to the exact place you last saw her?'

I head over to the little path. PC Reynolds and the male copper, whose name I have already forgotten, follow. Other people look down and clear the way as we walk. Like they are embarrassed because something bad has happened and they don't want to look me in the eye.

I stop at what I think is the right place. I look back to the tree where I was counting and try to work out exactly where she was when I heard her cry.

'Here,' I say. 'This is where she fell. She screamed and I ran over to check she was OK, and then I went back to that tree to count while she hid again.'

'And can you remember if you heard her footsteps running away? Or anyone else's voice?'

I shake my head.

'No. My phone rang, see. I had to answer it. Work, you know.'

I shrug, sure she does think I'm a bad mother now.

'And how long was it before you started looking for her?'

'I don't know. I mean I was talking on my mobile for a while, and then I shut my eyes and pretended to count in case Ella was looking, and then when I opened them I realised I'd lost her balloon.'

'Her balloon?'

'Yeah, a red one from the lad's party she went to earlier. I was looking after it for her. I only realised it was gone when I started looking for her.'

I look down at the ground, knowing how shabby it all sounds.

'So perhaps it was as long as five minutes altogether?'

'Yeah,' I say with a sigh. 'It was probably a good five minutes or so.'

She nods, walks a little distance away and speaks into her radio. I look around and see that there are three other coppers in the park now. I see the flashing lights in the car park and hear another siren from the road that runs alongside it. More coppers appear a moment later. They are running this time. I brush my hair away from my face, aware that my hands feel clammy. This is real. It is happening to me. I am not going to wake up from this.

I hear an out-of-breath voice say, 'Lisa.' There's a hand on my shoulder. For a moment I think it is Alex but turn to see Dad standing there in a grease-stained T-shirt and jeans which are belted too tight under his belly. He hugs me. I can feel him shaking. I have never known him shake before. Maybe that is why I start feeling sick.

'Why haven't they found her yet?' he asks.

I shrug, unable to produce any words.

He goes up to the male copper and points accusingly at his face. 'What are you doing standing around here? You should be out there looking for her.'

'Sorry,' I say to the copper. 'He's my dad.'

The copper turns to Dad. 'I can assure you both that we are doing everything we can but we have to go through set procedures in cases like this.'

'I don't care about your fucking procedures. She's four years old. I want everyone out there on the streets looking for her.'

'Dad, don't,' I say as PC Reynolds comes back over to us. 'They're doing their best.'

'Well their best's not bloody good enough. She's not here, is she? It's a waste of time looking for her here.'

'Sorry,' I say to both the coppers. 'He's a bit upset.'

'I understand that,' says PC Reynolds. 'But in a missing-persons case we always start with a thorough search of the area where the person was last seen. That's what the officers are doing now.'

She gestures across the park. There must be at least eight pairs of coppers searching now. It's as if they are multiplying every time I look up. It should make me feel better but it doesn't. It makes me feel worse.

Another copper is making his way towards me. He has one of those flat hats on. Maybe he has bad news for me. Maybe they have sent someone senior to tell me something terrible. He holds out his hand.

'Mrs Dale, I'm Sergeant Fuller from the Halifax station. I'm in charge of our operation here. More officers are being deployed as we speak and we have a thorough search going on.'

'She's not here,' says Dad. 'Someone's taken her.'

Sergeant Fuller looks at me. 'He's my dad,' I say, wondering if I should get some kind of sign to hang around his neck so I don't have to keep apologising for him.

'Right. Mister?'

'Benson,' says Dad.

'Mr Benson, I can assure you that officers have been deployed to a variety of tasks including containing the immediate area and taking details of everyone leaving the area. Several officers around the park also have recording cameras and we have a police search adviser on the way. In the meantime we are doing everything we can to make sure we find her.'

Dad shakes his head and paws at the ground with a foot, like some bull about to charge. I suspect it's only the fact that Sergeant Fuller is obviously local that has stopped Dad from letting rip at him.

Fuller turns back to face me. 'Were there any family members or friends in the park at the time?'

I shake my head.

'What about school friends?'

'She doesn't go to school yet. She's due to start reception on Monday.'

My voice catches as I say it.

Sergeant Fuller nods. 'Nursery friends then? Or other children she knows?'

'No. She went to a neighbour's party in town this morning, but none of them were here. She'd have said if they were. She doesn't miss a thing.'

'OK. We will need the names of all of those at the party though. My colleague mentioned that you lost a balloon which belonged to her.'

'Yeah. I had it when I got here. I'm pretty sure I had it when she fell over, but I must have let go at some point after that, maybe when I answered my phone.' My voice trails off. I'm aware that the phone is about the only thing I have managed to keep hold of.

'Right. Have you got a photo of her on your phone?'

I get out my mobile and start swiping through the photos.

'Anything taken today?' he asks.

I shake my head. I should have taken one of her climbing up to the slide. I didn't even think of it, though. He probably thinks I am a bad mum too.

'What about one wearing the same clothes as she has on today?'

I swipe further back, and my finger stops over a photo of her wearing the green and white striped dress on the beach at Bridlington last month. She doesn't have the leggings on but the dress is the same.

'Here,' I say, passing the phone to him. 'That's the dress she's wearing.'

'When was it taken?'

'Last month.'

'OK. And are you happy for us to circulate it to all officers and to the media too if necessary?'

I don't like the way he says 'if necessary'. I don't want
to even think about what that means. I nod anyway.

'Thank you. Can you email it to this address please?'
He pulls out a card and gives it to me. My fingers are
shaking as I type the email address. I attach the photo
and press Send. His phone beeps almost instantly.

'Right,' he says. 'If you'll excuse me I need to get this
out. You stay put and I promise to keep you informed of
any developments.'

I nod again. Feeling like a spare part in all of this.

'What can I do to help?' I ask.

'You could contact all your friends and family to
check that they haven't seen her. Does she know anyone
who lives within walking distance of the park?'

I think for a moment, but there's no one. No one at
all. I shake my head.

'OK, well, keep thinking. One of my colleagues will
be along to go through your phone contacts with you at
some point.'

He gives me what I presume is supposed to be a
reassuring smile and walks off, talking into his radio.

Dad looks at me. 'Does Alex know?' he asks.

'No. His phone's turned off. He's in a meeting. I've left
a message for him to call me when he comes out.'

'Right.' He is silent again for a bit.

'Do you remember seeing any blokes hanging about the playground?' he asks.

'Dad, don't.'

'What? If some bastard's taken her then he must have been in the park at the same time.'

I shut my eyes for a second and sit down heavily on the ground, aware that my legs don't feel capable of supporting me any more. Dad kneels down and puts his arm around my shoulders.

'Look, I didn't mean to upset you, love.'

'I know. I just keep hoping she'll come running across the grass any minute, laughing that we took so long to find her.'

Dad doesn't say anything because he knows, like me, that it's not going to happen.

'I'm going to go and look for her,' he says eventually, getting to his feet.

'Where?'

'Outside the park. In the streets around here. I need to do summat. Keep myself busy, like.'

'OK. Have you got your phone on?'

He nods. 'Call me if you need me, Lis. Are you going to be all right on your own?'

'Yeah. I'll get in touch with people, like the copper said. Just in case, like.'

Dad opens his mouth to say something but shuts it again. I watch him walk off, his footsteps heavy, his head low. A few seconds later I hear him calling Ella's name. It is half-hearted though. Like he knows she can't hear him.

I take out my phone. The sun has disappeared behind the clouds now so the screen is easier to see. Still nothing from Alex. I call his number again just in case he hasn't picked up the voicemail. I don't leave another message though. I don't know what else I can say. Instead I go to my contacts and start scrolling down the massive list of mobile numbers and email addresses. They're a mixture of friends, family and clients. There are people who I haven't spoken to for years. The gas man who fitted our new boiler. Clients who stopped their personal training sessions ages ago, whose faces I can barely remember. I can't bring myself to phone anyone, but I can text people. I can at least do that.

I start trying to compose a text. I keep deleting words because I don't want to worry people and then I remember that it is not the time to be stupid like that.

In the end I settle on 'Ella has been missing from Grange Park, Halifax since 3.10 this afternoon. If you have seen her anywhere since please text me asap. Please don't phone as trying to keep line free.'

I send the text, trying not to think about the looks on people's faces as they receive it. Within a couple of moments the replies start coming in. I read the first couple, both about how awful it is and that if there is anything they can do to help . . . I don't even register who they are from. It doesn't really matter.

I glance up, aware that someone is standing next to me. It is the woman who sent her son to look for Ella. She is holding a polystyrene cup.

'I got you a tea, but if you'd rather a coffee just say and I can go back and get you one.'

'No. Tea's fine. Thank you. How much do I owe you?'

'Don't be daft,' she replies, handing it to me.

'Thanks.'

'Dan's still looking,' she says. 'He's determined to find her.'

'That's really kind of him,' I say. 'But don't worry. The police are here now. You guys can get on home.'

She gives a little nod and walks away. I notice the police are grouped together having some kind of meeting. I wonder if I should go over and join them or if they will all stop talking when I arrive. I look at my watch again. I swear the hands haven't moved since the last time. The texts are coming in thick and fast now. I check each one in case, but they all just say how sorry they are and that they're thinking of me. No one has seen her. I wish I could turn the bloody thing off now but I can't in case Alex rings.

I sit down on the grass and try to summon up something obvious that I haven't thought of yet. A reason why she would have gone off with someone, an explanation for the fact that she has disappeared, and no one, least of all me, saw or heard anything. The only thing I can think of is the balloon. If she maybe saw it and went running off after it. If she's cross at me for losing it and upset enough to be hiding somewhere. I still don't think she would do that. But I also know that if I rule out the possibility, all I am left with is the horrible, scary explanations. I feel a bit lightheaded and put my head between my knees for a moment. When I look up the police meeting appears to have broken up, the officers walking off purposefully in different directions. Sergeant Fuller heads back over to me.

'OK,' he says. 'Ella's photo has gone out to all officers and to the media.'

'You think someone's taken her, don't you?'

'I think we need to get as many people as possible looking for her. It's pretty instant these days with Facebook, Twitter and whatnot. And very often in these cases a member of the public will find the child. If she has simply wandered off after her balloon, we need the public to be looking out for her.'

'I still think someone's taken her.'

'Have you talked to her about not going with strangers?'

'Yes . . . well, I mean as much as you can with a four-year-old without scaring the life out of them.'

'And if someone did try to take her, how do you think she'd react?'

'She'd shout and scream, make a big fuss. She's not a shrinking violet. She's got an older brother, she's used to standing her ground.'

He looks at me and nods.

'No one's being allowed to leave the park without us filming them. We're getting names and addresses, asking for statements.'

'Has anyone seen anything?'

He shakes his head.

'What about the people who left before you arrived? How are you going to find them?'

'We'll put out appeals through the media. I'm sure they'll come forward.'

I look down at my feet. 'I should have called you earlier, I feel so bloody stupid. She could be anywhere by now.'

'Come on. We need you to keep positive. Is there anyone who can come and be with you?'

'My dad's still here but he's gone off to look for her. He's not good at waiting around.'

He nods. Hesitates for a moment. 'Look, I need to ask about Ella's father. Do you live together?'

'Yeah. We're married. He's working in Manchester. He doesn't even know yet. I've left him a message.'

'OK. I'm going to send one of my officers over to you to take his details and the names and details of everyone in your family. Your friends too. And everyone at the kiddies' party earlier.'

'I've already texted everyone.'

'That's great, but we still need to contact them ourselves.'

'You think it's someone she knows, don't you?'

'We have to build up a picture of everyone she knows, everyone she's come into contact with. To be honest, the younger they are, the easier it is. When they're teenagers they've had contact with that many people on social media it's a nightmare.'

I think of Chloe. He's right. I wouldn't have a clue how many people she's chatted to online.

'Sure, whatever I can do to help.'

'We've got a lot of officers out there now, so please be assured we're doing everything we can.'

I nod. He walks away. I wish to hell I hadn't taken that call on my mobile.

Alex finally calls at five fifteen.

'Have you found her yet?'

'No. There's no sign. Police are searching everywhere.'

'The police?'

'Well, yeah. She's gone missing, Alex. I had to call them.'

'Oh Jeez.' I can picture his face, almost hear it falling down the phone.

'I'm sorry. I shouldn't have joked about it. I just didn't think she could actually have disappeared. I didn't see how that would even be possible.'

I hesitate, wondering if I should tell him about the phone call. I decide to wait to do it in person.

'I know.'

'Maybe she simply wandered off.'

'Maybe. I did lose her balloon from the party. I don't know exactly when, but I must have let go of it at some point.'

'That's it, then. She'll have seen it and followed. That's how she'll have left the park.'

I turn my head away from the phone so Alex doesn't hear me sigh. Usually his optimism is refreshing. Right now it seems ridiculously naive. I don't want to stick a pin in his bubble but at the same time I know we both need to be realistic.

'I don't think so, love. I don't think she'd have left the park without me. Not even for that.'

There is a moment's hesitation at the other end of the line.

'Well, I'm sure there's an innocent explanation of some kind. Look, I'm leaving now. I'll come straight there. It might take a while, mind, with Friday-night traffic. Is anyone with you?'

'Dad came but he's gone off looking for Ella. Mum's got Otis.'

'Right, well I'll be there as soon as I can.'

'I gave the cops a photo of her. They've sent it to the media. Just so you know, like.'

'Great,' he says. 'Hopefully someone will find her

pretty sharpish.' I wish he wouldn't sound so upbeat about this. I want him to scream and shout and swear down the phone. I want to know he is feeling the same pain inside as me.

'I'll let you know then, if I hear anything, like.'

'Yeah. Thanks. It'll be fine, I'm sure. They'll probably have found her by the time I get there.'

'Yeah,' I say, ending the call and wishing I could believe him.

Dad comes back half an hour later. Tony is with him, for once out of his overalls, in jeans and a T-shirt. He gives me a hug. I think it's that which upsets me most. The only other time I can remember him giving me a hug was at Grandma's funeral.

I look across at Dad. He shakes his head.

'We've done all the roads around here. Asked everyone we saw. Cops are all over the place too.'

'She's probably a long way from here by now,' I say.

Tony looks down at his feet, scuffs a trainer in the dry grass. Sometimes I swear he is still my ten-year-old kid brother, struggling with the news that he is going to be an uncle.

'Someone must have seen summat,' says Dad. 'They'll come forward when it's on the news tonight. Calendar TV van's outside the park. Their chappie was filming the search, like.'

'Did you talk to him?'

'Only to find out if it'll be on the teatime programme.'

I look up at the sky. My life has turned into a bloody soap opera in a matter of hours. People are going to be stuffing their faces watching the telly, seeing a picture of my little girl. My little girl, who isn't here any more because I wasn't fucking paying attention.

I walk a few steps away. I can't deal with this right now. Not here, in the middle of a park with loads of people everywhere.

'Why don't you go home?' Dad says. 'We'll stay here. We'll call you as soon as she turns up.'

I shake my head. 'No. I'm not leaving, not without her. I brought her to the park and I'll take her home again.'

Dad looks at Tony. They don't know what to say because I'm upset and they can't handle it. They used to leave all that stuff to Mum to deal with. I wish Mum were here but she can't be because she has to be with Otis, and the one thing I am sure of is that I don't want him to be here.

One of the coppers comes back over. The one who asked me for all the names on my phone. I can't remember what his name is. I've lost track of them all now.

'Is there anybody in at your house?' he asks.

I shake my head.

'Only we'd like to go and search it, if that's OK.'

I look at Dad. I know exactly what he is thinking but he doesn't give me a chance to say anything before he jumps in: 'She's not fucking there, is she?'

'I'm sorry, sir, but we need to search the missing person's home. It's standard procedure in these cases.'

'You can stick your standard procedures where the sun don't shine, sonny. Some pervert's got my granddaughter and you want to try and pin this one on us.'

'Dad, leave it,' I say. 'You'll only make things worse.'

'Worse? How can they be worse than this? Ella's missing and they think her own family's got summat to do with it.'

'Please understand that we have to rule out the possibility that she might have got back home somehow. She could be hiding somewhere in the house, thinking she's in trouble. We have to eliminate every possibility.'

I sigh and nod my head, knowing he's right.

'I'll go with them, if you want,' says Tony.

I nod, realising he'll be more use there than here. I fish my house keys out of my pocket and hand them to him. 'Thanks.'

The copper looks at me. 'We'd like your permission to search the whole property – garden, outbuildings, everywhere.'

'Fucking hell, what is this?' says Dad.

I grab hold of his arm. 'Enough.' I turn back to the copper. 'That's fine. Whatever you have to do.'

'And forensics need a toothbrush or hairbrush and something with her scent on too. An item of clothing.'

'Right,' I say, trying hard to keep my voice from

breaking. 'Tony, give them her red toothbrush from the bathroom and her *Frozen* pyjamas. They'll be on her bed.'

He looks at me, nods and swallows hard. I'm glad he's going now. I'm not sure I could cope if he started crying.

Tony walks off with the copper. Dad turns straight to me. 'I can't believe you let them do that.'

'They're trying to find her, Dad.'

'No, they're not. They're trying to pin this on us. Just because we live in Mixenden.'

'I don't live in Mixenden.'

'No, but we do, and that's good enough for them. You see this on the telly, don't you? Cops trying to fit someone up just because they come from the wrong side of the tracks. They've probably seen that your brother's got previous by now.'

'Jeez, don't be so bloody paranoid. They're just doing their job. I don't care what they do. They can turn the whole place upside down as far as I'm concerned. As long as they find her, I really don't give a shit.'

Dad looks down and scuffs the grass with his shoe. I know now where Tony gets it from.

It's nearly seven when Alex texts me to say he's here. Dad has gone off searching the streets again. I wonder if I should warn Alex that the park is still crawling with coppers. He probably won't have thought about that – I know I wouldn't have if it was me turning up like this when everyone else has been here for hours. But before I can do anything about it, I see a figure running up from the far end of the park. I know instantly it is him because he's crap at running, always has been. It's not lack of speed; he simply looks weird running, something to do with the way he brings his knees up. I used to take the piss out of the way he ran on the treadmill at the gym. Although as I look at him now, the only thing I feel is an overwhelming sense of love.

He runs straight into my arms, almost knocking me off my feet, and holds me, holds me tighter than he has ever done in his life. So tight that he manages to squeeze some fresh tears out of me. When at last I look up, I see that his eyes are red too.

'She's gone,' I say. 'Someone's taken her.'

'We don't know that for sure.'

'Then why are you crying?'

Alex scrunches up his face and looks up at the sky. 'I didn't want to think it; I wanted to believe she'd just wandered off. But when I got here and saw all the police . . .' His voice trails off and he shakes his head.

I look up at the sky again and blink hard. 'Someone's taken her.'

'Even if they have, we'll get her back. We need to be positive, to keep strong for her sake.'

'Well I've been trying to be strong since it happened

because I've had to deal with all this crap myself in the middle of the park with other people gawping at me, and right now I don't want to be strong any more, right now I want to bawl my fucking eyes out.'

He nods, pulls me back close to him and lets me do exactly that.

6

MURIEL

The sirens keep coming. I had no idea the mother would make such a fuss. She couldn't be bothered to look after her child when she had her, but now the girl has gone she is trying to ease her guilt. She knows it is her fault, you see. Knows that she has neglected her child and now she is trying to save face. That is what it is like these days. People don't care about their actions until they are caught. Until someone else is pointing the finger, and then all the excuses come out. Suddenly they are the doting parent who has had this terrible thing happen to them. She will insist it is not her fault – it never is. The police will find out though. It will take time, of course. The police won't say what they have found straight away. There will be a lot of sympathy for the mother at the beginning, but the truth will come out in the end. And when it does, and only then, I will take the child back. Will explain that I have been acting *in loco parentis*. They will thank me then. Too few people are prepared to do their public duty these days. Everybody walks by on the other side of the street. Not that I want thanks. I was simply doing the right thing. And as soon as they understand that, I will hand the child over. Not to the mother, for they will have found her unfit by then, but to the authorities. They will have to decide what to do with her. For now I am her guardian. And as such it is my duty to take care of her properly.

I move away from the landing window and go back downstairs to the lounge, where the child is playing with Melody. It is such a help that she loves the cat. I fear it would have been very hard to settle her otherwise.

'I want to go back to park now,' she says as I enter the room.

'Your mother has asked me to look after you for a little longer. It isn't safe for you to go back, you see.'

'Are the big boys still being naughty?'

'Yes. Yes, they are.'

'Is Daddy coming to pick me up?'

'Not this evening, no. They've asked me to look after you tonight. You can sleep in Matthew's room.'

The child starts crying. 'I want to go home.'

I walk over and crouch down next to her. 'You can stay and play with Melody.

'I want Charlie's birthday cake.'

'Who's Charlie?'

'Charlie Wilson. I went to his party. His cake is in my party bag. Mummy's got it in her car. And she's got my balloon. Did you see my red balloon?'

I shake my head, and the child's face falls further.

'How about I make you crumpets for breakfast in the morning?'

'I want my balloon. Mummy's got it.'

My hand is on her shoulder. Her body is shaking. I hold her to me. For a moment she resists, her body rigid. And then it gives. Her arms loop in turn around my neck as she sobs into my shoulder. Her warm tears dampen my blouse. My left hand is rubbing her back, the other tight around her. I smell her. Breathe her in. The sweetness of her youth mixed with the dust and heat of the day. I ache inside because I know that she needs me. Needs me in a way that Matthew doesn't any more.

'How about I run you a nice warm bath after tea? I'm sure you'll feel better after a bath.'

She nods, snot dripping from her nose.

'Let me get you a hanky,' I say. I return from the kitchen and hand her a pale blue cotton handkerchief embroidered with seashells. She looks at it and back to me, a frown creasing her brow.

'To blow your nose,' I say. The frown increases. I realise she has never seen a proper handkerchief before. 'Like a tissue,' I continue. I take it back from her and hold it over her nose. She sniffs rather than blows. I wipe her nose anyway, fold the handkerchief and hand it back to her.

'You can keep it in your pocket, in case you need it again.' She looks down. She hasn't got a pocket, of course.

'Never mind,' I say, taking it back from her. 'I'll look after it for you. Now, what would you like for tea?'

'SpongeBob Squarepants pasta,' she says.

'Right, well I have various pastas but not that one, I'm afraid. Would you like pasta tubes or twists?'

'Tubes,' she replies. 'With tomato sauce.'

I nod.

'And cheese on top.'

'I'll see what I can do.'

'Can I watch TV now?'

'I'm afraid not.'

'I always watch TV while Mummy's cooking tea. She lets me.'

'I don't have a television, my dear. I don't find I need one.'

The girl stares at me, incredulous. They use them as babysitters, you see. Dump their children in front of the box and do whatever it is that is more pressing than looking after them.

'Is it in other room?' she asks, looking towards the door.

'No, I really don't have one. Go and see for yourself.'

She gets up and trots through to the other room. A few minutes later she returns, tears streaming down her face.

'Good heavens, let's not get into a state about it. It is possible to survive without television, you know.'

The crying intensifies. Clearly I need diversionary tactics.

'Why don't I go and get you one of Matthew's toys to play with?' She looks up momentarily. I take this as a yes.

'I'll go and have a look upstairs and see what I can find. You stay here with Melody.'

I walk up the stairs and past Matthew's bedroom. There are no toys left in there, of course. But as he grew out of things I took them up to the box room, partly because I couldn't bear to part with them and partly for my grandchildren. Older toys are so much better than the rubbish you get nowadays. And quality lasts, unlike all of that plastic tat people's houses are full of today.

I pause at the top of the next flight of stairs. It is a long time since I have gone into this room and I have to steel myself to do it.

I open the door halfway and squeeze inside. It is like entering a museum of Matthew's childhood, albeit a rather chaotic and muddled museum in desperate need of a curator. The exhibits may not be neatly labelled and displayed in cases but they are organised inside my head. And I have a clear picture in my mind of each thing being used or played with by Matthew. Why, I can practically date them all: Rocky the rocking horse (Matthew was admittedly not very original with names), with him sitting astride it wearing a cowboy hat, Christmas 1999; pair of stilts, Matthew standing on them in shorts and black plimsolls, a huge grin on his face, summer 2002; Monopoly, Matthew staring intently at the board, desperately trying to work out how to beat his father, 2004. The list goes on, the shutter firing inside my head as each captured image comes sharply into focus. I stop and catch my breath, run my hand across his little easel before glancing down at the chalk dust on my fingers. It all comes to dust in the end. Memories and dust.

In the distance I hear more sirens. I peer out of the tiny window. I can't understand where all the police are coming from. You certainly never see them in Halifax town centre when you need them. The park is usually quieter at this time in the evening, a lull in activity while the children have their tea before a final play outside. Matthew will be worried. He doesn't like noise or upset, changes in routine. I know he will be hiding in the trees, seeking sanctuary in the folds of the cloak they provide. He may be rocking and singing to himself, but no harm will come to him there. I wish I could go to him but I can't. The child needs me. And I need to stay here to protect the child.

I turn, and a flash of red ribbon in the corner of the room catches my eye. The bottom half of my face breaks into a smile. The top half, still preoccupied, reluctantly allows itself to follow. I step over an abacus and the easel and reach out to grab the extended paw. The rest of it comes out easily. Mr Boo. It has been such a long time. I hold the bear to me before examining him more carefully. The red ribbon around his neck is frayed a little, the stitching is loose around his left arm, and the fur is worn in places but probably no worse than I remember. And that was always part of his charm. Matthew adored him, right from when he was tiny. It was my mother who gave the bear to him, I think on his first Christmas.

I pick my way back towards the door and down the stairs. When I get to the landing I hear the child crying, having obviously worked herself up into a state. I hurry down the last flight of stairs and back into the lounge.

'Now, if you dry your eyes and stop this nonsense,' I say with the bear still behind my back, 'I've got a present for you'. The tears stop instantly. I produce Mr Boo and hold it out to her. A smile breaks across her face. They are as maddening and inconsistent as our weather, children. But this is one of those rainbow moments. And I feel a satisfaction from having quelled the deluge. A satisfaction I haven't felt for a long time.

'His name is Mr Boo,' I say. 'He was Matthew's favourite toy when he was your age.'

She takes the bear and hugs him to her. 'Will Matthew want him back?'

'No. He's yours to keep. You can take him to bed with you tonight.'

'Iggle Piggle,' she says in an uncertain voice. 'I take Iggle Piggle to bed with me.'

I look up at the ceiling to compose myself. 'Not here you don't. Here you will have Mr Boo.'

She hesitates before replying.

'Can I take him home with me tomorrow?'

It is my turn to hesitate. I believe in being honest with children where possible, but having stemmed the flow of tears, I have no desire to start it up again.

'Like I said, he's yours to keep.'

She hugs him to her and lowers her head to talk to him in the same sing-song voice which Matthew used. I watch for a moment – the curl of the fingers, the dimples, the very colour of the hair.

'Right, well, you tell Mr Boo a story while I go and make your tea.'

I go to the kitchen, fill the kettle and flick up the switch, before going through to the dining room and laying the table, aware of the enormous pleasure it gives me to be laying it for two.

Later that evening, while the bath is running, I go to the guest room and start going through the large chest of drawers. I kept some of Matthew's clothes as well. Most of them, actually. Certainly the ones from when he was little. I know the exact pair of pyjamas I am looking for. White cotton with stars and rockets on them and red cuffs which I always worried would run in the wash but never did. I find them at the back of the bottom drawer. They are rather crumpled. Normally I would iron them but I do not want to delay things any longer. The child is still playing with Mr Boo, but I have a feeling that the dam could burst again at any moment and it is therefore best to whisk her along from one thing to the next. To not give her the time to dwell.

I turn the light off and head back to the bathroom, where I pop the pyjamas over the radiator as I always used to do for Matthew, only to remember that, being August, the heating isn't on. That is the trouble with summer. The evenings may be balmy but there is nothing like having your pyjamas warmed on a radiator.

I pull up the sleeve of my blouse and check the bath water. I am not a believer in having the water cooler because it is summer. Matthew always liked a hot bath, even in the middle of a heatwave.

I turn the tap off and give the water a swish with my hand. I think it is fine but if the child complains I will add some cold.

I go back downstairs and take her firmly by the arm, not giving her the chance to protest.

'It's bath time now,' I say.

'Have I still got germs?'

'No, but a bath will do you good.'

'Will my hands sting?'

'Only for a second. And they'll feel better afterwards.'

She follows me into the bathroom and peers into the water as if she half-expects the Loch Ness monster to rear up at her from beneath the bubbles.

'What's that?' she asks, pointing at the bottom.

'It's a bath mat. To stop you slipping.'

'Why is your bath slippy?'

'All baths are. That's why it's safer to have a bath mat.'

'We don't have a bath mat.'

'No,' I reply. 'I don't expect you do. Your mother doesn't appear to give safety a very high priority.'

She stares at me then starts to undress without saying anything further. I fold her clothes and put them neatly on the stool. When she is ready I take hold of her under the arms and lift her into the bath. I had forgotten how light children are at this age. They may eat like horses but they are still nothing more than puffs of air. Matthew was always the lightest one in his class, mind. Malcolm used to worry about it. Say he needed feeding up a bit. I used to tell him the boy was not a turkey being fattened up for Christmas. Besides, I liked the fact that he was light on his feet and I always equated it with swiftness of thought too. There are some complete lumps of children being raised now. You see them in Halifax town centre on a Saturday afternoon, being shepherded around by complete lumps of adults who feed them in the street as if they were animals at a zoo. I sometimes think that if you built a cage around them and supplied a constant stream of food they would not think to complain.

'Where are your toys?' asks the child.

It is the one thing I do not seem to have kept, bath toys. Probably because of the mould and mildew.

'Here,' I say, picking up the jug and a plastic beaker from the sink. 'This is what Matthew used to play with. He used to pour a drink for all his toys.'

'Did he pour one for Mr Boo?' she asks.

'Oh yes, all the time.'

She takes the jug from me and immerses it in the water, before struggling to lift it out.

'A little bit at a time,' I say. 'Just enough to pour a cupful.'

She empties some and tries again, smiling at me when she manages it. I have quite forgotten what it feels like to be smiled at like that. As if someone has installed central heating in my bloodstream.

I scoop up some bubbles and put them on her nose. She screws her face up and giggles. I think maybe we are over the worst and she will stop making a fuss now. Will realise that she is better looked after here than she ever was at home.

And then she lifts her hands out of the water to examine them and it's as if her past is etched there. Her face drops as she scans her pink palms for the grazes from earlier.

'Have they gone?' she asks.

'Almost. The water is helping them heal.'

'Did you put Deathol in the bath?'

'Dettol,' I correct, smiling at her. 'Just a capful. That will make them better.'

'Will Mummy need to put a plaster on when I get home?'

'No,' I say sharply. 'You won't need a plaster. You need to let the air get to it.'

It is when I am drying her hair with a towel afterwards that I realise what must be done. She won't like it. But sometimes you have to be cruel to be kind when you are a mother. And the sooner this is done, the sooner the child can start her new life. Can learn to put the past behind her.

I go to the bathroom cabinet and take the hairdressing scissors from the top shelf. I haven't used them for a long time. Matthew got to the age, as all boys do, when he no longer wanted his mother to cut his hair. He went to a barber in the town centre one Saturday without me knowing. I cried when I saw what they'd done. It was too severe, it didn't suit him. I think even he realised that, although of course he didn't acknowledge it at the time. But he did let it grow back longer, and when he went to have it cut again he went somewhere different and they were kinder there, gentler. They seemed to understand that it was necessary for someone with such a gentle face.

I comb the child's hair through. The fringe completely covers her eyes when wet.

'I'm just going to give your fringe a little trim,' I say.

'Here?' she asks.

'Yes.'

'Mummy takes me to the Treehouse in Hebden Bridge. The lady dresses up as a fairy and she lets me watch DVDs and gives me chocolate ladybirds afterwards.'

I sigh, wondering how things ever got this complicated. Maybe if mothers learned to cut their own children's hair instead of paying others we wouldn't have all this silly nonsense.

'Well, I am quite capable of doing it myself, thank you. And you shall be rewarded by being able to see properly afterwards.'

I take the hair cape from the bathroom storage tub and put it over the towel wrapped around her. I pick up the scissors in my left hand and feel her shoulders tense beneath the cape as I make the first snip.

'There. That wasn't too bad, was it?'

She shakes her head. I snip again, watching as the damp clumps of hair fall on to the cape. She shuts her eyes without me having to ask her to. I cut briskly along the fringe. And when I have finished the fringe I continue down and round the side, leaving just enough to cover the child's ears. Matthew never liked having his ears showing. Not when he was her age, anyway.

I wait for her to say something, to shriek or scream,

but she is oddly quiet. As if the rhythmic snipping is calming her, sending her half to sleep after the rigours of the day. I follow the line around the back of her head. I do not do layers. It is simply a straight cut. It is easier to maintain like that. Malcolm used to ask me what basin I had used. He had a dry sense of humour like that. Most of the time it was OK. But not always.

I make it to the other side without a whimper from the child. When I am done I step back to check for any bits I have missed. There is nothing obvious but it will be easier to check once I have dried it.

I usher the child into my bedroom and pick up the hairdryer from the bedside cabinet.

'Is it noisy?' she asks. 'I don't like noisy ones. Or the noisy hand driers in toilets. The ones that roar at you when you walk past. I like the ones like a toaster you stick your hands in.'

'I'll put it on the low setting for you. That should be OK.'

To be honest, her hair is half dry anyway and the low setting is all it needs. It is fine, like Matthew's. And it falls similarly into place without guidance from me. Clearly it knows its own mind.

'Can I see?' she asks when I turn the hairdryer off. I hesitate, aware she doesn't realise what I have done, then guide her gently over to the dressing-table mirror. I watch closely as she catches her reflection in the mirror. Her eyebrows rise as she lets out a gasp before a frown settles on her face. I brace myself, waiting for the inevitable tears.

'I look like a boy,' she says, but in a calmer voice than I had expected, a voice which is apparently not offended by the idea. He gaze flits from her own reflection to that of the photograph on my bedside table. It goes back and forth a couple of times before she speaks. When she does so, she speaks directly to the mirror, rather than to me.

'I look like Matthew.'

7

LISA

We say nothing for a while. Just stand huddling together in the same spot in the park where I have been all afternoon. I feel close to Ella here, simply because it is the last place that I saw her. It's almost as if, if I wish hard enough, I might be able to make her rematerialise in front of my eyes at any moment. She won't, of course, but somehow it feels like the right place to be.

'I took a call on my mobile,' I say as we watch the toing and froing of the coppers in the park.

Alex looks at me. 'What do you mean?'

'When she disappeared. My phone rang and I answered it. I was too busy talking to some dickhead trying to arrange training sessions to hear anything.'

'You would still have heard if she'd screamed.'

'Yeah, but she didn't, did she? And I don't know why because I was on the fucking phone.'

'It's not your fault,' he says, taking my hand. He means it too, which is what makes it worse. Usually when Alex puts up the scaffolding around me I am grateful. Today it simply makes me feel even more of a cow than I already feel.

I shrug. 'I wanted you to know, that's all.'

He is silent for a moment. 'You said she fell over, just before.'

'Yeah, there,' I say, pointing. 'And I ran over and saw to her, although I didn't have any wipes or plasters or whatever, and I said we should go and get Otis and go home to get it sorted but she still wanted her turn to hide. And that's when I turned my back and started to walk away. That's when my phone rang.'

'Was she upset about falling over? More than she was letting on, I mean. Might she have run off somewhere in a state?'

'No. She'd stopped crying. She wanted to hide. She's bloody won this time, hasn't she?'

Alex shakes his head. 'It must have been the balloon then, she must have seen it. It's the only thing I can think of.'

'Let's hope you're right,' I say, nodding in the direction of Sergeant Fuller, who is on his way over to us. 'He's the one in charge.'

Alex holds out his hand, 'Alex Dale, Ella's father.'

Sergeant Fuller shakes it firmly. 'Please be assured we are doing everything we can to find your daughter, Mr Dale. I came over to give you both an update.'

We both nod, waiting for him to go on. I think for a second it is going to be bad news. If it is, I wish he would just get on and tell us.

'You may have noticed we've sealed off the park.'

I look around. I hadn't noticed. I just thought it had gone very quiet.

'We're satisfied that your daughter is no longer in the park but we have sealed it off for forensic purposes. Your daughter has been classed as a high-risk missing person.'

'What does that mean?' asks Alex.

'In operational terms, it means that a detective superintendent is being put in charge of the case. Our police search and rescue team are also involved. We tried to call in the sniffer dog but unfortunately we've got a problem in that it's on holiday with its handler and not due back until a week tomorrow.'

'Well, what about the other dogs?' says Alex.

'I'm afraid there aren't any other dogs.'

'Of course there are other dogs,' I say. 'The police force is full of dogs.'

'Not highly trained search-and-rescue ones like this.'

'Can't you get one from another part of Yorkshire?' asks Alex.

'This dog covers the whole of Yorkshire.'

'Jesus, that's ridiculous,' Alex says, pulling his fingers through his hair.

'I'm sorry. We've got plenty of other strategies and options open to us and, as I said, we've got all available resources working on the case.'

'You think someone's taken her, don't you?' I ask.

'Third-person involvement is one of the scenarios we're looking at but not the only one.'

'So what are the others?' asks Alex.

'It's still possible that she may have had an accident, clearly not in the park but somewhere outside.'

'She wouldn't have left the park on her own, though,' I say.

'I understand what you're saying but we can't eliminate it at this stage of our enquiries. I can tell you that we've finished searching your property and nothing has been found. We've removed items for DNA as we agreed.'

I feel sick inside. They have my daughter's DNA. That can only be used for one thing. I don't want to think about it. I don't want to hear any of this.

Sergeant Fuller looks at me and Alex in turn and shuffles his feet. 'I'm sorry to have to ask this,' he says, 'but is there anyone you can think of who might have a grudge against you or your family?'

I stare at him. 'You're not serious?'

'We have to look into every possibility at this stage.'

'No,' says Alex before I can say anything else. 'We're not that sort of family. I'm a small-business adviser and my wife works in a gym. Not exactly turf-war territory.'

'No, I appreciate that. It's just something we have to consider. The other thing we need to ask you for is a list of every adult your daughter knows.'

I stare at him. The thought that it could be someone we know hadn't even occurred to me until this point.

'But she hardly knows anyone. She's only four. Anyway, one of your officers has already been through my phone and taken the numbers of family and friends.'

'I know. I'm talking about adults who may know your daughter, rather than family or friends. Acquaintances, if you like. People she might recognise, even if she doesn't know their names. If you could have a little think and email me the names of anyone you can think of and the place of work or organisation which she knows them from, that would be a great help.'

'Right,' I say, getting out my phone as Sergeant Fuller walks briskly away. I look at Alex. The expression on his face mirrors mine.

'I don't know how to do this,' I say. 'It feels wrong, writing down the names of people who we are basically saying could have taken her.'

'I know,' says Alex, running his fingers through his hair. 'Let's not think of it like that, though. Let's just write a list of people she knows who we don't know very well.'

I look up, frowning as I think. 'Well, I suppose there are the other parents at nursery, she'd recognise them. Charlie's dad Dean, Mr Humphreys on the corner who always says hello to her.'

'What about the instructor at Gym Tots, the young lad with red hair?'

I shrug. 'I don't know. I suppose so. He's always been so bloody great with her, mind.'

'Jesus,' says Alex. Normally I would make a quip about Ella not knowing him but this is not normal. It is far from it. 'What?' I ask instead.

'This. It's doing my head in. It's not right. It shouldn't be happening.' I see him swallow. If Alex crumbles I have got no chance. I am well aware of that. I reach out and take hold of his hand.

'Come on,' I say. 'We can do this together.'

He swallows again and nods. I get out my phone and start typing names. Ten minutes later I email Sergeant Fuller a brief list comprising parents, neighbours, a shopkeeper and the lovely young guy from Gym Tots. If we do get her back, I know I'll never be able to look him in the eye again.

A few minutes later Sergeant Fuller comes back over to us.

'Thanks,' he said. 'That's really helpful. If you think of anyone else, please just let me know.'

'So what can we do now?' I ask.

'We appreciate your help,' he says, 'we really do, but

there's nothing more you can do here. I'd suggest that you go home. It's probably the best place to be. We've got your numbers and we'll let you know as soon as there's any news. And we'll be sending a family liaison officer round first thing in the morning so you've got someone who can be with you and answer any questions.'

We both nod but neither of us moves. Sergeant Fuller hesitates before leaving.

'We'll be working through the night on this,' he says. 'Most of us have kiddies ourselves. We won't stop till we find her.'

'Thanks,' says Alex. Sergeant Fuller nods and walks away.

I turn to look at Alex. 'How can we go home?'

He puts his arm around me. 'He's probably right. I mean we can't sleep out here, can we?'

'It doesn't matter. I'm not going to sleep wherever I am. I may as well be here.'

'You know what I mean.'

'I can't leave her.'

Alex squeezes my shoulder. 'You're not leaving her; she's not here. And when they find her, she'll want to come straight home.'

I sigh, trying not to be irritated by his continued optimism. 'OK. I suppose so.'

'What shall we do about Otis?' asks Alex.

I feel a stab of guilt for not having thought about that myself.

'I'll go and get him.'

'You don't have to. He could stay at your mum's tonight. I could nip his stuff round.'

I shake my head. 'No, I want him home. I want at least one of my children with me.'

Alex nods slowly and looks down. I realise too late that I said 'my' instead of 'our'. He knows it's because I was referring to Chloe as well. And I know how much that still hurts him.

'What are you going to tell Otis?' he asks.

'I don't know. I don't think we should lie to him though.'

'Maybe just be economical with the truth.'

'He'd see straight through that.'

Alex sighs. He knows I am right. Otis is way too sharp for that. 'Well, just say she's got lost or something. Let's try and make out it's not a big deal. At least till the morning.'

'OK. I'll ring Mum. Let her know I'm on my way.'

Alex hesitates. 'Are you going to be all right driving?'

'Course I am. You get straight on home. Just in case, like.'

He nods and gives me a hug. 'She'll be fine. They'll find her.'

I do one of those little mouth-closed smiles you do when someone has said something nice to make you feel better and turn and head off in the direction of the car park. All I can hear as I walk is the sound of people calling out Ella's name and me screaming it over the top of them. Followed by the silence.

Mum opens the door before I even knock. Her usual smiling face is trying hard to put in an appearance but it is her eyes which give her away. She grabs me and gives me a hug. I am transported back to being sixteen again. Standing in the kitchen telling her I'm pregnant, desperate for her to be able to take all the fear away.

'Your dad and our Tony are still out looking,' she says. 'They won't come home till they find her.'

I shake my head. 'She's gone,' I say. 'Someone's taken her.'

'You mustn't say that.'

'Why? Because it's true?'

Mum bites her bottom lip and looks up at the ceiling.

'He's very quiet,' she says softly, nodding towards the front room, where I can hear what sounds like a Dalek.

'What have you told him?'

'Just that his sister's hid in such a good place that no one can find her.'

'And has he bought that?'

'I don't know,' she says with a shrug. 'He's not said much. I've let him watch *Doctor Who* DVDs to try to take his mind off it, like.'

I go through to the front room, fighting like mad

with myself to find a voice which doesn't sound worried.

'Hey, how did football camp go?' Otis is sitting on the sofa staring at the screen, his knees pulled up to his chest. He has ridiculously long legs, courtesy of Alex's side of the family.

He looks up at me. He knows, I can see it in his eyes straight away. He knows that this is a big deal and that I am only doing this bright and breezy crap because that's what grown-ups do.

'Where's Ella?' he asks.

'We don't know,' I say, sitting down next to him on the sofa. 'Grandad and Uncle Tony are out there looking now.'

'Can I come and help?'

'Not now, love, it's too late. We need to get you home to bed.'

'But Ella goes to bed before me.'

'I know, but it's different tonight.'

'You can't just leave her out on her own, can you?'

I swallow hard and take a moment to reply while I try to steady my voice.

'The police are looking too. They say there's nothing more we can do tonight. They want us at home so they can bring her home when they find her.'

'What if they don't find her?'

'Well, let's hope they do.'

'Yeah, but it they don't, where will she sleep?'

'Let's not worry about that, eh?'

'Will she have to sleep on a park bench like tramps do? Will someone give her a blanket to keep her warm?'

I swallow hard again. For a boy who has spent most of the summer holidays arguing with his sister, he is doing a very good job of tearing me apart with his love for her.

I lean over and pull him in towards me. 'I'm sure she'll be OK. Try not to worry.'

'But she needs to come in now. It's started raining.'

Otis points to the window, where the first drops of rain are splattering the glass. They are big drops, the type you get when the weather breaks suddenly.

'I expect she'll be keeping dry somewhere. She'll be fine.'

'But we can't just leave her outside, she'll go rusty.'

It is the one which breaks me, which starts my own tears falling. I hug Otis tighter as he sobs into my shoulder. When I look up, I see Mum standing watching in the hall, her puffy red eyes mirroring my own. And this time she can't tell me that it'll all turn out fine. No one can.

Otis is quiet on the journey home. What I miss most of all is the sound of the two of them bickering in the back. I pull in to our cul-de-sac. I see curtains twitching, faces peering out of windows. It will have been on the telly by now. They'll all know. And they'll have seen the coppers here earlier. Things like this aren't supposed to happen in a nice village like this. It puts everyone on edge, makes them realise that winning a silver award in the Britain in Bloom competition does not guarantee a crime-free existence. I wonder if they think we're under suspicion. Maybe people have been talking, saying it is someone in our family. Mixenden may only be a few miles away but it may as well be on a different planet as far as they are concerned.

I park badly on the kerb but for once don't care. I get out and hurry to open Otis's car door but all I can see is Ella's empty car seat on the other side. He gets out, his eyes firmly fixed on the ground, and I follow him up the front path, wishing I hadn't noticed that the wheelie bin has been moved from its usual place at the end of the drive. The police must have looked in that as well.

I usher Otis indoors and shut the front door behind us. Alex comes straight out from the kitchen. He shakes his head slightly at me as a way of letting me know there is no news without saying anything in front of Otis.

'Hey, Otis, let's see this medal of yours, then.' He smiles. Otis looks at him as if he has lost the plot.

'Why aren't you looking for Ella?'

The forced smile disappears from Alex's face. 'Because the police are looking for her,' he says, crouching down to him. 'They're the experts in things like this. We'd only get in the way.'

'Grandad and Uncle Tony are still looking.'

'I know, but we wanted to be here with you. Ella wouldn't be very happy if we weren't all here when she came back, would she?'

'Is she still in the park?'

Alex glances at me but I can only manage a shrug.

'We don't know, son. They've done a big search but they haven't found her there.'

'Only I know the best hiding places. I could go and show them.'

Alex pulls Otis to him. I look up at the ceiling, desperately trying to hold it together for Otis's sake.

'Thank you,' Alex says to Otis. 'Tell you what, how about you draw a map of the park and put a cross at all the places to look?' Otis appears to brighten a little.

'Yeah,' he says. 'Like a treasure map. Only Ella will be the treasure.'

He disappears upstairs to his bedroom where his pens and paper are. Alex looks at me blinking back the tears.

'Sorry,' he says. 'I just wanted to let him think he's helping.'

'I know. Thank you.'

He comes up to me and hugs me. 'It was on the radio news,' he says, 'when I was driving home. Just so you know.'

'What did they say?'

'Just that a major hunt has been launched for a four-year-old girl who had gone missing from the park. I kept thinking it was going to be someone else until they said her name. It just doesn't seem real.'

'I know.'

'And it's on the BBC News website, her photo and everything.'

I nod again before I realise. 'Shit,' I say, closing my eyes for a second.

'What?'

'I'd better let Chloe know. Someone might text her or post on Facebook. I don't want her hearing from anyone else.'

'No. No, of course not.' He shakes his head slowly, understanding how much I do not want to do this to Chloe.

'I'll do it now,' I say. 'Can you go up with Otis? Keep him occupied with the map.'

'Sure. Tell her not to worry, OK?'

I nod, although I know full well that will be impossible for Chloe.

I dial the number, wondering whether they are still an hour ahead of us in France and trying to prepare the right tone of voice for when she answers.

'Hi,' she says. 'I was going to text you later. We're just on our way back to the hostel.'

She thinks I'm checking up on her. She has no fucking idea, poor kid.

'Chloe, it's about Ella.' My voice doesn't come out how I want it to at all.

'What?' She is listening now, not trying to get rid of me.

'She went missing in the park today. We haven't found her yet.'

There is a pause on the other end of the line. I imagine her standing there, trying to take it all in.

'What do you mean missing?'

'We were playing hide-and-seek. When I looked for her I couldn't find her anywhere. I had to call the cops in the end.'

'Well, where did she go?'

'We don't know. The police are still looking. I just wanted to let you know because it's been on the news here and they've put her photo out and that.'

'Has someone taken her?' Her voice is wobbling. I imagine her brushing away the tears.

'We don't know, love. We don't know what's happened to her, but she's not in the park any more.'

I can hear her crying now. I shut my eyes and screw them up tight. I hate this. I hate having to do this to her.

'I'll come home,' she says.

'No, you don't need to do that. I just didn't want you finding out from anyone else, that's all.'

'Well I can't stay now, can I? I can't stay here when my little sister's gone missing.'

'What about Robyn?'

'She won't mind. Anyway, I haven't got any choice, have I?'

I sigh. I suppose she's right. Maybe I should have thought of this before I phoned. Maybe I've done the wrong thing again.

'Well, it's too late for you to come home tonight. Let's wait till morning. She'll probably be back by then, eh?'

'OK. Phone me though, won't you? If you hear anything, like?'

'Course I will. I'll let you know straight away.'

I hear her whimper slightly at the other end.

'Love you,' I say.

She ends the call. I imagine her standing there in the street, telling Robyn what has happened. The two of them hugging, crying. I don't even know where they are. They were heading towards Nantes last I knew, but I'm not really sure.

I open my eyes to find Alex looking at me from the top of the stairs.

'It's Otis,' he says. 'He wants you to see his map. And he's upset because the police have moved some of the stuff in his bedroom.'

I nod and slowly make my way up the stairs, counting each step as I go to try to stop myself crying.

Later, much later, when the house is quiet, I lie in bed listening to the rain drumming against the window. Alex is lying next to me. I do not think for a moment that he is asleep but it is too dark to see. It was his idea to go to bed. He said rest was important, even if we couldn't sleep. I went along with it mainly because it was a change of scenery from the kitchen and would at least stop me drinking coffee for the entire night. I haven't slept a wink, of course. I haven't even shut my eyes. All I can do is cling desperately to the hope that Ella is lying injured or stuck somewhere and getting drenched in the rain. Because the alternative is far too scary to even contemplate.

8

MURIEL

Matthew is poking my legs. I do not know what the time is but the air is heavy with the scent of early. I pretend to be asleep at first. It often works. He will prod and poke for a bit, but if I do not stir he will eventually give a deep sigh and pad back to his room to look at a book or play with his toys. He knows better than to jump on my bed, of course. I hear other parents tell me that happens in their house and I look at them and shake my head. They may think it is sympathy but it is not. It is pity. Imagine allowing that to happen. And then, when their child turns thirteen, they'll complain that they don't take a blind bit of notice of a word they say. At which point I will sigh and shake my head again. And they still won't have the nous to work out why.

He is still poking me. Gradually working his way up

my body. He gets to my shoulders and stops. We don't poke people in the face, he knows that. But he shakes my shoulders a little. There is even a hint of a whimper. Followed by a very distinct one.

I open my eyes. The face of a child with pale skin and red-rimmed eyes framed by short fair hair stares back at me. The child is wearing Matthew's pyjamas. The ones with the red cuffs – which strangely mirror the red eyes. The child's bottom lip trembles before it opens its mouth to speak.

'Can I go home now?'

It takes a minute for me to be able to formulate a response.

'Let's have breakfast. I promised you crumpets if I remember.'

The child looks at me solemnly. For a moment I think I might have done enough to stop any further tears. But it is only a moment.

'I want my mummy. I want to go home.' The tears run freely. I sit up in bed, glancing at the alarm clock as I do so. It is only six thirty but clearly there is no chance of any further sleep.

'Let's not get into a state,' I say. 'We'll go downstairs and I'll get your crumpet. Some warm milk too, if you like. You'll feel much better after that.'

The child looks at me doubtfully but there is a momentary lull in proceedings.

'Where's Mr Boo?' I ask. A hand emerges from the

sleeve of the pyjamas, which are a little too long, and points back towards Matthew's bedroom. 'You go and get him, then, while I pop to the bathroom. Just wait in there and I'll dig you out some slippers.'

The child leaves the room. I stand up and hurriedly make my way to the bathroom. I have to heed nature's call straight away in the mornings. Often it is the thing which actually wakes me. If Melody's miaowing hasn't already accomplished it. I do remember the days, pre-pregnancy, when I could go and make a cup of tea first if I wanted. And I remember being able to hold it for ages during a lecture when I was at university too. It is one of the things they never tell you at antenatal classes. That you will lose all dignity in that department. I read an article once in one of the women's magazines they have in the dentist's waiting room. It was about some-one who'd gone to have it seen to. She'd visited a physiotherapist who specialised in such things, after having unsuccessfully tried some kind of weights you had to insert in yourself in order to try to rebuild the pelvic floor muscles. Quite why someone would tell any-one this, let alone a journalist, I have no idea. The very thought of people reading about my private parts in dentists' waiting rooms up and down the country turns me cold.

I make it to the toilet just in time. On numerous occa-sions, particularly in the early days after having Matthew, I didn't. Once Malcolm complained about the wet patch on the toilet mat where I'd tried to mop up my accident. I told him the stiff tap in the basin had gushed out water when I'd finally managed to turn it on. He said he'd take a look at it. I knew he wouldn't though, which is why I didn't feel bad about lying to him. It's amazing what you can conceal from a husband. All those years and he never knew about my little accidents. Mind you, it's amazing what a husband can conceal too. Or at least try to.

I wash my hands and apply hand cream – my skin is like paper without it – and go through to Matthew's bedroom.

The child is sitting on the bed cuddling Mr Boo. She has stopped crying at least, though her face still looks as though it may break into a fresh wave of tears at any moment. I wonder how much sleep she actually got. She cried for a long time after I switched the light out. And once during the night her crying woke me and I had to go in to her. Maybe it was twice, actually – it is difficult to recall now.

'Let's find you something to wear on your feet then.'

'Slippers,' she says. 'You said you would find me slippers.'

'So I did. Now, let me see which cupboard they will be in.'

I never moved Matthew's shoes to the guest room. They tended to stay at the bottom of the wardrobes when Matthew outgrew them, and he never complained about having them there. I didn't keep all of them. Certainly not anything with scuffs on or which had worn through the sole. But Matthew's slippers were generally in good condition when he grew out of them. Plenty of wear left. Certainly worth saving for another pair of tiny feet.

'Ah, here we are,' I say, rummaging among the plastic bags at the back of the furthest wardrobe on the left. 'Do you know what size you are?'

'I'm four but I'm five next month,' she says.

'No, shoe size. You could be a size 10 or 11. Or you might know it as twenty-something, the European way they do it now. Unless your mother gets you measured in Clarks. They still do the traditional sizes. Do you go to Clarks?'

The child's face is resolutely blank. She has probably never even had her feet measured, poor mite. I remember her Crocs on the shoe rack by the front door.

'I'll nip downstairs and find out,' I say. I recoil as I see the bright splat of green on the shoe rack. They are fine for the beach but that is about it. I turn them over. They put both the UK and European sizes on them. I brush the dirt off one of the soles to be able to read it properly before going back upstairs.

'You're a size 10 in children's,' I tell her.

'Have you got them in your shoe shop?'

I smile at her. 'It's not exactly a shop but I should have. Matthew would have been the same size as you at some point.'

'What size is he now?'

'Nine in adults,' I reply.

'Will my feet grow that big?'

'No. Ladies' feet are smaller. Not to mention more fragrant.'

I have another rummage. The sizes have rubbed off on some of them so I try to gauge the size just by looking.

'Here, try these,' I say, handing her a pair of blue slippers. She puts them on her bare feet, but when she takes a step they slip off her heels.

'OK,' I say, taking another look. 'What about these?'

She tries the red pair I hand her. Matthew was not fussy about colours at that age.

'I like them,' she says putting them on and taking a few steps. 'Did Matthew like them?'

'Oh yes,' I reply. 'They were his favourites.' She seems placated for the moment.

'Right, let's go downstairs. Have you been to the toilet this morning?'

The child nods her head. 'In the green bathroom.'

'For a number one or a number two?'

She bites her lip, a frown starts to gather on her forehead and she fiddles with a strand of hair.

'I don't know,' she says finally. 'We don't do numbers, but I had a wee.'

I nod at her. 'That's a number one in this house,' I say.

'And is a p—'

'Yes,' I interrupt. 'Now let's go down for breakfast. Melody will be wanting feeding too.'

Her face brightens a little. 'Can I feed her? Can I give her some biscuits? I haven't got Germolene on my fingers.'

'You may do. And then we'll have breakfast together.'

'And then Daddy will come to take me home.'

I look at her and away again without responding. Cruel to be kind, I tell myself. Cruel to be kind.

Melody comes to meet us at the foot of the stairs. She rubs around my ankles but appears confused because she's missed the opportunity to wake me.

'It's OK, we're up earlier than usual this morning, you haven't missed out on anything.' The child squats down to stroke her. I make sure she smooths the fur in the correct direction.

'Biscuit time, Melody,' the child says in her sing-song voice. Melody's ears prick up. I think she will like it. Having a young child in the house. I think we both will.

I leave the two of them together and go through to the kitchen, fill the kettle and flick the switch before busying myself with the crumpets. For a brief moment my mind wanders to what will be going on in their house. I don't suppose either of her parents will have slept much. I see tired faces, hands clutching coffee mugs. I get no satisfaction from other people's suffering.

But I also know I must stay strong for the child's sake. She deserves a better life than the one she had there, and in time even she will understand that. One day, when she has grown up, she may even thank me. Not that I am doing this for gratitude. I am doing it because it is the right thing to do. So often these days people shy away from doing the right thing. They want it easy, you see. They want everything handed to them on a plate, washed, prepared and ready to consume. They sell carrot sticks in Marks & Spencer, for goodness' sake.

My mother lived through the war in London. She understood the true meaning of hardship. Of fighting against the forces of evil, how you must never let your guard drop, even for a minute. Because it is a slippery slope, oh my, how slippery, once your standards start to fall. Before you know it you end up on the wrong side. Justifying behaviour which you know to be wrong, all because it is the easy thing to do.

I warm the pot for a moment before measuring in the loose-leaf tea, the scent of Earl Grey rising with the steam as I pour the water in. I give it a stir then pop the lid on, followed by the cosy. I knitted it myself, I think around the time I was knitting bootees for Matthew. Things last a long time if you take care of them.

Melody walks into the kitchen closely followed by the child.

'Can I give her the biscuits now?' she asks.

'You may do. I'll get them for you.' I bend down and

open the bottom cupboard, take out the pouch and hand it to her.

'Just pour some into there,' I say, pointing to the ceramic bowl in the corner. The child follows my instructions, glancing up after a moment to check if she's poured the right amount.

'That's right. A few more should do it.' Melody dives in without waiting for her to finish. The child hands the pouch back to me.

'I want to go home now,' she says.

'Breakfast,' I reply. 'We're going to have crumpets, remember?'

As soon as she finishes her last mouthful I take her by the hand and lead her upstairs. Keeping busy, that is the key to this. If I talk to her while I am getting her dressed she won't be paying as much attention to what I am saying.

We go into Matthew's room together. I open the curtains and the early-morning sunlight catches the child's hair. Every strand a different shade to the one next to it. I reach out and stroke it, finding myself humming as I do so. Schubert. I used to stroke Matthew's hair sometimes as he played it on the piano.

'Will Mummy be cross about my hair?' she asks.

'Your hair looks lovely. And it is far more practical to have it out of your eyes.'

'Tell Daddy that you did it when he comes. Mummy doesn't let me play with scissors.'

I snort. That's a first, a safety concern in the child's household.

'The thing is, dear, Daddy won't be coming for you today. He's asked me to look after you a little longer. Your Mummy's poorly, you see. She's not really up to looking after you.'

'Daddy can look after me.'

'I expect he'll be working. He does work, I take it?'

The child nods. 'Grandma looks after me when Mummy and Daddy are working.'

'Well, not today she isn't. They've asked me to take care of you.'

I am aware of the sharpness in my tone as soon as I say it. It is hard. She doesn't understand that this is for her own good. The child starts crying.

'I want to go home.'

'Come along now, there's no need for that. We can have lots of fun together.'

'I want to go home.'

'You can play with Melody.'

'I want my mummy.'

'I'm sure we'll have a lovely time together.'

'I want to go back to the park. I want my mummy.' She is shouting now, on the verge of screaming. It is like firefighting in the Australian bush. Every time you think you have put it out you turn round and another one has started. I go to embrace her but she pushes me away. She is not an attractive crier. Few children are.

Matthew was an exception. He cried so elegantly. One dainty tear, dripping down his face, followed by another. The rest of his face remaining calm and still as if he was one of those baby dolls which you can make cry by turning a wheel at the back.

'Let's get you dressed and then we can go upstairs and find Matthew's toys.'

'I don't want to get dressed.'

She is simply opposing everything I say now. But the tears are diminishing ever so slightly. If I can get her up to the toys it might just break it. I bring over the green dungarees, beige top and white briefs and socks which I dug out from the spare room earlier.

'I want to wear my striped dress,' she sobs.

'Well you can't, I'm afraid. It's gone in the wash along with your leggings. Covered in dust and grass stains from the park they were.'

'I don't care. I want to wear them.'

I take off her pyjama top before she has even realised what I am doing and manage to get Matthew's top over her head. His face smiles back at me, a bit of Marmite smeared on the corner of his mouth. I get a wet flannel and dab it. He giggles. Always a smile. Always a cheery face.

'I don't like them. I don't want to wear them.'

'Right, pyjama bottoms off and on with your knick-knacks.' When she doesn't move I whip the bottoms down myself. She steps out of them without a protest and I hold the pants for her to step into.

'They're boys' pants not knickers,' she says.

'Well, they're the best I can do for now, I'm afraid. They're clean, that's all that's important.'

She gingerly raises one foot at a time and steps inside. I pull them up for her. They are a bit baggy but will do the job. The dungarees are obviously going to be more difficult to get on. She fidgets and pushes my hand away as I try to clip the straps.

'I want my stripy dress. I don't want to wear these.'

I take deep breaths and say nothing. If I ignore her protests she may get tired of them. So many people give in to their children's demands. And then they wonder why they keep pestering them.

Finally I manage to clip the straps into place. The dungarees suit the child. I do not hold with this urge to differentiate between genders so early. They are children and should be treated as such, not dressed as pink princesses or Premiership footballers. No wonder they start having sex so early. They are being primed for it from the time they are toddlers.

'There we are,' I say. 'That wasn't too bad, was it? We'll just pop your socks on and I'll take you up to see Matthew's toys.'

The child looks up at me, a combination of anger, resignation and curiosity in her eyes as she points her toes to allow me to pull the socks on.

'What toys has he got?'

Curiosity has won out. I smile and take her hand.

'Let's go and see. You can choose three toys you'd like to play with today and I'll bring them downstairs.'

'Won't he mind?'

'No, not at all. He'll be pleased someone else is enjoying them.'

'Mummy says I have to ask Otis before I borrow his toys.'

'Yes, well, he lives with you, doesn't he?'

'And Matthew doesn't because he's a big boy.'

'That's right.'

She comes upstairs with me without any further protest.

'Why have you got two lots of stairs?'

'It's an old Victorian house. They often had three floors. The servants' quarters would have been up here.'

She looks at me blankly.

'Servants are people who clean and cook for you.'

'Do you have servants?'

I smile down at her. 'No, dear. I use it as a storeroom. It's where I keep Matthew's things.'

We reach the top of the stairs. Matthew is in the box room. I can hear him playing on the glockenspiel. I wonder for a moment if he is doing it in protest. If he does not want some other child trampling over and playing with his things. I don't think he is though. I think it is more of a welcome. I turn and look down at the child. She can't hear the music, but it is enough for me to know that he was playing.

I turn the door handle and the music stops. We walk into a silent room. Only in my ears is the music still ringing.

I hear an intake of breath from the child. I look down and her face has brightened considerably. The tears dried and forgotten.

'You can have a look at them,' I tell her. 'Just be careful with things and ask if you'd like me to get anything out.'

She squats down in front of me and peers into the mass of toys.

'There's a rocking horse,' she squeals. 'Matthew has a rocking horse.'

'Yes, that's Rocky. Would you like a ride on him?'

She nods vigorously. I step over a few things to reach him and manage to slide him out so that she can climb on board. She sits tall in the painted saddle and rocks gently back and forth a few times before gaining in confidence and rocking more vigorously. The child's face is beginning to blur. The lips are fuller, nose slightly broader. He rocks so hard I fear he is going to tip over and fly off, either that or grind himself through the floorboards. He doesn't though. He always come back to me smiling. Always.

The doorbell rings downstairs. I hear it only faintly at first but then it rings again. Whoever's finger is on the bell sounds impatient. It will probably be the postman – he never stops even to pass the time of day. I glance down at the child. She is in a world of her own. She will not notice if I slip away. But if he keeps ringing the bell she may hear it and run downstairs. I back out of the room and silently close the door behind me before hurrying down both flights of stairs. It suddenly occurs to me that it could be the father. That someone could have seen me with the child yesterday and told them. My throat tightens as I reach out and open the door. It is not the father though. It is a police officer. My fingers grip the door handle tightly. So tightly that I fear I might snap it clean off. I can't work out how they know. How they found me so quickly. And then I look at his face and see that he is smiling, and I look down and see the pile of leaflets in his hand. Further down the road there are other police officers knocking on doors. He doesn't know at all. I let go of the handle, put my other hand on the door frame to support myself, relieved that the shoe rack is safely out of view behind the door.

'Hello, I'm a police community support officer,' he says, flashing an ID card at me. 'Sorry to disturb you so early on a Saturday morning. We're doing house-to-house enquiries regarding the little girl who's gone missing. You may have heard about it on the news.'

I shake my head. 'No.'

'Oh. Well, her name is Ella Dale, she's four years old, and this is what she looks like.' He holds up a flyer with a photo of the child on. She is wearing the stripy dress. The same one she had on yesterday. The one which is in

my washing machine. I ease the door closed a little, try
ing to work out how I will stop him if he asks to come in.

'Right. Well I haven't been out so I'm afraid I can't
help.'

'Do you have any outbuildings? Only we need to
check any sheds or other buildings which are left
unlocked. Places she may have climbed into.'

'Only a garden tool store. It's there,' I say, pointing to
the corner of the front garden. 'And it has a padlock on.'

He goes up to it and checks the padlock before coming back to me.

'Well, thank you for your time, and if you do see or
hear anything suspicious please do call us.' He hands
me a flyer as he says it. I take it without looking and
manage to force the corners of my mouth up slightly.

'Thank you, officer,' I say, shutting the door quickly. I
turn and start as I see the child peering down through
the banisters at the top of the stairs.

'Why did the policeman come?' she asks. I keep my
left hand, the one with the flyer in, behind me. I try to
stop my other hand shaking.

'Just to tell us it's still not safe to go to the park.'

'Because of the naughty boys?'

'That's right.'

'Why doesn't he tell them to go home?'

'He does, but they keep coming back.'

'The big boys are always naughty. Otis is sometimes a
bit naughty but not as naughty as the big boys.'

I am aware that I need her to go away so I can hide the flyer.

'Would you like me to bring the rocking horse down so you can play on it?'

She nods.

'OK, you run upstairs and tell Rocky, and I'll be there in a minute.'

She turns and hurries up the stairs. I wait until I hear her get to the top of the second flight before I bring my left hand out from behind me and look again at her photograph.

She looks very different now, with her haircut and Matthew's clothes. Almost unrecognisable in fact. I fold the flyer in half and put it in the pocket of a jacket hanging on the coat pegs. I stand still for a moment. There is no way back now. I know that. I have to wait until they dig deep enough to find out the truth about the mother. I have no idea how long that could take.

I pick up my mobile phone from the hall table and turn it on. I very rarely use it. It is more for parents to leave messages than anything. They all seem to want to text these days. Anything to avoid conversation, it seems.

I type in the message. It takes a long time as I have one of those older-style phones. It doesn't have the predictive thing. I keep the message brief and impersonal. 'Apologies, all piano lessons cancelled for the next week due to illness. Miss Norgate.'

I send it to the list of parents in my address book. I realise belatedly that Olivia Harper's lesson is at two o'clock this afternoon. It is very short notice. I should ring her parents and apologise in person. But if I do that they will ask me what is wrong and I will have to make something up and then it will all get difficult. And it is difficult enough as it is.

I climb the stairs, pausing on the first landing to look out of the window. There are three police cars parked further up the road. There appears to be a lot of activity in the park. Matthew will not like it. I know exactly what he will be doing. Covering his ears and singing 'la, la, la' at the top of his voice.

MATTHEW

Monday, 3 March 2014

It's like Mum has done something to piss off God (yeah, I know there isn't one but just go with it), and he's decided to throw a whole load of crap down to see how she copes with it. Nan's died. She was eighty-five so it's not like it's a big deal or anything, but I guess it's still a bit of a shock – it has been for Mum anyway. I mean Nan didn't have cancer or anything and she still had all her marbles, and I have the feeling Mum thought she was just kind of invincible, like one of those old bids who goes on till she's one hundred. Only she wasn't.

It was Mum who found her. I've never seen a dead body, not in real life anyway. I guess it must freak you out a bit. Mum went to see her as usual on Thursday morning and let herself in, and Nan didn't call out or anything and she wasn't in her armchair so Mum went upstairs and found her dead in bed. She didn't say much about what happened after that but it can't have been very nice. She's been really quiet since, even at meal times when she usually does that making-conversation thing. I don't think she's really got over Dad leaving and now this. I mean this has to be one of the crappiest starts to a year ever. The funeral's next week. I've never been to a funeral before. I was only nine when Grandad died and Mum said it wasn't the done thing for children to go to funerals. Valerie next door but one looked after me. I remember we played board games and she let me watch *Newsround* because she didn't know that Mum didn't usually let me see it.

I don't know if Dad's going to be there. Mum probably hasn't even told him and I can't ask her because the 'We don't talk about your father' rule still applies. I suppose I could tell him. I mean I've still got his mobile. But there would be a big scene if he went, and Mum would probably have a breakdown or something so I'm just going to keep quiet.

The trouble is, Nan dying means I'm like the only family Mum's got left now (apart from Auntie Jennifer, and she's in Middlesex so that doesn't really count), which freaks me out a bit. I mean she is so in my face anyway, always wanting to know who I'm with or what I'm doing if I'm not at home or school. And now she's got no one else to worry about she's going to be fussing over me even more. Always in my hair and checking what I'm up to.

The whole uni thing has been hard enough. It's a bit of luck Leeds had a course I wanted to do (and that Sparrow wanted to go there) because Mum wouldn't hear of me going anywhere a long way away. She said she wanted me somewhere where I could be back home on a Friday evening. Maybe she thinks all the sex and drug-taking only happens at weekends or something.

And now I'm going to be on a massive guilt trip if I don't come home every weekend because I know she'll be on her own and she hasn't even got anyone to visit or talk to any more (apart from Melody). Which means I won't be able to be with Sparrow as much as I'd like but I can't even complain about that because Mum doesn't know about me and Sparrow. It's gonna be a real pain in the arse. I hate having to do all this secret stuff and it's going to get even harder now because Mum used to go and see Nan twice a day so I knew she was always going to be out in the afternoon and that was when Sparrow came round. Mum would go ape if she knew. It's not like we've been shagging or anything. We just kiss and stuff. Nice stuff, but she doesn't want to go any further than that at the moment, which is fine by me. I mean, fucking hell, it's not like I'm gonna complain or anything, is it? Sometimes I just look at her and I can't believe she's actually lying next to me. I mean she's so beautiful, proper beautiful, like in an old oil painting or a statue, not that fake beauty like the girls the other lads look at on their phones, all huge arses and tits and false smiles and faces plastered in make-up. She doesn't wear make-up because she doesn't need to. Her eyes are so dark and her lips are absolutely perfect, like the lips on a doll or something. And half the time I just lie there and look at her and wonder why the hell she bothers with a skinny geek like me. I mean she could have any of the lads at school if she wanted. They might pretend they're not bothered when they see us together but I bet they wouldn't say no to her. That's why they take the piss out of me more when she's around – they're trying to show me up in front of her. She doesn't care though. She really doesn't give a toss about what they say. She says they're all arseholes, which they are. Maybe I should get a T-shirt which says something like, GEEKS GET BETTER GIRLS THAN ARSEHOLES. No, actually, that doesn't sound quite right. Anyway, what matters is that we're together. I know Sparrow hates it as well, all this creeping around. She doesn't let on, but I see her do this look sometimes and I just get the sense that she thinks I'm making it up about Mum, that she can't really be that bad. I mean you can tell people about someone but unless they actually live with them, they can't understand what they're really like. And her family seem really nice, not that I've ever met them, mind, but the way she talks about them, they seem really laid-back.

I guess one day I'll have to introduce her to Mum. I

mean I can't expect her to marry me or anything without actually having met my mum. I'll wait till the last minute though. Like when we've got engaged, and then Mum won't be able to do anything about it. She'll just have to smile and say congratulations like everyone else. I suppose she'll be on her own then. Maybe that's what she's scared of, although it's stupid really because she spends so much of her time slagging off other people and saying how awful they are you'd think she'd actually prefer to be on her own, it would make life easier for her.

I shouldn't say that really. I know it sounds a bit mean. And I know she only goes on at me because she wants the best for me – that's what she always says anyway. But she does bang on so much about what a lovely little boy I used to be that sometimes I can't help thinking that she didn't want me to grow up, that she'd have preferred it if I'd stayed a kid for ever, like Peter fucking Pan or something.

Anyway, I guess we'll get through this like we did with Dad going, and things will all settle down again. And in the meantime all I'm going to think about is Sparrow and how brilliant it's going to be when we're at uni together next year.

9

LISA

I watch the light fighting its way through Ella's curtains, signalling the end of the longest night of my life. I gave up trying to sleep at 4 a.m. and came in here. I wanted to be close to Ella. It is only a small room, barely enough space for a single bed and a tiny wardrobe. It's the downside of being the youngest child, what Dad used to call the 'last to arrive gets crappiest room' policy whenever Tony complained about his. He got my old room when I moved out, of course. To be fair, Chloe did offer Ella her room when she went to university. Ella didn't want it though. She said she liked her bedroom and she didn't want to move. I remember saying at the time that she might change her mind when she was older. Now I don't know if she'll ever get the chance.

I clutch Ella's dressing gown tighter to me, bury my

face in it, trying to breathe her in – what I have left of her, at any rate. And the thing I can't get over is the complete ridiculousness of the situation. I am lying in my four-year-old daughter's bed and I don't know where she is. She's not even started school and I don't know where she spent the night. How can that even be possible? Yesterday I was playing with her in the park and today I do not know if she is dead or alive. How did that happen? I don't know the answer. I don't have answers for any of the questions in my head. All I have is an ache deep inside me, a feeling like morning sickness and an empty bed belonging to my daughter.

I sit up, trying to fight away the images I have in my head, but they keep coming. More than anything I am worried that she is scared and suffering. Or that she was scared and she did suffer – if she is no longer alive. If you offered me a quick death for Ella without suffering and without her knowing what was going to happen to her, I would take that right now. It is the idea of her being subjected to things that no child should be subjected to which is killing me. I think I might be about to throw up.

I run to the bathroom and retch over the sink. There is very little to come up, probably because I haven't eaten since midday yesterday. All that is left is liquid fear, and I appear to have that running through my body. I wash my face and stare at the mirror. I look like shit, which is hardly surprising in the circumstances.

I go back to our bedroom, which is empty – clearly Alex couldn't sleep either – and pull on a pair of jogging bottoms and a fresh T-shirt. I am about to go downstairs when I have the urgent need to check on Otis. I push open his door and shut it quietly behind me. It takes a moment for my eyes to adjust to the gloom. Otis used to get woken up by the light in the mornings when he was little so we got him blackout curtains. I can't make out his body on the bed. There is no head on the pillow. I feel a slight breeze on my arms and remember that Otis insisted I leave the window open a little last night, even though it was raining. The realisation hits me so suddenly I hear myself gasp. Someone could have taken him. Maybe the same person who has taken Ella. Perhaps they have been watching us; perhaps all this has been planned. I feel my way along the bed, patting the mattress and duvet as I go. He is not there. He has gone too. They have taken everything I have. The gasp becomes a faint whimper. My legs buckle beneath me. And then I come to the pile of scrunched-up duvet at the bottom of the bed, and my hand finds something hard. I pat my way along it, feeling feet, knees and at last a head, tucked right into the bottom corner against the wall, Otis curled up like a foetus in a duvet womb.

I start to cry, while inside the torrent of relief meets the dam which is the knowledge that no amount of patting Ella's bed will bring her back. I pull down the duvet slightly and stroke Otis's tangled mass of hair. I wish he could sleep until all this was over. I don't want him to wake up and find his sister still not here. I don't want to hear the questions he is going to ask and I don't want to have to find the words to answer them.

I hear the door open and a second later feel a hand on my shoulder. I look up to find Alex standing there. He puts his hands under my arms and helps me to my feet, guides me out of the room and into our bedroom, shutting the door behind us, before allowing me to sink to my knees and sob.

'I thought he was gone. I thought they'd taken him as well.'

'It's OK,' he says, kneeling down next to me and putting his arm around my shoulders. 'Otis is fine.'

'Yeah, but Ella's not, is she? Ella's still out there. If she's still alive, that is.'

'Hey, come on. You mustn't talk like that.'

'Why not? It's what I'm thinking, it's what you're thinking, it's what Mum and Dad and Tony are thinking, but no one fucking says it, do they?'

'We have to keep positive.'

'Why? How is that going to help anyone?'

'Because we need to keep functioning for Otis's sake if nothing else. Come on, come downstairs. Let's let him sleep while he can.'

He lifts me to my feet again. I'm conscious of the softness of his dressing gown against my skin. I've never been able to understand how he can wear something like that in hot weather, but he doesn't sweat, not when he's at the gym and not when he's under pressure. He has a secret reservoir of coolant somewhere in his body. I wish I had access to it right now.

We reach the bottom of the stairs and Alex leads me though into the kitchen and sits me down at the table. His laptop is open in front of him; there is a picture of Ella on the screen, and both of our mobiles are on the table.

'No word?' I ask.

'Nothing from the police. It's all over the Internet, mind. And your phone's been beeping like crazy with messages.'

Alex puts the kettle on. I pick up my phone. There are sixty-three unread texts and a hundred and three messages on Facebook. I know without looking that none of them are important. If something important had happened we'd have had a call or a knock at the door.

I put my phone down and scroll through the story on the BBC News website on Alex's laptop. It's like reading about someone else's life. Or watching one of those three-part dramas on TV. I wonder who would play Alex and hope fleetingly that James Nesbitt isn't available. I have no idea how this became real, how the story became us and our daughter.

Alex strokes my arm.

'It still doesn't make sense,' he says. 'I just don't think she would have gone off with someone she didn't know, not without shouting and screaming her head off.'

'I know, I keep going through it all too. Maybe she hid somewhere on the other side of the park, so I wouldn't have heard if she'd screamed, even if I hadn't been on the phone.'

'I told you, stop blaming yourself.'

'Well who else can I blame? It happened on my watch, didn't it? If you'd been looking after her I'd be screaming blue murder at you; the only difference is that you're too bloody nice to do it.'

The kettle boils. The steam which rises feels like it is coming from my ears. I want to scream again, a massive scream like the one I produced in the park. I can't though, in case it wakes Otis.

'For what it's worth,' says Alex, 'and I know you won't believe me because you're too busy beating yourself up as usual, I don't blame you. I blame the bastard who took her.'

I look up and frown at him. 'You think she's been abducted too?'

He shrugs. 'I'm trying really hard to think of another scenario, something innocent, but I can't think of one. I think our best hope is that she followed the balloon, but I still don't think she'd go out of the park without you.'

'We're not going to get her back, are we?' I say, my voice breaking. 'Think of all those little girls who have been abducted. Their parents never got them back, did they? I can't think of a single one who was found alive.'

Alex puts a mug of coffee in front of me and sits down opposite with his head in his hands. I stare at the mug. It is the one Ella made me at the pottery shop for Mother's Day. Alex catches my eye and realises.

'Shit, I'm sorry,' he says. 'I wasn't thinking.'

Before I can say anything my mobile rings. Sergeant Fuller's name comes up on the screen. I look at Alex and back at the screen. I have never wanted to answer a phone call and not answer it so much in my life.

My hand reaches out and picks it up, seemingly acting entirely on its own. I swipe the green arrows and put it to my ear.

'Mrs Dale?' I try to work out from the tone of his voice if it is bad news, but I don't know if they put a voice on to disguise it if it is.

'Yeah,' I manage.

'It's Sergeant Fuller. Still no news, I'm afraid.'

I shake my head at Alex and watch him trying to decide whether to be pleased or gutted.

'We've got alerts set up at all ports and airports. As soon as it's a decent hour we're going to start house-to-house calls, radiating out from the park. What we'd really like to do later is a press conference. You don't have to be there – we can simply read a statement from you if you'd prefer – but if you are up to it, it would create more media interest to have you there.'

'We'll do it then,' I say.

'OK, thanks, that's great. We've got a family liaison

officer for you. Her name's Claire Madill. She'll be with you in half an hour and will keep you up to date on what's happening.'

'Sure,' I say.

'And she'll be your point of contact from now on.'

'Right, thanks.'

I think I hear a note of relief in his voice. That he won't have to be the one who tells us. I do not blame him in the slightest.

Even though I have been warned to expect her, I still shudder when the knock comes and I see the figure of someone I know to be a policewoman through the glass in the door. As I go to open it, I hear a woman's voice call out.

'Hi, Lisa. It's Claire. Stand behind the door and open it out of view. There are photographers outside.'

Are there? I had no idea. It hadn't even crossed my mind. I do as I am told and pull the door back in front of me.

A tall woman with a blonde bob steps into the hall and immediately shuts the door behind her. She smiles briefly in a way which suggests there is no need to force myself to smile back, holds up an ID card and offers her hand.

'Claire Madill, I'm your family liaison officer. I'm here to offer any support I can. Like keeping you out of the way of that lot.'

'Thanks,' I say, shaking her hand. 'I hadn't even real-ised they were there. How do they know where we live?'

'Are you on the electoral register?' she asks.

'Yeah.'

'There you are then. There's a box you can tick on the form to keep your details off the public register, but most people don't even notice it. Mind you, it probably wouldn't make that much difference these days. You can find out pretty much anything about anyone through Facebook.'

Alex comes into the hall and introduces himself. Claire shakes his hand.

'Did you know there are photographers outside?' I ask him.

'No. I haven't even drawn the curtains. Are they allowed to do that?' he asks, turning to Claire.

'I'm afraid so. As long as they're not on private prop-erty or obstructing the public highway, which they're not.'

'So there's no way we can get rid of them?'

'The best way is by having a press conference. Once they've got their pictures of you, they should leave you alone. And we'll be making it clear later that any media organisation which uses photographs taken without your consent will not be invited to future press confer-ences. That usually does the trick.'

I stare at her, still not able to take it all in. I am not

ready for this. All I want to do is get Ella back. I don't want photographers outside our house, everyone knowing our business.

I blink back the tears. Alex puts his arm around me.

'Come on,' says Claire. 'Let's go and put the kettle on and you can ask me anything you want to know.'

Alex leads her through to the kitchen and closes the door behind us.

'Our son's still asleep,' he says.

I glance around. Yesterday's breakfast things are still on the counter, the debris of a life put on hold scattered all over the place. 'Sorry about the mess,' I say, hurriedly clearing a corner of the kitchen table.

'Don't be daft. I'm here to help you, not inspect your kitchen.'

I manage a hint of a smile and sit down.

'Tea or coffee?' Alex asks her.

'Coffee, but I'll do it. The last thing you need right now is to be looking after strangers in your own home. Just show me where everything is – you can never find anything in kitchens these days – and I'll get on with it.'

Her eyes meet mine for a moment. I know I look like shit, but she is either kind enough to pretend not to notice or if she has, it really doesn't bother her.

Alex opens the cupboard where the teas and coffee are kept and pulls out the cutlery drawer.

'Great,' she says. She walks over, picks up the kettle

and, finding there is enough water in it for three, flicks up the switch.

'Right,' she says, turning to us, 'what do you want to know first?'

I look at Alex. It is hard to know where to start.

'Just exactly what's going on, I guess,' he says. 'How you're trying to find her.'

'OK. Well the detective in charge is called Detective Superintendent Johnston. He's good. I know you probably think I would say that about anyone, but believe me I wouldn't. I've only worked in West Yorkshire for a year but he's one of the best ones I've come across.

'He's leading the detectives on the case, but we've also got police search and rescue people on it. They're specialists in missing persons cases and they go through all the possibilities very methodically, ruling things out, looking at all the possible scenarios.'

'Like what?' I ask.

She looks at me and Alex in turn. 'I'm going to give it to you straight,' she says 'It's how I work. If that's OK with you?'

We both nod.

'Well, the first thing they have to consider is whether the person wants to be missing. Obviously with a child as young as yours, that's highly unlikely to be the case. Then, whether they are missing but don't know it, such as someone with Alzheimer's. Again, your daughter doesn't fit the profile for that. They also look at whether the person might be missing due to an accident, which is one of the scenarios they're actively considering, and lastly whether there is third-party involvement.'

She stops, the words hanging in the air. I hate that she makes it sound like an insurance case. This is Ella we're talking about. Ella's life.

'Someone took her,' I said.

'OK. Why do you think that?'

'She wouldn't leave the park on her own, she just wouldn't.'

'I know it seems unlikely, but we still have to examine that possibility. We can't rule things out until we know they haven't happened.'

'I'm her mum. And I know she wouldn't do it.'

'What about the balloon?'

'Not even for that.'

Alex puts his hand on my shoulder. 'The trouble is,' he says, 'we can't work out how someone could take her and nobody saw or heard anything. That doesn't make sense either because we're both sure she would have kicked up one hell of a row.'

'Which is why we're examining all the possible scenarios. Such as whether it might be someone she knew.'

'I gave them a list of everyone she knows yesterday,' I say, 'but I can't believe for a minute any of them would have anything to do with it.'

'Sometimes it's like that,' says Claire. 'Sometimes

nothing makes sense. It's like looking for the missing piece of a jigsaw.'

'Do you ever find them alive?' I ask. 'The kids that go missing, I mean. It's just that you only ever hear about the dead ones.'

She pauses and looks at us both again. 'We do,' she said. 'You'd be surprised how often we do, but it's like you say, that's not news, is it? And when you go to the press conference this afternoon, you've got to be thinking that she's alive, you've got to appeal to someone who might have taken her to bring her back, you've got to get people looking for her, believing that they can actually find her.'

'Do you believe she's still alive?' I ask.

'Yes,' she replies without hesitation. 'And I'll be here for you until we find her, OK?'

Alex's phone beeps with a message. He picks it up and checks it.

'Anything?' I ask.

He shakes his head. 'Just Otis's piano teacher. She's ill, says there'll be no lesson next week.'

I nod, thinking that there will at least be one piece of good news for him when he wakes up.

'The first thing I need to ask you to do,' says Claire, looking at me, 'is to get together what we call a go bag. Basically, it's a bag with Ella's essentials in it – a change of clothes, pyjamas or nightie, underwear, that sort of thing. And your stuff too. So, if we get a call and we think we've found her you can just pick it up and go, wherever she is and whatever time of day or night it is.'

'Right,' I say, trying not to think about what state she might be in if that happened. 'I'll go and do that then.'

'Do you want my stuff in it too?' asks Alex.

Claire looks down before answering. 'No, thanks. We usually advise just the mother to go in these cases.'

'But I'd want to go too,' says Alex.

'I understand that. But sometimes children might not want to see a man, even their own father. Depending on the circumstances.'

Alex looks at me, hurt colliding with blind fear on his face. He gets up from the table and walks slowly out of the kitchen.

The dull ache in my abdomen turns into a stabbing pain.

Chloe texts me at seven thirty, which for her is ridiculously early. 'Have they found her yet?' She knows of course that I would have told her if they had. What she really means is *Can you give me a call and tell me what the hell is going on, only I haven't got much credit left?*

I call her straight back. She answers almost before the end of the first ring.

'No,' I say. 'Not yet.'

'I'm coming home then.'

'You really don't need to, Chloe.'

'Of course I do, my little sister's missing.'

'OK, we'll transfer you some money for your ticket. What about Robyn, what does she want to do?'

'She says she'll come back with me.'

'Well tell her we'll pay for her ticket too. And say sorry. The last thing we wanted was to ruin the holiday for both of you.'

'People have been texting and putting stuff on Facebook. It's like everyone knows.'

'I know. The police say the more people are looking for her the better.'

'They're going to find her, aren't they?'

'I hope so, love.' There is a silence on the other end of the phone. 'Right, well as soon as you've got your trains sorted let me know. One of us will pick you up from the station.'

'What are the police saying, like? Do they think someone's taken her?'

'They can't say for sure. It's one of the things they're looking at though.'

Another silence. I imagine her screwing her eyes up tight, the wind blowing her long brown hair across her face. She shouldn't have to be dealing with this. I'm not sure she's strong enough to cope, really I'm not.

'They've asked us to do a press conference this afternoon. Just so you know.'

She manages a muted noise of some kind. She is trying hard not to cry. Trying to hold herself together. If I

say what I want to say to her it might just push her over
the edge.

'I'll let you know as soon as we hear anything, OK?'

Something akin to a strangled squeak travels down
the phone before she hangs up and I am left standing
there with the phone in my hand, wondering how the
hell I made such a hash of my relationship with my
daughter. Possibly the only daughter I have left.

I don't even hear Otis get up. He simply arrives in the
kitchen in his *Dr Who* onesie with his hair sticking up
all over the place. He stares at Claire, who is sitting at
the kitchen table with a coffee in her hand.

'Morning, love. This is Claire,' I say, going over and
putting a hand on his arm. 'She's a policewoman and
she's going to help us find Ella.'

'Hello, Otis,' says Claire.

He looks up at me with a scowl. 'Hasn't Ella come
home yet?'

'No. But the police are looking everywhere for her.'

'We're doing our best, Otis,' says Claire. 'And we won't
stop looking until we find your sister.'

'Can I show her my map?' asks Otis. It takes a second
for me to remember what he is talking about.

'Yes, of course. Why don't you go and get it?'

He runs off upstairs. I turn to Claire.

'He did a map last night,' I explain. 'Of all the hiding
places in the park.'

Otis bursts back in brandishing the map and thrusts it in front of Claire. 'It's like a treasure map,' he explains, 'only the crosses are all good hiding places and the treasure is finding Ella in one of them.'

Claire takes it and studies it before looking up at Otis. 'This is brilliant. Would you mind going through it in detail with me and then I can pass it on to the detective in charge?'

Otis has the nearest thing I've seen to a smile on his face since he found out. He sits down next to Claire as she takes out her notebook. I nod at her and manage a little smile. She is good at this, I think.

The press conference is in Bradford; Claire says there isn't enough room at the police station in Halifax. I don't understand what she means until we pull up outside and I see the rows of TV vans.

'Jesus,' I say, 'is that all for us?'

'Yeah,' replies Claire. 'They're all inside though. They've been asked not to take any pictures until the press conference.'

I look at Alex, who squeezes my hand.

'Are you two both sure about this?' Claire asks, glancing in the rear-view mirror. 'You can back out now if you want. Everyone will understand.'

'No,' I say. 'Not if it's our best chance of getting her back. We'll do it.'

'Great,' says Claire. 'They might seem a bit scary when

you walk in, but remember they're actually there to help us – they're on your side.'

We get out of the car and Claire leads us into the building and along a maze of corridors until we're outside a room marked B8. She knocks on the door and we go in. A middle-aged uniformed copper is sitting inside, next to a young woman in plain clothes. Claire introduces us.

'DS Johnston,' the copper says, standing up and offering his hand. 'Thank you so much for agreeing to this. I appreciate it can't be easy.'

I look at him and nod, not knowing what to say. Alex holds my hand a bit tighter.

'This is Joanne Anderson, our head of media relations,' he continues. I nod at her. She doesn't look old enough to be head of anything, to be honest.

'I'm sure Claire will have explained the whole process,' continues DS Johnston, 'but we're here to help you prepare. Have you written a statement? Would you like us to go through it with you?'

Alex hands him the folded sheet of A4 paper from his pocket that we wrote with Claire's help earlier. I notice that his hand is shaking.

Half an hour later DS Johnston leads us into a large conference room. It is hard to work out what hits me first, the blinding flashes of the cameras or the noise of the shutters going off. It's like they are actually shooting at us. For a moment I am expecting Alex to fall to the ground, clutching his chest. He doesn't though. He follows DS Johnston to the table and sits down. I sit down next to him, blinking, Claire and Joanne on my other side. As I raise my head when Joanne starts talking, the flashes go off again. It is me their lenses are pointing at, my pain they are trying to capture. I want to scream at them, tell them to fuck off and leave us alone. And then I remember that we are here because we need them, because they are our best hope of finding Ella, and that, as DS Johnston has explained, they are giving us the opportunity to appeal directly to someone who may have her or know where she is.

I take a deep breath, look up and stare straight at them, as if down the barrel of a gun. I hear the shutters firing and squint a little at the flashes, but I am not going to give the person who took Ella the satisfaction of seeing me in tears or of breaking down in public. I am not going to be intimidated and crack up in front of all these people. I am going to be strong.

DS Johnston is reading through his appeal for information, asking for the public to help fill in the gap between the last time I saw Ella and the moment I called the police. He mentions the balloon. They ask a lot of questions about that. And about the police investigation. To be fair, they are better than I expected. None of them has a pop at us. They ask what the public can do to help find Ella. I feel that Claire was right, that they are actually on our side. I make eye contact with a couple of them, a woman with hair almost as scruffy as mine, a guy wearing the same Fat Face shirt as Alex has at home. I realise for the first time that they probably have kids and that they are thinking what everyone else is thinking – thank God this didn't happen to me. DS Johnston takes the last question and then turns to us. I know it is our turn. I stare straight in front as Alex unfolds his piece of paper and starts to read,

'Ella is a very special little girl. She is cheeky, mischievous and ridiculously competitive. She likes trying to beat her big brother at things and was hugely proud of the fact that she had just learned how to climb the frame to the big slide in the park all by herself.'

I swallow hard as he continues.

'She is chatty and friendly, not at all shy, and she is forever asking questions. She also loves playing hide-and-seek, which is what she was doing in the park yesterday.'

I dig what is left of my nails into my palms.

'If you saw her at any point yesterday and have not yet spoken to the police, please come forward. We believe someone must have seen her leave the park, whether that was with someone else or on her own. If you did, please, please come forward and tell the police what you saw, even if you think it isn't important.'

I continue staring straight ahead, I'm not sure I even blink. I want the man who has Ella to see my face, to know that he is not going to break me. And I won't give up until I get her back.

'And if you are holding Ella, please understand that you need to let her go. She belongs with us, her family. She has an older brother and sister who are worried sick about her. Just let her go, drop her off somewhere and let her come home to us.'

I hear Alex's voice falter for a moment, I bite my bottom lip, determined to hold it together, while the barrage of flashes lights up the room.

Alex folds the piece of paper up and puts it back in his pocket. I squeeze his hand under the table. They are not going to ask questions; DS Johnston thinks that will be too much for us today. I glance across at Claire. She nods at me, gives a tiny hint of a smile. I get to my feet. For a second the room sways in front of me. I worry that I might collapse in front of them and then he really would know what he has done to me. I must not give in to him, I must not let him see my pain. I take a deep breath and walk slowly out of the room, staring straight ahead.

10

MURIEL

'Are you taking me to school today?' The child looks up at me with hopeful eyes as I pour my second cup of tea of the morning.

'It's a Sunday. There's no school on a Sunday.'

'Does Monday come after Sunday? I'm starting school on Monday.'

'It is Monday tomorrow but we're not going anywhere. We'll be doing your lessons at home.'

'Is Miss Roberts coming here?'

'No, I'll be teaching you.'

'But you're not my teacher. Miss Roberts is my teacher and I've got a coat peg with my name on it at school.'

The child's voice is starting to get hysterical again. She must get it from her mother. Younger women seem to do a lot of shrieking. It is one of the reasons I don't have a television.

'Well, I'm going to be your teacher for now.'

'I want to go to school with the big boys and girls.'

'The big boys have been naughty. You know that.'

'Is that why I can't go to school?'

'It's not safe outside. The policeman asked me to keep you in.'

'Will Otis have to stay in too?'

I take another sip of tea. I do not like doing this, but it is just going to be easier all round.

'I expect so.'

'And Charlie?'

'Who's Charlie?'

'I told you. Charlie Wilson who lives next door to me. His name is on the coat peg next to mine.'

'Charlie too.'

She sits swinging her legs. I wonder if I have managed to placate her sufficiently for now.

'When are they going to catch the naughty boys?'

'I don't know. The important thing is that we keep safe inside until they do.'

'Is Mummy still poorly?'

'Yes, she is.'

'Will she be able to go to work?'

'I don't know.'

'If Mummy doesn't go to work we won't have enough

money to put dinner on the table and pay for me to do nice things.'

I look across at her and raise my eyebrow. Clearly someone in her family works very hard to justify her actions.

'Well, you can do lots of nice things here with me. And I'll teach you everything you need to know.'

'Did you teach Matthew?'

'I taught him a lot of things.'

'But did he go to big school?'

'Goodness,' I say, finishing my tea and putting the cup gently down in the saucer. 'You do ask rather a lot of questions.'

I hear the rattle of the letter box.

'Is that Daddy?' she asks.

'I've told you. Daddy's not coming. He's asked me to keep you safe here with me.'

I stand up and hand her the ball of string on the dresser. 'Why don't you see if Melody would like a game with this?' She slides down from the stool, takes the string from me and hurries over to Melody.

I go to the front door. I am concerned it may be another flyer but it isn't. Only the newspaper. The paper boy always has a real struggle to get it through the letter box. They don't think about practical things like that, the people who produce these newspapers. They simply keep adding supplements, as if we all cannot function without knowing ten things you can do with aubergines.

I pull the newspaper from the letter box and unfold it. For a moment I don't understand. I think they must have put the local paper through by mistake. They haven't though. There is photo of the girl on the front page of the *Sunday Times*. The same photo which was on the flyer. The one of her in the stripy dress. The dress which was on my rotary washing line in the backyard yesterday. The dress which I ironed last night and is now in the airing cupboard upstairs. I hold on to the banister to steady myself. It is national news. I feel a clawing sensation inside. It is me. I have done this. I am the cause of this whole kerfuffle. Half the police force is searching for this child, and she is here with me, playing with a ball of string with Melody. It would be funny if it wasn't such a huge waste of resources. I wonder for a second if I should phone them. Tell them that I took the child but only for her own good. I know they won't understand though. They will probably arrest me or even charge me with something. I remember reading about a woman who was arrested shortly after that toddler was taken by those boys in Liverpool. She'd spotted a little girl crying because she'd lost her mother and all she did was take her by the hand, and the next thing she knew the police grabbed her and accused her of child abduction. People get so hysterical about these things. All common sense goes out of the window.

I open the newspaper. There is a photograph of the parents too. They made an appeal for her safe return at a press conference. The mother looks awful. Her hair is straggly and she doesn't appear to be wearing make-up. The father is unshaven. He is not even wearing a collar and tie. And then I read what she said, the mother. About how she only turned her back for a minute and her daughter was gone. Well, she is lying. It was a lot more than a minute. And she says that after the child fell over, she cleaned her up. She didn't. She barely brushed the dirt off her hands with her fingers. There was nothing clean about it. I was the one who cleaned her up, and maybe if the mother hadn't been so busy on her mobile phone she would have realised that she hadn't looked after her properly at all. And now she is expecting people to feel sorry for her. The gall of the woman.

They won't buy it. The police will see through this charade very quickly. Once you start lying you are in trouble. And when the police dig deeper it will all come tumbling out. The lies. The neglect. Everything. I will simply hold the fort here until the police are ready for me to return her safely to them. I will not be swayed from my duty by this emotional blackmail. I will give the child the protection she needs. Provide a place of safety. Be the mother that her own mother is clearly not capable of being.

I hide the newspaper in the magazine rack and hurry back to the kitchen. The child is still playing with Melody.

The ball of string has pretty much unravelled. Melody is tangled up in it. The child is smiling, the delight dancing in her eyes as she flicks one end of the string. It is good to see her laughing after all the tears. She will be happy here, I know that. And I will be happy too.

'How would you like to start learning the piano?' I ask her later, when Melody finally tires of playing and retreats to her basket.

She turns to look at me. 'You mean like Otis does?'

'Yes, proper lessons.'

'Will I be better than him?'

'You might if you practise harder.'

'Otis doesn't like practising. He says it's boring, and sometimes he goes outside to play football and Daddy gets cross about it.'

'Doesn't anyone else in your family play?'

'My nanna plays and she bought Otis the keyboard and piano lessons for Christmas. Otis wanted a Lego Hobbit house.'

'Yes, well, we don't always get what we want, do we? We have to be grateful for what we receive.'

'Nanna gave me a painting stand.'

'An easel?'

'Yes,' she says, obviously pleased I knew the right word. 'And Grandma gave me Lego Friends, and Mummy said she didn't understand that I wanted the same Lego as Otis, not the pink one.'

'But I'm sure you still thanked her nicely for it in your letter.'

'What letter?'

'The thank-you letter you wrote.'

The child looks at me blankly. I shake my head and sigh. I shouldn't be surprised by now, I really shouldn't.

'Right. Come and sit on the piano stool and we'll make a start.'

The child looks up at me. Her face is serious, her voice almost a whisper. 'I don't know what those little squiggles on lines in Otis's piano book mean.'

'It doesn't matter, dear. I'll teach you.'

She nods. The corners of her mouth turn up a little.

'Can I play to Daddy when I get home?'

'Let's see how we get on, shall we?'

She sits on the stool, her legs dangling. I pull out the footrest for her.

'What about those?' she asks, pointing to the pedals.

'There is no need for pedals yet. It's your hands we need to start with.'

She holds out her hands as if for inspection. 'Have my germs gone now?'

'Yes, they're fine.' Her fingers are reasonably long but slightly chubbier than Matthew's were at her age.

'Now, shape your hand like a bridge, with your fingers curved and on their tips. Like this.'

She looks at my hand and then copies. 'Like I'm going to tickle Melody,' she says.

'Yes. I suppose that is another way of looking at it. Tickle the piano keys then. Very gently.'

'The black ones or the white ones?'

'It doesn't matter for now. I just want you to get used to having your hands in the correct position.'

The child's fingers curl gently over the notes and she produces the most delicate of tinkling noises.

'Wonderful,' I say. 'Now always remember to hold your fingers curved like that. Never let them flatten out. Flat fingers don't produce the right sound.'

'Does Otis have flat fingers?'

'Not now he doesn't. But it took a long time for me to get him to stop.'

'Am I going to be better than Otis?'

'Let's hope so, shall we?'

She nods and tinkles some more. I hear Matthew playing, his fingers so delicate he sometimes barely seemed to touch the keys. He hums along to the tune. He thinks he is only humming inside his head. I don't tell him that he is humming out loud. The world is full of people who only hum in their heads. He will have the rest of his life for that. I want him to hum out loud while he can. I want his heart to sing with the music. His body to vibrate to the notes. Sometimes, while he is playing I am able to forget the world outside. To simply close my eyes and immerse myself in the moment. To breathe in the very essence of aliveness.

'Piano lady, are you asleep?'

The child's voice cuts through to me. I open my eyes.

I see the outline of Matthew. Matthew's clothes, his hair, his pale skin.

'Just resting my eyes,' I say to the child. 'Now, we're going to learn all about the different notes on the piano. Do you know your ABC?'

'I don't know.'

'Your alphabet, dear, from A to Z. Do you know it?'

She shakes her head.

'Right, well you can start now. We only need to know A to G. I think we can manage that. Point to the black keys for me.'

The child points.

'They are grouped in twos and threes. Show me the two black keys together in the middle.'

She points again.

'Now, the white key to the left of those is middle C. That's very important to remember. You can always find the other notes if you can find middle C.'

I glance down at the child. She has a glazed look in her eyes. I'm not sure any of this is going in.

'Where's middle C?'

She hesitates then points to the white key to the right of the two black ones.

'You don't know your left from right, do you?'

She shakes her head. 'Mummy says they'll help me with them at school.'

'Matthew knew them before he started school, you know.'

She looks down. Her bottom lip is trembling.

I sigh, knowing full well what is about to happen.

'I want my Mummy,' she sobs. 'I want to go home. I don't want to play piano any more.' She screws up her face as she wails.

'We'll leave it for now then,' I say, standing up.

'I want to go home.'

'You know why you can't do that.'

'I don't care about naughty boys.'

'Well the police do and your parents do. Besides, I told you, your mother isn't well enough to look after you.'

'Has she got a poorly tummy?'

'No. It's a different sort of poorly. Her head's poorly.'

'Did she bump it?'

'No, but she's not thinking straight. She doesn't know how to look after you.'

She frowns at me. 'Will the doctor make her better?'

'It's not something the doctor can mend. It's inside her head.'

The frown deepens. I think it's right that I do this now. I need to prepare her for what is going to happen. It will make it easier for her in the long run, even if it is going to be hard now. I sit back down next to her on the piano stool.

'Your mummy hasn't been looking after you very well, I'm afraid. Remember when you arrived here? The mess your hands were in? Your mummy should have taken care of them.'

'She said we had to go and get Otis first.'

'Yes, well. It seems your mother is often in a rush. No time to cut your hair or your nails. Or even to feed you properly.'

'Mummy doesn't let me have ice creams. She says they make your teeth go bad and people get fat if they eat too many ice creams.'

'Well, I've never heard such nonsense. Matthew used to have ice creams in the summer, and they never did him any harm.'

'Are you going to get me an ice cream?'

'I will do but I can't go to the park at the moment.'

'Because of the naughty boys?'

'That's right.'

'Grandma gets them from her freezer. She has choc ices in there.'

I stand up straight away, cursing myself for not having thought of that earlier.

'And so do I.'

'Can I have one? Can I have a choc ice?'

'I'm not hearing the magic word.'

'Pleeease.'

I smile at her, stand up and leave the room with her following behind me like a faithful Labrador. There is a lightness in my step as I go through to the kitchen. And a smile on my face when I hand the plate with the choc ice on it to her and watch her slowly unwrap it, pop a broken piece of the chocolate into her mouth and then take a bite of the soft ice cream below. I can do this. I can make her happy. I can be the mother she needs. And she does need me. Even if she doesn't know it yet.

She cries less at bedtime than the previous two. Only by ten minutes or so, but it is something. She is coming to accept it. That her place is here with me. Little by little, the resistance will wane. The important thing is not to listen to the crying but to the gaps between. I remember that from when Matthew learned to go to sleep by himself. Some mothers would crack after a few minutes. Would go in and cuddle them, try to soothe them. They didn't understand that once you had done that, there was no going back. The baby would cry and cry until you went into them again. You have to be strong about these things. Know that you are doing the right thing and not be swayed by your emotions. Matthew learned soon enough. Five nights and then I barely had a whimper from him. And babies taught to go to sleep without a fuss grow up to become children who go through life without a fuss. Matthew was never a needy child. Never.

I picture him outside in the park now. Wrapping himself in the tree canopy. Understanding that I cannot come to him. Knowing that it doesn't mean I love him any less. Simply that the bond between us is such that he does not need me fussing over him all the time.

I go to the guest room and switch on the computer which I keep in there. It is a desktop model, rather old and no doubt obsolete by now. It does not matter to me though. I use it very rarely. Only for the occasional email and a bit of online shopping. Mostly the grocery order. Ocado is a godsend for those who can't abide the weekly shop. The very thought of stepping inside a supermarket turns me cold: the screaming children, the frazzled mothers, the cashiers who don't even make eye contact with you during the entire transaction. No, I don't miss that one iota.

And the Ocado drivers are so polite too. It's like they have been to some sort of finishing school which the rest of the population of Halifax doesn't have access to.

I check my weekly trolley and am about to press Place Order when I realise that my normal shop will not be sufficient. I need to order for two. For a child. My finger hovers over the mouse. I am not at all sure what young children eat these days. Crumpets obviously and pasta – she has mainly eaten pasta since she arrived. And she asked for tomato ketchup and fish fingers, neither of which I had in. I do a search for fish fingers. It comes up with twenty-three different products. I have no idea which ones she prefers. I choose Birds Eye because Matthew liked them and because I can't bring myself to order anything with Jamie Oliver's name attached. Tomato ketchup is just as bad: twenty-seven products, though at least Mr Oliver's name isn't featured on any of them. I go with Heinz, again on the basis that Matthew liked it. I add some more things she has asked for: baked beans, cheese slices, little sausages, Coco Pops, Magnum ice creams – the little ones, because the full-size ones are so expensive and far too big for a child that age anyway. The only thing that comes up when I search for SpongeBob Squarepants are some cartons of orange juice drink. I put them in my trolley. I won't give the treats to her all at once. I will ration them to one or two a day. That will give her something to look forward to, and I can use them to stop the tears when they come. Not that there will be so many tears as the days pass. I am quite sure of that.

I place the order. The amount I pay is both alarming and satisfying at the same time. Shopping for one is not something anyone ever aspires to.

I am about to turn off the computer when I remember the press conference. It will probably be on the Internet somewhere. I hesitate, unsure whether I should watch it. The media are good at wringing the emotion out of these things. Everything is always painted as black or white. Life is not like that, of course. Life is about all the shades of grey in between.

I go to the BBC website. It is the only news one I ever bother with. Matthew showed me how to find it. I like the fact that you only have to click on the stories you want to read. Not like listening to the ten o'clock news, when you have to listen to all the stupid things that stupid people around the world are doing before you get to the bit at the end about the royal family, or whatever it is you are actually interested in. That's why I decided we didn't need a TV. It is bad enough that these people exist without inviting them into my living room on a regular basis.

It is there. The photo of the child in the stripy dress is at the top of the page. I scroll down the story until I get to the video of the press conference and press Play. I recognise the father instantly, though he has always been clean shaven when he has come with the boy. Usually he has a very casual, couldn't-care-less air about him but that has gone too. His body is taut, his fingers twitchy. She, on the other hand, sits there with a scowl on her face. Looking for all the world as if it is everybody else's fault, not hers.

A police officer introduces himself as the detective leading the enquiry. There are two other police officers, both women, sitting next to the mother. The detective introduces the parents as Lisa and Alex Dale. I watch as he outlines the 'facts' of the case. It is ridiculous, of course, because they aren't facts at all. They are her version of events. A version which she has carefully crafted to give the best possible impression of herself. So it comes across as if she is some poor innocent victim who just happened to be in the wrong place at the wrong time. The policeman doesn't mention the way she neglected her child when it fell over. Or the fact that she was more interested in answering her mobile phone than keeping an eye on the child. He has clearly accepted her version of events. If this is the detective leading the case, I dread to think what the others are like.

Every now and again they go to a shot of the mother and father. They are stony-faced, as if they are assuming the worst. The mother looks awful. Her hair is lank. She appears to have put a bit of lip gloss on but it only succeeds in accentuating how pale and lifeless the rest of her face is. Guilt does that. Sucks the life out of you.

The policeman says the father is going to read a prepared statement. I watch as he gets a piece of paper out and holds it in front of him, hands shaking, his voice trembling as he starts to read.

I try not to listen to the words. He will have written what he was told to write by the police or what she told him to write. The mother sits next to him, her jaw set, her eyes staring straight ahead. She doesn't appear in the slightest bit sorry for what she has done. She does at least draw the line at crying. Maybe she knows that she couldn't do it convincingly. When the father gets to the bit where he asks for anyone with information to get in touch with the police she looks up. As she does so, she is greeted with a battery of flashes. She doesn't even appear to blink; simply stares out at the photographers, her face hard and uncompromising.

When the father finishes reading he folds up the

piece of paper and gives an audible sigh. I watch as they stand up, the mother still staring straight ahead. You can see it in her eyes, the fear. They probably think she is frightened of what has happened to her child. Only I know that she is scared of being found out. Scared of the truth.

11

LISA

We are all sitting at the kitchen table. It has become like some kind of war cabinet, each of us waiting for news from the front while trying desperately to think of something constructive to do or to come up with the important piece of information which hasn't been thought of yet.

Mum gets up to put the kettle on; she makes the most of the opportunity to be useful when Claire isn't here. I say that like Claire is part of the family. In reality we have only known her for twenty-four hours, but real time doesn't exist any more. It is like we are living in an alternative universe where one earth day equates to about a year of our lives. If we do get Ella back, I wonder if it will turn out that she was only actually missing for a few minutes in real time, if maybe this has only stretched into days in my head. It is a big if, though. There are lots of big ifs.

'We've done pretty much every lamp post within about a two-mile radius of the park,' says Dad. 'We're going to go further out today, do the main roads out of Halifax and that.'

I look at him, his eyes dull and heavy, sitting there thumbing through the pile of MISSING posters one of Tony's mates had printed yesterday. His face wasn't the best-preserved thing before the start of all of this; I dread to think what it's going to look like by the end. If there is an end, that is. Sometimes they don't find missing children. I know that. I can't imagine what kind of hell that must be, having this be the state in which you exist for the rest of your life. I wonder if the parents of those kids ever sleep again or if they simply run on anxiety.

I've been thinking about them a lot, the other parents. The ones I remember from the news. I wonder if I'll end up as one of them, if people will say, 'Ahhh, poor cow,' whenever someone mentions my name or they see my face on the television. Or whether they will say, 'I think she did it, you know. I think it was her, the hard-faced cow.' Someone said that on Twitter after the press conference – that I was a hard-faced cow. I don't know why I looked. It was stupid of me. I don't even like Twitter; I'm only on it for work. But Ella's name was trending and I clicked on it to see what people were saying. And that was one of the things they said. It seems I'm the wrong sort of mother. Apparently I should have been bawling my eyes out, and not doing so was 'not human' according to some people. Like someone has written a book about how mothers of missing children should behave and I forgot to read it. I haven't told Alex. It would only wind him up. Maybe he looked too and decided not to tell me. Maybe people all over the country are having conversations about whether they think we are guilty or not. Whether the cops are going to end up digging up our patio. I want to scream at everybody to piss off. That it is none of their fucking business. It is though. We are everyone's business now.

It was the main headline on the news last night. Mum told me – we couldn't bear to watch it. I mean, why would you choose to watch yourself going through hell when you're doing it anyway? There's no point, is there? The weirdest thing was thinking about other people watching it, people who know us, not close friends like, but the other mums at school, clients from the gym. I can't help wondering what they were thinking. It doesn't matter, of course, I don't give a toss really. But I still can't help wondering.

'Thanks,' I say, remembering what Dad has just said. To be honest, I can't help feeling that lamp posts should be reserved for posters of missing dogs, not children. I think of all the dogs which will piss up those lamp posts while their owners look at the photo of Ella. I can't say anything though. Dad is trying his best, and doing this is his way of coping. I am not going to discourage him.

'I was thinking maybe we should set up a Facebook page too,' says Tony. 'Call it Find Ella and get people to like it. I mean more people probably use Facebook than buy newspapers, and they can share it to people all across country, across world even.'

Mum puts the tray of mugs down heavily on the table and gives Tony a look. She doesn't think he should have said 'world'. I can see this from her face. She doesn't want to think that Ella might not even be in this country any more. To be honest, I am not that bothered. I don't care if they find her in Mablethorpe or Marrakesh; I just want her back.

I look at Alex, who is always allowed a veto when it comes to my family. It's only fair because he does the same for me with his family. The sign is a nose scratch, although they don't know this of course. Alex's hands stay firmly around his mug of coffee.

'Yeah, thanks. It's worth a try,' I say. 'Anything's got to be worth a try.'

Mum squeezes my hand. She has been doing that a lot since Friday. That and looking as if someone has taken hold of all her internal organs and is squeezing them incredibly tightly.

'What time is Otis coming back?' she asks. Otis has gone to play with Ben, his best friend from school. His mum texted me to offer. I asked him before I replied but he said yes pretty much straight away. I think he was just grateful for the chance to escape the house for a bit.

'Four o'clock. He wants to be here when Chloe gets home.'

'Ahh, that's nice. And what time are your parents getting here, Alex?'

'About two. Depending what the traffic's like on the M1.'

She nods and smiles. Sylvia and Graham do not come up very often, maybe two or three times a year, if that. It is, as they always say, a long way from Surrey.

'Ah, well it'll be lovely to see them.'

It won't, of course. They're only coming because Ella is missing and they told Alex they feel they should offer their 'emotional support'. It feels like everyone is gathering for a family funeral: Chloe returning from abroad, the in-laws up from Surrey. I'll have some long-lost second cousin from Aberystwyth turning up next. I want to tell them all to piss off – not Chloe, obviously, but pretty much everyone else. I want to shout at them that Ella isn't dead and they should stop gathering around her graveside waiting for her body to appear. But I can't do that because actually I don't know if it's true.

There is a knock at the front door. Claire texted me to say she was on her way but it still turns my stomach. Mum gets up to answer it.

'No, I'll go,' I say. She sits back down again. I go into

the lounge and peek through a crack in the curtains first to see if there are any photographers outside. The road is empty, as it was when Mum and Dad and Tony arrived earlier and when we got back from the press conference yesterday. Maybe it's done the trick, maybe they won't bother us again. Surely there are only so many photos of me looking like shit that people will want to look at.

When I open the door I look at Claire's face. I made her promise to tell me straight away if it is ever bad news. She does that little sympathetic half-smile thing so that I know it isn't.

'Manage any sleep?' she asks.

I shake my head. 'I think Alex might have got an hour or two.' She nods and follows me through to the kitchen. She met my family last night after the press conference. Mum greets her like an old friend.

'Hello, Claire, love. This is an early start for you. and on a Sunday too.'

Claire glances at me. I shrug. Mum makes it sound like she is doing us a favour. Maybe she doesn't want to admit to herself that Claire is a police officer, sent to deal with a possible child abduction, not some Avon lady who has popped by on the weekend with her order.

'We've had a lot of calls following the press conference,' Claire says. 'More than a thousand so far. Nothing in the way of major leads at the moment, I'm afraid, but the detectives are sifting through all of them, identifying possible leads to chase up.'

'Anyone who saw her in the park after I did?' I ask.

'Not yet but, like I say, they've got a lot of information still to sift through.'

I nod. Maybe it will be the last call they come to, like it's always the last place you look that you find the thing you've lost. Maybe it will all be over in a few hours. I brighten for a moment but then realise I might not want it to be over. Not if over is my worst nightmare.

Claire is still standing looking at us. She fiddles with her glasses.

'What is it?' I ask.

'I'm afraid they need to interview all family members today,' she says.

'Why?' I ask.

'It's standard procedure in these cases. They want to double-check every single detail and piece of information. Make sure there's nothing they've missed.',

Dad slams his mug down on the table and looks up at her. 'And if you think we believe that crap you're a damn sight dafter than I had you down for.'

'Dad, don't.'

'Well, it's bloody obvious, isn't it? They're trying to pin it on someone in our family. They think one of us did it.'

'I can assure you that isn't the case,' says Claire. 'On an investigation like this we have to do things systematically to make sure nothing gets missed.'

'So you do think we did it,' says Dad. 'Who's in the frame then? Well it's not him, is it,' Dad says, pointing at Alex, 'because he wasn't anywhere near here, and if you think Tina's capable of hurting so much as a fly, you want your head seeing to, so that only leaves me and our Tony. Why don't you just admit that and leave the others out of it?'

'Dad, stop it!' I shout.

Claire looks at me. 'It's OK, Lisa. I understand. I'd be pretty racked off if it was my family, to tell you the truth. I know this is the last thing any of you need right now, but we wouldn't be doing our job properly if we didn't do it, and it might be that if we take detailed statements from all of you, one of you might just think of something that you've forgotten or we haven't thought of, and suddenly we've got a new line of enquiry which could just lead us to Ella.'

Everyone is quiet for a moment before Alex stands up.

'Do me first then,' he says.

Claire looks at him.

'You might be too nice to say it,' he continues, 'but I know how people think and how they point the finger, and that's the last thing we need right now, so the sooner we can all clear our names, the sooner you can concentrate on looking for whoever took Ella.'

I stare at him. I think he probably has read the same stuff I have on Twitter. And maybe other stuff too. He looks across at me. I give him a little smile.

'Thanks,' says Claire. 'If you're sure, I'll run you down the station now.'

Alex nods. Tony stands up too. 'Come on, Dad,' he says. 'We've got nowt to hide. We'll get this out of the way and then go and do leaflets and Facebook and that.'

'Great,' says Claire. 'What are you going to do on Facebook?'

'Tony's setting up a Find Ella page,' says Dad. 'Unless we're not allowed to do that now.'

'Course you are. It's just important to keep me informed, that's all. I can get our press office to link to it from their page, you see.'

Dad looks at her. It is his grudging-respect look, though I'm not sure Claire realises that. Dad stands and picks up his mug of tea. 'Right you are then. Let me finish this and we'll be off.'

Mum lets out a long sigh when they are gone. It is like the war, just the womenfolk left at home to wring their hands. I know full well what she's thinking.

'Try not to worry. Tony'll be fine,' I say.

'I don't like them knowing, that's all. People make judgements. He'll be a bad apple in their eyes.'

'Yeah, well. It was a long time ago. And it wasn't exactly crime of the century, was it?'

'He's my son, though, Lis. I don't like people thinking badly of him.'

'I really don't think they'll be bothered, Mum. All they want to do is find Ella. They're not going to be interested in trawling up his past, are they?'

Mum nods. I think she is about to squeeze my hand again. I'm not sure I can cope with that right now.

'I'd better cancel my clients for tomorrow,' I say, standing up and reaching for my phone.

I am on my own when Alex comes back. Mum has gone home to start on Sunday lunch. If a nuclear bomb went off, when the dust cleared, you would still see Mum doing Sunday lunch for anyone who had survived.

'You OK?' I ask as he comes in and sits down at the table. It is a stupid question. I must get it from Mum.

He simply shrugs.

'What did they ask you?'

He runs his hands through his hair and looks up at the ceiling.

'I had to give them the name and contact number of the client I was meeting. They wanted my car park ticket to prove I was there and everything.'

'Jesus.'

'Yeah, I know.'

We are silent for a moment. 'You've seen what they're saying, haven't you?' I ask. 'On Twitter and Facebook and that.'

'Yeah,' says Alex. 'I didn't say anything in case you hadn't seen it. I didn't want to upset you.'

I look at him and raise my eyebrows. He looks down at his hands.

'Maybe they're right,' I say. 'Maybe I am a crap mother.'

He looks up straight away. 'Come on, you mustn't let them get to you. They're sad bastards with nothing better to do than take a pop at other people. It doesn't matter what they say. None of this is your fault.'

'I bet your mum and dad don't think that. Did they say anything on the phone?'

'Of course they didn't. All they care about is finding Ella. They're not blaming anyone.'

I make a noise and look away. The look of disappointment on Sylvia's face at our wedding still haunts me. Alex tried to claim her discomfort was due to the prawn cocktail disagreeing with her, but it was pretty obvious to me the only thing she had a disagreement with was his choice of bride.

'Did they ask why I didn't cry? Yesterday, at the press conference.'

'No. They asked how you were, that's all.'

'Only because they didn't want to rock the boat by saying anything to you. I bet it's what they wondered when they watched it, though – why their daughter-in-law is some lowlife cold-hearted bitch who doesn't even cry when her own daughter goes missing.'

Alex gets up and comes to me, kneeling down and hugging me as my tears start to fall. Because I am crying now. Away from the lights and the cameras I'm bawling my fucking eyes out.

'Stop it,' he says, brushing away the tears. 'Stop it right there, because I am not going to let you do this to yourself. I know how much you love her and I know what a brilliant mum you are, and I really don't give a toss what anyone else says or thinks.'

'So why didn't I cry at the press conference? That's what I was supposed to do. That's what everyone wanted.'

'And that's probably why you didn't cry. Because I've never known anyone who's less of a victim than you are. And I've never known you do anything simply because it's expected of you. You're your own person, it's one of the things I love about you. And I also love the fact that you don't normally give a toss what anyone else thinks.'

I sniff loudly. 'I didn't want him to think I'm weak,' I say. 'Whoever's got Ella. I didn't want him to think that I'm going to crack.'

I feel Alex's tears mix with my own on my cheek and run down my neck. We stay like that for a long time, huddled together against the world.

'Do you think we'll get her back?' I whisper as he strokes my arm.

'I don't know. I keep wishing I'd told you to ring the police when you first called. I can't believe I took the piss out of you. I feel so stupid. I mean that ten or fifteen minutes could have been crucial.'

'Come on,' I say. 'Don't you start beating yourself up – you'll probably be better at it than me for a start.'

He manages a hint of an upturn at the corner of his mouth. His stubble is rough against my face. I actually like him with stubble, although it feels stupid even to be thinking that right now. I wonder if he won't shave until Ella is found, whether her absence will be recorded unofficially in the length of his facial hair. I am reminded of one of Ella's favourite books, *Mr Follycule's Wonderful Beard*, in which the previously clean-shaven Mr Follycule wishes for a beard and by the next morning has one which grows at such an alarming rate it stretches halfway across town. She once asked Alex if he could wish for a beard to see if his would do that. Maybe that is what he is doing, trying to grow a Mr Follycule beard for Ella. Maybe I will have to stop him when it gets to a foot long. Gently sit him down and tell him that it's no good, it won't make her come back.

'I can't bear to think about what might have happened to her,' he says, closing his eyes for a second.

'I know. Me neither. I think I'd know, though. If it were the worst, like.'

'Do you?'

'Yeah. I'm not sure how. Maybe it's a stupid mum thing, but I think I'd know.'

He pulls me in and buries his face in my hair.

'Let's hope you're right then,' he says. 'Because I'm not sure I could bear it otherwise.'

*   *   *

Sylvia and Graham arrive dead on two. Normally this would irritate the hell out of me. Today I do not give a shit. Sylvia glides in, her silver hair looking immaculate as ever, the scent of lilies impregnated in her skin. She holds my shoulders (possibly the first time she's ever done this in my entire life) and says quietly, 'Hello, Lisa. How are you bearing up, dear?'

I slap her across the face and tell her to take her composed compassion and stick it up her arse. At least I do in my head. In real life I manage to say, 'Oh, you know,' and smile weakly at her.

Sylvia turns to Alex and kisses him on both cheeks, 'This must be so awful for you. I still can't quite believe it.'

Alex nods in acknowledgement and goes to help Graham, who is struggling up the path with their overnight bag. He walks with a slight limp. Did something to his knee years ago while playing golf; nothing they can do, apparently. We go through the same excruciating greeting routine. Now I wish I'd said no when Alex asked if it was OK for them to come. I couldn't though, not really. They are trying to be nice, to say and do the right things. That is the problem though, that is what I am sick of already. Everybody being so bloody nice, behaving so damn reasonably.

Graham struggles to bend down and take his shoes off. When the children were little I made Alex say something about the fact that most people had the courtesy to remove their shoes without being asked to, except he said it in a nicer way than that of course. There was a bit of a do about it. Sylvia said it must be a 'northern thing' as no one did it in Surrey. Dogs not being capable of crapping on the same pavements people walk on in the south of England apparently.

'Don't worry,' I say. 'It's fine.' Graham looks up at me, opens his mouth as if to say something before closing it again, presumably having thought better of it.

'Good journey?' asks Alex.

'Yes, straight through,' says Graham. 'I thought it would be much busier, to be honest. What with it being the end of the school holidays.'

He pauses, having caught my eye. Ella should be starting school tomorrow. Her new uniform is hanging upstairs in her wardrobe. Right now I don't know if she will ever get to wear it.

'Otis is at a friend's,' says Alex, obviously keen to move things on. 'He'll be back about four. We're going to Lisa's mum's for lunch if that's OK. We weren't really up to cooking or going out anywhere.'

'No. No, of course not,' says Sylvia. 'You must both be exhausted, you poor things. We watched the press conference. It didn't feel real, to be honest, seeing you both on the television.'

I try to imagine her watching me, wonder if she criticised what I was wearing. I can't even remember what I was wearing.

'I know,' says Alex. 'It didn't feel real to us either.'

'Do the police have any leads?' asks Graham. 'Anything at all to go on?'

'Nothing major. But there were lots of calls afterwards apparently. They're still going through them all.'

'Well that's something,' says Sylvia. 'Let's hope it's not too long.'

I nod. Although I'm no longer sure exactly what I'm supposed to be hoping for.

'You're looking well, Sylvia,' says Mum as she shows them into the living room. The carpet has been freshly vacuumed; you can smell it and almost see the lines, like when people cut the lawn with those old-fashioned mowers. She has plumped the cushions too. Not even Ella going missing can stop her doing that.

'You really shouldn't have gone to this much trouble,' says Sylvia. 'Not in the circumstances.'

I take it that is the phrase which is going to be used all the time here. This is starting to feel like when someone has cancer and no one dares say the C-word.

'It's no trouble,' Mum says. 'Can't have you driving all that way and not having a decent meal waiting for you; it wouldn't be right.'

I roll my eyes. I can think of a lot of things which aren't right at the moment – being denied a hot meal is not one of them.

'Well, it's very much appreciated,' replies Sylvia. 'Alex always says you do a lovely roast.'

Alex glances at me, perhaps sensing that I might not be able to take much more of this.

'Shall we go through, Tina?' he asks.

'Yes, I'm about ready to serve up. Vince, will you get a bottle of wine out of the fridge.'

'We haven't got one in there, have we?'

'Yes, we have, love,' she replies through gritted teeth.

'Why?'

Mum fixes him with a look.

'We've got guests, haven't we?'

'I've never had wine with my Sunday lunch. Couple of pints of Stella to wash it down, maybe.'

'Really,' says Graham, 'there's no need to go to all this trouble on our account.'

'Don't be silly,' says Mum. 'It's not often we get the chance to entertain.'

'Oh, so it's a fucking social occasion now, is it?' They turn to stare at me. I can't put the cork back in now, though. It is too late for that. 'Ella is missing or has everyone forgotten that?'

'I didn't mean—' starts Mum.

'Yeah, well, whatever,' I say, blinking back the tears as I walk out of the living room and go through to the kitchen. I imagine their faces behind me; Sylvia's raised eyebrows, whispered sympathy, someone saying I'm not coping very well. Maybe I'm not. I don't know what coping is in this situation, mind. As I see it, you either get through each day or you slit your wrists, that's about the size of it.

Alex is the first to make it into the kitchen. He puts his arms around me and kisses me on the top of the head.

'I'm sorry,' I say. 'I shouldn't have lost it like that, but this is doing my head in. It doesn't seem right, us sitting down to a meal when we have no idea where she is.'

'I know. They're hurting too, though.'

'Then why don't they show it? Bawl their eyes out or whatever. It's this pretending everything's fine and avoiding the subject I can't stand.'

'I should have told them not to come.'

'My lot are worse than yours, to be honest.'

'We can go home if you want. We don't have to do this. They'd understand.'

'No,' I say, running my fingers through my hair. 'Mum's gone to a lot of trouble, and your parents haven't driven all that way not to see you.'

'You sure?'

'Yeah. Let's just get it over with.'

Alex goes back into the living room. A few minutes later he returns, followed by Mum.

'I'll get it all dished up now, love,' she says, her eyes moist. 'I'll save a bit for Chloe for when she gets home, mind.'

I nod and manage a hint of a smile. The others come

in and sit down silently at the table. Sylvia appears to still be in shock.

'Vince, give our Tony a shout, will you?' says Mum before turning to Sylvia. 'He's upstairs doing the Facebook thing.'

Sylvia and Graham look blankly at her.

'We've set up a Find Ella Facebook page. Tony says it's got thousands of likes already.'

'Right,' says Graham, seemingly unimpressed.

'Her picture's being shared all over the Internet,' says Dad, coming back into the kitchen.

'And that's a good thing, is it?' asks Sylvia. 'Only I thought parents usually tried to keep photos of their children off the Internet.'

'Yeah, well, this isn't usually, is it?' says Dad, glancing in my direction.

'No,' says Sylvia as I dig my nails into the palms of my hands, 'I suppose it's not.'

Both Alex and Dad offer to pick Chloe up from the station but I am having none of it. I need to get out of the house; I need to breathe, to be with people who aren't trying so hard not to upset me that they are doing so in the process.

I get in the car and glance in the rear-view mirror as if I half-expect to see Ella sitting there, smiling back at me. The empty car seat mocks me for my stupidity. It is so ridiculously silly, losing a child. I've never even been one of those people who mislay little things – bus pass, keys, purse – and yet here I am having lost the most valuable thing in my world.

I drive off, wondering what the hell Chloe must think of me. I sent her off to France with advice about being careful and not doing anything silly and I manage to lose her little sister while she is gone.

Chloe should be my mother really: in so many ways she is more sensible than I am. And she was right about one thing too. Why should she ever listen to my advice again?

I pull into the station car park and find a space at the far end. I look at my watch. I am early. I momentarily rest my head on the steering wheel. All I really want to do is fall asleep. Tiredness is eating away at me from the inside. I thought I'd put sleep deprivation behind me after Ella was through the first few months. Not so, it seems. I'm aware that the only thing which is keeping me going is adrenalin. I have visions of myself deflating into a quivering mess on the ground at the point where that adrenalin is taken away from me. And if she's never found at all, I guess I'll look like those other mums, the ones who have a haunted expression on their faces and deep, dark layers of sadness running through every breath, every movement, every word they utter for the rest of their lives.

Another car pulls into the car park a little further down. I think I recognise Robyn's father at the wheel. I offered to run her home too but Chloe said not to worry as her dad was going to pick her up. I haven't seen him for well over a year. To be honest I hardly ever saw him once Robyn and Chloe went into sixth form, only the odd pick-up or collection, a wave of acknowledgement from the doorway or the car. If he has spotted me I know he won't come over. He was never a great talker and I can't imagine that he'd relish the prospect of having to make small talk with me. He will sit in the car staring straight ahead until Robyn arrives and then drive off without glancing over, thanking God it is not his daughter that this has happened to.

I go to put the radio on then stop myself when I realise it is nearly four o'clock and the last thing I want to do is listen to the news. I'd put a CD on but the only one in the car belongs to Ella and somehow I am not in the mood for the Tweenies at the moment.

I ponder whether to get out of the car and go to meet them on the platform or stay where I am. Having been through the thing of being made to feel like a mortally embarrassing mother (even though Robyn apparently once said that she thought I was pretty fit for a mum), the obvious thing to do is to stay in the car. But if I do, she will just get in, put her belt on and we will probably drive home with barely a word said. I want to touch her, to hold her, to talk to her, even if she doesn't want to do any of those things to me.

I wait until I see the train coming into the station

before getting out of the car, walking through the foyer and along the walkway to the top of the steps. They are already coming up them when I get there, looking somewhat dishevelled with huge rucksacks towering over their backs, faces serious, eyes fixed firmly on the steps. Robyn manages a little smile when she gets to the top and sees me. Chloe is trying to blink away the tears and I decide not to say anything so I don't make it worse.

'Hi,' I say. 'Your dad's in the car park, Robyn.'

She nods.

'I'm so sorry you've had to come home early.'

'It's OK. I hope . . . you know.'

It is my turn to nod.

She gives Chloe a hug. They are a mass of hair, hurt and rucksacks. I remember them on their first day at school, walking in hand in hand, all smart in their school uniforms, that same hair in neat bobbles.

Robyn walks off towards the car park. And then we are standing there, me and my eldest daughter, who still hasn't managed to look me in the eye, and I am overwhelmed with love for her and an enormous sense of having failed her entirely.

'Sorry,' I say again. 'I feel so bad about this – messing up your holiday.'

Chloe shrugs. Her bottom lip is quivering. I am desperate to throw my arms around her but am not sure if I'm allowed to do that any more.

'It's not your fault, is it?' she says. She is only talking about Ella – I understand that – but it is all I need to hear. I step forward and hug her, which isn't easy with the rucksack. At first her body is rigid, but after a few seconds I feel her arms closing around my back, feel her body shaking in time with mine.

'What's happened to her, Mum?'

'I don't know, and I guess I'm trying not to think about it. It's the only way I know how to cope. But the police are looking everywhere for her, they're being really good. We've got this woman, Claire, a family liaison officer. She thinks Ella's alive. Says we can still get her back.'

Chloe sniffs loudly in my left ear. 'I don't understand. How can she just have disappeared?'

'I don't know. I only turned my back for a minute.'

'And you didn't hear her scream or anything?'

'No. I had to take a call on my mobile. For work, you know. I still think I'd have heard her, though. If she had screamed.'

Chloe pulls away and looks at me, her face different now. Her eyes colder and unforgiving. The same as they have been for most of the past year. She says nothing but walks off towards the car park, her purple rucksack bobbing up and down behind her.

12

MURIEL

The child has wet her bed. The smell of urine hits me as soon as I enter Matthew's room. Matthew was never a bed wetter. He was far too careful a child to do that. She is curled up on the other side of the bed, away from the wet patch. Her body shakes as she sobs. Her crying woke me. Although I did go to the bathroom before I came in.

'Never mind, dear,' I say as I open the sash window a little. 'These things happen. We'll whip off the bedclothes and get some fresh ones on.' The crying intensifies. I walk around to her side of the bed. The pillow is almost as wet as the bed sheets. I wonder if she wet the bed at home too. Some children do, even when they are of school age. Perhaps her mother scolded her for it.

'I need to get you up now so I can change the bedclothes.'

She shakes her head. 'I want to go to big school,' she wails, snot running down onto her top lip.

'I told you. I'm going to be teaching you here.'

'I want to go to big school with the big boys and girls. I want to go with Otis.'

'That may well be the case, but it's not possible at the moment.'

A fresh round of sobbing. I sigh and close my eyes for a second. When I look down again the tears have dried. The eyes are wary but resigned to what is about to happen. There is a slight tremble in the lower lip but the upper one remains firm. He is not going to let me down. He is not going to make a scene, however difficult we are both going to find this. Silently I unbutton his pyjama top, as he still finds it tricky to do it himself. The buttons on his shirt aren't as stiff and he can do them up himself; we have practised. He takes down his own pyjama bottoms and steps out of them. He picks up the pants I have laid out on the chair next to the bed and puts them on, followed by the vest. No words pass between us. There is no need for any. We both know this is simply something which has to be done. I take the shirt off its hanger and hold it out for him to put one arm in, followed by the other. I watch as he does up the buttons by himself and nod approvingly when the last one is closed. The school tie is one of those elastic ones. It makes him look about five years older as soon as he puts it on. The short trousers have been pressed and have a crease down the front. His tiny legs look sparrow-like in them. They are still a bit loose around his waist too but there is nothing I can do about that now. Perhaps the school dinners will cause him to fill out a little. All those stodgy puddings. I have never cared for date and syrup sponge and custard myself.

Finally the blazer and cap. Another five years added to him. I'm aware that my little boy is somewhere in there, fighting desperately but wordlessly to get out. I nod again. Letting him know that I understand his anguish but I also appreciate his cooperation in this.

I shepherd him towards the mirror. He is visibly surprised at the reflection which stares back. He peers hard as if trying to spot his other self, the one which was poured into that uniform only a few moments ago.

'Right,' I say, glancing at my watch. 'It's time to go.' I reach down and take his hand. Tiny pale fingers curl around mine.

'You'll be a good boy for Mummy, won't you?'

I look down and a face stares back at me. A face full of fear and confusion.

'Is Mummy coming? Am I going home?'

It is the scent of urine which finally brings me back. That and the dampness of her hand in mine. Matthew never had sweaty palms.

'No,' I say firmly. 'We're going to school downstairs. I've got Matthew's old desk out of the box room for you. We will start with writing. Just as soon as I've got this sorted.'

The face crumples. The hand slips out of mine, I start to strip the sheets off the bed.

The desk is one of those traditional ones, wooden with a hinged lid and an inkwell. The child eyes it with interest, raising the lid and peeking inside.

'Is it a desk like they have at big school?'

'Oh yes. The big boys and girls use ones like this.'

She runs her hand over the lid and sits down gingerly on the stool, like Goldilocks trying out Baby Bear's chair. She looks up, raises half a smile.

'Stay there a moment,' I say. I return with my camera. It is one of those digital ones. Matthew showed me how to download the pictures and print them out myself. I like that I can do that. So much more personal than taking a film into Boots. I never liked the idea of other people looking at my photographs. I used to imagine the staff chatting about the images in front of them. Laughing and pointing maybe.

'Let's have a nice big smile,' I say. 'Everyone has their photo taken on their first day at school.'

She hesitates but then obliges, one of those toothy grins children produce before they become self-conscious.

'Can I see?' she asks.

'It's not like phone ones – I can't show you. I'll print it for you later when school's finished.'

She nods. Fidgets a bit on the stool.

'Right, I'd better give you a pencil case then, hadn't I?'

She looks up as I hand her the case which I found in Matthew's room earlier, seemingly uncertain whether she is allowed to open it.

'Go on,' I say. 'Everything you need is inside.'

She gets everything out in turn: pencil, coloured pencils, rubber, ruler.

'Are these Matthew's?'

'Yes, but he won't mind you having them.'

'Thank you,' she says, lining the pencils up on her desk. I hand her the only unfilled exercise book I could find. Matthew has written on the first couple of pages but the rest of it is blank.

'It hasn't got my name on it,' she says. 'Miss Roberts said we would get a writing book with our name on it.'

'That's because you're going to write your name on it.'

She looks up at me doubtfully.

'My E for Ella is a bit wonky.'

'Well, practice makes perfect. Let's see how you get on.'

The child picks up the pencil and starts to carve her name onto the front of the book, her fingers gripping the pencil tightly. When she is finished she holds it up to me for inspection. The letters are all of different sizes but she is at least consistent in using capitals.

'There, you've got the letters right. I expect you found it easier without your hair getting in your eyes.'

She shrugs. Releases her grip on the pencil a little.

'Right. Well, before we progress to the whole alphabet,

we're going to learn about pencil control. I've got some writing exercises here for you to practise. Just copy the lines you see onto your page. It doesn't matter if you go wrong; simply start again.' I remember all this from when Matthew started at The Grange. The hours he spent at home following lines with his pencil. He was always such a meticulous child and so conscientious. Not the easiest of combinations, either for him or me as a mother. A lifetime of worry, that is what Malcolm used to say we had in store. He was right too. Although I don't suppose he would even remember that now.

I look down as the pencil lead snaps. It is not surprising considering how hard she is pressing. She is looking up at me, unsure how I will react.

'Never mind. I'll sharpen it for you. You don't need to press so hard, though.'

'My fingers hurt. Can we do something else now?'

'You've hardly started.'

'Miss Roberts has an aliens' corner in her classroom. She has lots of pants pinned up on the line, like in the *Aliens Love Underpants* book.'

This is why I sent Matthew to The Grange. For a proper education. Rather than fill his head with all this other nonsense. It is too late to get the child in there, of course. You have to put their names down early. Before they are born even. Baby Thornton, that's what they wrote down for Matthew. I had to make it clear that I was Miss Norgate only professionally. As a parent I was to be known as Mrs Thornton. It was a little confusing. School fees to pay as one person and music teacher salary paid to me as another. Some of the mothers in Matthew's class didn't even know that I was one and the same person. I liked keeping things strictly professional though. Even Matthew had to call me Miss Norgate when I taught his class. He came out one afternoon in tears, saying one of his classmates didn't believe I was his mother. I remember being touched that it mattered so much to him that they knew.

I miss it sometimes. Being in that professional environment. You command far more respect as a school teacher than you do when giving private lessons. But what's done is done. I do at least still get to call myself Miss Norgate to my private pupils. There is far too much informality around. These teachers who ask the children to call them by their first names and then wonder why they don't show any respect for them.

I look down at the child, realising that she is still waiting for a response. 'We will play in the afternoons. The mornings are for working.'

'Are we going to make an aliens' corner?'

'No. We shall play the piano and perhaps do some sewing cards or baking.'

The child is looking at me. It doesn't appear to be the answer she was hoping for.

'We'll still have lots of fun,' I add, 'but it will be the right sort of fun.' I think for a minute she is going to

have another meltdown but when I hand her the sharp-
ened pencil she looks at it closely and goes back to her
writing.

A moment later the lead has snapped again.

'Oops,' she says.

'What has happened to those delicate fingers which
played the piano so beautifully?'

'It hurts my fingers to write.'

'Because you are gripping too hard.'

'Are we going to have break time? Miss Roberts has
break time and you get to play in the sand pit and there
are swirly patterns on the playground you can run
round but they haven't got a slide.'

'When we've done some more writing you can have a
break time.'

'Will we play outside?'

'You know we can't do that.'

'Because of the naughty boys?'

'That's right.'

'What will we do then?'

'You can have a glass of milk.'

'Do they have milk at big school?'

'Not now. They used to, though.'

'Did Matthew have milk at school?'

'No. Only at breakfast and when he came home.'

'Will Melody have milk too?'

'I expect so. You can pour it for her if you like.'

'Does Otis ever give her milk?'

'No.'

'Is it milk time yet?'

'Do you ever stop asking questions?'

She gives a little shrug.

'You will have your milk break when you've finished your writing.' The child looks down at her broken pencil.

'Here,' I say with a sigh. 'Let me sharpen it for you.'

I give up after another twenty minutes. There is no point in pushing the child on the first day. Their fingers and thumbs are used to touch screens these days, not holding a pencil.

She drinks her milk in silence. Her mind appears to be elsewhere. At the school she was due to attend perhaps. There will be an empty desk in her classroom. An empty coat peg on the wall. It is a shame, of course. That we have to do it this way. But sometimes the end justifies the means, and this is one of those occasions. It is such an underrated skill, parenting. People think it is instinctive. That the second you give birth to a child you will know the right thing to do. You don't though. I can still taste the fear of when I first held Matthew in my arms, realising that this little person was utterly dependent on me and no one was going to provide the answers; I had to work them out for myself. It is easy for the father. They have to provide for children, yes, set a good example and be there to play ball games with them when they are older, but essentially it is the mother's responsibility to raise them. To ensure they know right from wrong. Keep them from straying onto the wrong path. I realised that as I held him. That his future lay in my hands. I told him there and then, bent down and whispered in his ear. That I would do right by him. That if he listened to me, did as he was told, he would be fine. All he had to do was keep listening to me. I wasn't to know, of course. That someone would try to drown my words out. Shout in his other ear. Attempt to turn him against me. Because she wanted him for herself. If I had known that I would have added one final piece of advice: never trust anyone apart from me. Because no one can ever love you more than your own mother.

The child finishes her milk.

'What are we doing now?' she asks.

'Your numbers,' I say.

'I can count already. I can count up to one hundred. Mummy was counting to one hundred when we came to hide at your house.'

I print the photograph out after lunch, while the child is playing with Melody. I use the proper photo paper and for once the printer doesn't leave any smudges, which is good. I want it to be special, this first photograph. One to treasure. I do not have any spare frames so I go to the landing and look at the pictures on the wall. I find the duplicate photograph of Matthew quite quickly. We gave it to my mother, and when she died I brought it back here along with the others. We already had the same photograph downstairs, so I put it up here on the landing. I'm not sure Matthew ever noticed. If he did, he never said anything. And Malcolm was gone by then. Not that he'd have noticed either.

I take the frame down and turn it over, easing the catches out with my thumb and lifting out the back. I take the photo out and turn it over. Matthew smiles back at me uncertainly. I think the school photographer used to scare him. He was one of those men who was over-jolly with children. Loud and more than a little ridiculous. I suspect he reminded Matthew of the clowns at the circus. We only ever went to the circus once. We left before the interval.

I put the photograph to one side and replace it with the new one. I put the back on, forcing down the catches to secure it, before turning it over and looking. The child smiles back at me a little uncertainly. But in time she will trust me. Learn to listen to me and only me. And to ignore the other voices.

MATTHEW

Saturday, 10 May 2014

This is getting so hard now it's starting to do my head in. Mum has got no one left apart from me so it's like she's following me with laser eyes and BFG ears and some sort of sixth-sense thing. Sometimes I feel like I can't breathe without her permission. I mean I'm eighteen, for fuck's sake. I could be married or working or fighting for my country. I'm not some little kid, but she still acts like I am and expects me to be home for every single meal, and if I'm not I get the evil eye and this huffy silence from her and then I feel like I've been a real bastard, cos of everything that's happened to her, like. So then I tell Sparrow I can't see her out of school for a day or two and she gets pissed off with me (not that she tells me, but I kind of know she does because it feels a bit awkward when I'm around her and it's never felt awkward before) and I want to scream at Mum and tell her to stop being so fucking needy, only if I did that I'd be a serious bastard so I just sort of do deep sighs and go to my room.

So what do I do? I really don't know. I can only see Mum getting worse, to be honest. It's like her world's becoming smaller and smaller. At least she's still got her work – that's the only thing which saves me at the moment. And it helps that I kind of know her timetable at school because I don't think anything has changed at The Grange since I was there (actually, I doubt if anything has changed at The Grange since about 1452), so I know what days her piano lessons are and sometimes I even go on to their website and see what special assemblies and concerts and stuff they're doing because she always goes to those. And that's the only way I get to see Sparrow out of school because at least with our A levels coming up we've got study leave in school time when Mum's at work so we're managing to get to see each other. And it has to be here really because Sparrow lives two bus rides away and there's nowhere else to go.

But I know it's crazy and I hate having to creep around behind Mum's back like this and I get a bit paranoid and smooth out the duvet about twenty times before we go and sometimes I look at Melody and wonder if Mum has fitted her with some kind of recording device and she's like a sort of KGB cat because I wouldn't put it past her and then I realise that I'm comparing Mum to Putin and that makes me feel like a real git and it all just gets dead stressy. I try to pretend it's like being in a modern-day version of *Romeo and Juliet* only it's not like that because our families have never met, it's just that we know they'd hate each other if they did. Actually, that's not strictly true. My mum would hate them but they probably wouldn't hate her, they'd just think she's a bit weird. And anyway it's not like *Romeo and Juliet* at all really cos Sparrow has told her mum about me. Apparently she was pretty cool about it. She told her that as long as she was sensible and I didn't get her in trouble and she didn't let it affect her exams then it was OK.

If I told Mum she'd go ballistic, absolutely fucking mental. That's why I don't have any choice really other than to keep it all secret.

I'm already worried about what we're going to do in the school holidays when Mum's not at work. It's going to be a nightmare. I am so sick of all this. I can't wait till we get to uni. At least then we'll be able to be together every evening and Mum won't know anything about it and I'll just send her text messages telling her I'm studying and she won't know any different. I am so counting down the days. That's the thing I'm looking forward to most about uni. I mean I'm sure the course will be good and that but it's not really why I'm going. I'm going because it's the only way I can escape from all this and be with Sparrow without having to worry about Mum finding out. Three years of being with Sparrow all the time, that seems like the most amazing thing in the world to me. It's what keeps me going through all this crap. I am so counting the days.

13

LISA

I must have fallen asleep at some point. The realisation hits me as I open my eyes and see dawn creeping into the room uninvited. I seize on the hope that the whole thing might have been a nightmare. There is nothing in our bedroom to suggest otherwise. Alex's back is to me but light snoring suggests he too is asleep. There is one obvious way to find out. I slide out from under the duvet and pad through to Ella's room, opening the door gently so as not to wake her. I know instantly that she is not there because of how light the room is. Her curtains are not closed. There didn't seem to be any point. It is not a nightmare from which I have woken; it's a nightmare in which I finally fell asleep.

I climb into Ella's bed and pull the duvet up over me. I feel bad for sleeping, as if it is somehow disloyal to her.

'I do care,' I whisper into the duvet. 'I care very much, you know that. I just couldn't keep my eyes open any longer.'

I lie there for some time, wondering whether she has managed to sleep at all – if she's still got the opportunity to, that is. But this slips too uncomfortably into thinking about him, the man who has taken her. Thinking about how old he is, what he looks like, whether he is one of those loners you hear about in these cases. Maybe he still lives with his mother. Although if he does, he can't have taken Ella back home with him. Maybe he's already got rid of her. Maybe he did it on the same day and went home for tea with his mum. Maybe she doesn't even know.

Ella's pillow is soggy against my face. I hadn't even realised I'd been crying.

'Bastard,' I whisper. 'Dirty, fucking bastard.'

I get up and pace up and down Ella's bedroom, which, due to its size, only involves four steps each way. Maybe the cops were right. Maybe it is someone I know. Someone who I haven't thought of yet. A client who came to the gym years ago, one of those over-muscly sports-supplement guys to whom I gave a hard time. Maybe they saw Ella. I had to take her there once or twice when Mum was ill and Alex was working away. Maybe they remembered her. I try to see their faces in my head, every single client who has ever been through the gym. I can't though. I see a blur of faces merging into each other, smell a range of body odours, take a towel and wipe away the sweat which one of them has left on the bench press. This is not helping. I am not helping. Ella could be screaming for me at this very moment and I am no fucking help at all.

I catch sight of her school shoes in the corner of the room and realise what day it is. I open the wardrobe door. It is there, hanging at the end of the rail, her school uniform, white polo shirt, red sweatshirt and grey trousers. She was adamant about having trousers rather than a skirt. I remember doing a discreet little air punch when she said so. She won't get to wear them now. Not today at any rate, maybe not tomorrow, perhaps never.

I reach out and touch the sweatshirt. I should really have given her Otis's old one, which I still have, but she was so excited about the whole uniform thing that I decided to get her a new one. The other one will do as a spare when she gets spaghetti down the front of the new one, that's what I told myself. What I would give to see her getting spaghetti down the front of anything right now.

I am in Otis's room, standing just inside the door, when he wakes. I'm not one of those mothers who gets over-sentimental about how beautiful their kids are when they're sleeping. But this morning I needed to see him sleeping peacefully before he has to deal with what the day will bring. I sit down on the edge of the bed and stroke his hair, which is always a complete mess in the mornings.

'Did you sleep OK?' I ask.

He rubs his eyes and nods.

'It's not too late to change your mind, you know.'

'No. I want to go.'

'If you're sure,' I say. 'But if at any point it gets too much, or anyone says stuff which upsets you, tell Miss Farrell and I'll come and get you, OK?'

'Why would someone say stuff to upset me?'

'I'm not saying they'd mean to upset you but sometimes children can be a little bit . . . you know, insensitive. Speaking first and thinking about how it might make someone feel later.'

'Will they all know about Ella?'

'I expect so. It's been on the news a lot. Their parents will probably have talked to them about it.'

'What will they have said?'

'Just that she's missing. That the police are trying to find her.'

'Will they know where she was hiding? Only they might know hiding places at the park that I don't know.'

I swallow hard and pull Otis's body towards me.

'You're a brilliant big brother, you are,' I say.

'Are you sure you don't want me to take him?' asks Alex for the third time. I look at him and notice that he has finally shaved. I don't know if that means he has given up or if he is just trying to look presentable. I decide not to say anything.

'No, I told you. If he's got to go through this I don't see why I shouldn't have to.' Mum has texted twice this morning to offer to do the school run too. To be honest, I can't think of anything I would less like to do right now, but that is not the point. If I don't show my face, people will think it's because our family has got something to hide. I'm going to walk into that playground with my head held high.

'OK, but why don't you let me come too?'

'Because I don't need my hand holding, all right?'

I know as soon as I say it that I shouldn't have. The look on Alex's face simply confirms this.

'I'm sorry,' I say. 'I know you're trying to help but I can't do with all this fussing right now, OK?'

'I'm not fussing. I'm trying to support you. To support our family. Please don't push me away, Lis. I have to be able to do something.' He walks out of the kitchen. I screw up my face. I am making such a pig's ear of this. It's like I'm the wrong kind of wife as well as the wrong kind of mother.

Otis comes downstairs a few minutes later in his uniform. His trousers are too short; I probably should have bought some new ones in the holidays. Not that anyone is going to complain about them. Alex comes back into the kitchen and ruffles Otis's hair, as if he needs it to be any messier than it already is.

'Hey, here's the man. Do you think Year Five is ready for you?' he asks. Otis looks at him blankly. You can almost see the hurt dripping off Alex's face. The fun-dad routine isn't working any more and he knows it.

'All set then?' I ask Otis.

He nods.

'Right, let's go.'

I open the front door and we step out just as Charlie bounds out of the house next door. He looks older in his uniform. Smart too. He looks like Ella would have looked. In my head I see her running up to him and holding his hand, telling him she is going to look after him because she is nearly a year older than him. All those things which she would have done.

'Where's Ella?' he asks, looking behind us.

I glance across at his father Dean, who visibly winces. I don't know what he has told Charlie so I'm not sure how to answer.

'She's not coming today.'

'Is she poorly?' he asks.

'Yes. Yes, she is.' Otis looks up at me enquiringly. I give a little shake of my head.

'Did she like my birthday cake?'

'It's in the fridge,' I say. 'I'm saving it for her.'

'Did she get a bit with a chocolate button on?'

'I'm not sure, Charlie. I haven't actually unwrapped it.'

'Only if she didn't I've still got some left in the packet and she can have one of mine.'

'Thanks, Charlie,' I say. I see Dean blinking hard as his grip tightens on Charlie's hand. I know what he's thinking: *Thank God it wasn't my kid.* That's what everyone will be thinking today. That and other stuff I'd probably rather not know about.

I usher Otis in front of me and we walk off briskly towards school as I'm not sure I can cope with any more of Charlie's questions right now.

The nearer we get to the school the more people I see. They all do the same thing: look at me then look away quickly. Some of them manage a little sort of smile before they do so; most of them don't.

I want to hold Otis's hand but I know he is beyond that now. I put my hand on his shoulder as we approach the school gates.

'You'll be fine,' I say. 'And if you want to come home at any point ...'

He nods and goes off to join his line. He has a new teacher. Miss Farrell has only just joined the school and I should probably say something, at least hello, but I don't think I can.

Mrs Dewhurst, his teacher from last year, comes up to me. 'We'll keep a special eye on him,' she says, taking my hand. 'If there's anything we can do ...'

I nod and turn to go but as I do so I see the line-up of reception children being taken off towards their classroom, Charlie skipping along at the back of the line, and a cluster of mothers dabbing their eyes with tissues.

I want to yell at them to stop blubbing because they have nothing in the world to cry about. Their child is growing up and starting school, it's what every parent wants. And I would give anything to see Ella disappearing into that classroom at the moment.

I turn and walk away, my breath shallow, struggling to hold myself together. I overhear one conversation as I leave. A whispered 'That's her, that's the missing girl's mum' followed by 'They've questioned the girl's uncle – it's in the paper this morning. He's done time apparently. Bet it turns out to be him.'

I spin round. 'For your information they were taking a routine statement. So why don't you mind your own business, eh, seeing as you know fuck all about any of us.'

I don't even wait for a reaction. I start running. I run all the way home.

Alex and Claire look up from the kitchen table as I come in, the *Sun*'s front page with UNCLE OF MISSING ELLA QUESTIONED and a grainy photo of Tony going into the back door of the police station in front of them.

'Sorry,' says Claire. 'I wanted to tell you in person but I didn't get here in time.'

'Fucking arseholes,' I say, throwing my keys into the pot on the table. Alex stands up and comes over to me.

'Did anyone say anything to you at school?'

'Oh just the usual playground shit stirrers. Reckon it's only a matter of time before Tony's charged.'

Alex gives me a hug. 'Do you want me to go down to the school and have a word?'

'No point, it's nowt to do with them. It's how the bloody paper got that photo, that's what I want to know. Did you see anyone there?'

Alex shakes his head. 'Me and your dad went in first with Claire. Tony was a bit behind us.'

'I'm so sorry,' says Claire. 'We tried to be careful, that's why I used the back entrance, but it seems like they had a photographer in the building opposite. I didn't see anyone at the time. I had no idea this would happen.'

'How did the paper know who he was, though?' I ask.

'They ask around. And people talk, I'm afraid. Especially . . .'

Claire breaks off. 'What?' I ask. 'What were you going to say?'

'It could have been an ex-con. Someone who knew him when he was inside. A lot of them know the tabloids are after that sort of stuff.'

I sit down at the table with my head in my hands. 'Great. So now everyone thinks it's Tony and they'll all stop looking for Ella.'

'We're not going to let that happen,' says Claire. 'We've issued a strongly worded statement to the media making it clear that this was routine questioning and no members of your family have been arrested or are due to be questioned any further.'

'Bit late for that,' I say. 'How many million readers has the *Sun* got?'

'I know,' says Claire. 'I'm really, really sorry.' I look at her face properly for the first time and realise she looks awful, not nearly as awful as me, obviously, but she is clearly cut up about it.

'So what happens now?' I ask.

'We get the focus back on finding Ella. Which is why we'd like to do another press conference with you this afternoon.'

'Oh great,' I say. 'You may as well just line us up against the wall and let them shoot us.'

Alex looks at Claire. 'She's got a point. Are you sure that's a good idea? Won't they just want to muck-rake about this stuff?'

'Not now we've made it clear to them that we do not suspect any family involvement.'

'Yeah but mud sticks, doesn't it?' I say. 'My brother's an ex-con so in their heads we're all lowlife scum now. They won't want to know.'

'Lisa, your little girl is missing. That's what they're interested in. They've run photos of her under headlines saying OUR ANGEL. We need to keep her photo on the front page of every newspaper for as long as possible. It's our best chance of finding her.'

I sigh. 'Will they ask us questions this time?'

'Yes, but only if you're up to it, mind. We won't let them ask anything about Tony and we will call a halt to it if we think any of them have overstepped the mark.'

'What do you think?' I ask Alex.

'I'm not sure. It might be asking too much of you right now.'

'Nothing's asking too much of me, is it? I'm her mother. It's the least I can do.'

Claire looks down at the table.

'I was only—' Alex starts.

'Yeah, I know, but please don't. If it's the best way of getting Ella back I'll do it.'

'But what if it just gives more fuel to the press and the nutters out there?'

'I want to do it,' I say. 'I want to do everything that's asked of us. That way I won't beat myself up about what might have happened if we had done it.'

'Done what?' asks Chloe, walking into the kitchen bleary-eyed in her dressing gown. I didn't think she'd wake up for ages yet. Not after that journey. She starts as she sees Claire sitting at the table and pulls the dressing gown more tightly around her. And then her gaze falls on the front page of the paper.

'It's complete rubbish,' I say. 'And if we'd have known it was going to happen we'd have told you.' I see Chloe glance across at Claire again. 'This is Claire – she says the police have put out a statement saying it's a load of crap.'

'Hi, Chloe,' says Claire, offering her hand. Chloe shakes it as if she is worried about catching something.

'You never told me they questioned Uncle Tony,' Chloe says, turning back to me.

'They interviewed him before you got back yesterday. And Alex and Grandad too. I didn't tell you because it wasn't a big deal; they were just taking statements, that's all.'

'Well the paper shouldn't be allowed to print that, then,' says Chloe.

'We've made the situation very clear to the media this morning,' Claire says. 'And we've told them that anyone who acts in a way which hinders our enquiry from now on will be banned from press conferences.'

'Will they be there today, though?' I ask Claire.

'Yes. Because unfortunately they're still the biggest-selling newspaper and we need their help with this.'

'What's happening today?' asks Chloe.

'Claire has asked us if we'd be prepared to do another press conference. One where they ask us questions.'

'What sort of questions?'

I look at Claire.

'Mainly about Ella,' she says. 'What sort of girl she is, what she likes doing. Maybe about how you're all coping.'

'I'll do it if you like,' says Chloe.

'No,' I say quickly. 'I don't want you involved in any of this.'

'Why not? She's my sister.'

'I know, but you don't need this right now.'

'Says who?'

'Your mum's got a point,' says Alex. 'It's not a very nice thing to go through.'

'I don't care, I want to help find Ella.'

'You could help Grandad and Uncle Tony with all the Facebook stuff,' I say. 'You'd probably be better at it than they are.'

Chloe gives me a look. 'Stop treating me like a kid. I'm nineteen remember? I want to do this. Ella might see it on the telly. I want her to see us all together, like. So she knows we're all looking for her. You have to let me help.'

I sigh. Alex shrugs. I know what he's thinking. That she's her mother's daughter and therefore there's no way on earth we're going to get her to change her mind.

'OK,' I say. 'You can be there with us but I'm not going to let them ask you questions.'

'Fine. When is it?'

'One o'clock this afternoon,' says Claire.

'Right. I'm gonna go and have a shower then.'

Claire looks at us both when Chloe has left the room.

'Tough cookie,' she says. 'Wonder where she gets it from.'

'It's more a front, to be honest,' I reply. 'She's got a pretty soft centre.'

'Well, I'll make sure they're briefed not to ask her anything. Thanks, anyway. I know this isn't easy for you.'

My phone rings. I look at the screen. It's Dad. And I'm pretty sure I know what he's calling about.

I answer straight away. I may as well have put it on speaker because the others get to hear every single expletive.

'Have you seen the front page of the *Sun* this morning? What the fuck is going on? Your mum's in a right state.'

'Is Tony there?'

'No. He went to work early this morning. He's just rung to say his boss wants to see him and the other lads are giving him grief about it.'

'Right. Just hang on and I'll come straight round,' I say. 'I'll explain everything.'

'There's a couple of photographers outside the house now. I've told them where to go and drawn the curtains so they don't bother your mother, like.'

'OK,' I say. 'I'm on my way.' I put the phone down.

'Are you sure that's a good idea?' asks Alex. 'With the press outside, I mean.'

'No,' I say. 'But I sure as hell don't want Mum and Dad having to deal with them on their own.'

'Do you want me to come?' asks Alex.

'No, I'll be fine.'

I look at Alex's face and realise I have done it again.

'One of us should stay here with Chloe,' I add quickly.

'OK, if you're sure,' says Alex. 'I'll call Mum and Dad.

They said they'd like to come round for a while before they head back this afternoon.'

'They're going already?'

'Yeah. They texted while you were out. I think they feel like spare parts, to be honest.'

I feel a twinge of guilt, knowing I haven't exactly been welcoming. I don't know what they thought they could do to help, mind. Maybe they just thought they ought to show their faces. To be fair, it's not as if there are any books on this subject, *What to Do When a Child in Your Family Goes Missing*. The truth is, nobody knows what to do; you simply muddle through the best you can.

'Sure. Say goodbye from me and thank them for coming. And make sure Chloe says goodbye properly too.'

I turn back to see Claire taking her car keys out of her pocket.

'What are you doing?'

'I'll come with you,' Claire says.

'There's no need.'

'Well, I'd like to. I feel responsible. And I can have a word with the press for you while I'm there.'

'OK,' I say with a shrug. 'But I'll drive.'

'I just thought—'

'No, thanks. I'm quite capable of driving a car.'

Claire and Alex exchange a look. Claire nods before putting her keys back into her pocket.

*   *   *

I glance at Claire as I drive off. 'Sorry,' I say. 'It's all getting on top of me, that's all.'

'It's OK. I don't blame you, to be honest. And for what it's worth, I've had a lot worse.'

'Why do you do this?' I ask. 'I mean there must be better jobs in the police force?'

'What, like getting your head kicked in by some drunken oik on a Saturday night in Manchester?'

'Did that happen to you?'

'Not to me but one of my colleagues. I went into policing to help people, not watch them beating up one of my friends. And then I had a guy pull a knife on me and that was the final straw.'

'So why didn't you settle for a cushy desk job instead of having to deal with people like us?'

Claire smiles. 'Because I want to help people. Try to, at any rate. The way I see it, if people have to go through awful things, the least we can do is be there to support them and treat them with the respect you'd expect if it ever happened to you.'

I nod, hoping Dad's not going to be too hard on her.

'Have you got kids?' I ask.

'No. Married to the job, I am. I've got two cats for company, mind, and if I'm after stimulating conversation I just watch *Corrie* on catch-up. Damn sight better than putting up with a husband, from what I hear.'

I manage a little smile. We drive on for a bit in silence.

'You knew about our Tony's previous, didn't you?'

Claire nods. 'Yep, not that it matters to me. A lot of people do pretty stupid things when they're young.'

'He was pissed,' I say, 'and the bloke he beat up had been having a pop at his girlfriend.'

'I hope she appreciated him doing time for her.'

'She dumped him while he was inside actually and went off with one of his mates.'

'Ouch.'

'I know. So much for chivalry, eh?'

As soon as I turn into the road I see the photographers, three of them, with bulky bags on their shoulders and cameras around their necks, standing outside Mum and Dad's house. There are a group of teenage kids hanging about on the other side of the road as well, no doubt enjoying the free entertainment.

I pull up outside. The photographers turn and start taking pictures through the windscreen. 'Stay here a second and let me handle them,' says Claire, jumping out.

She goes up to the nearest photographer and shows them her ID.

'Claire Madill, West Yorkshire Police. I'd like to see your press card, please,' I hear her say.

He rummages in about six different pockets before producing a card and holding it out for her to see.

'Freelance are you?' she says.

'Yeah.'

'Who you working for?'

'Local agency.'

'Right, well we will be contacting all the agencies, newspapers and websites to let them know that if any of their employees harass members of Ella Dale's family they will not be admitted to the police press conference this afternoon.

'So I suggest you all get yourselves down to Bradford now and we'll look forward to seeing you at the press conference. Unless you want to come in and explain to the girl's family why you're adding to their suffering right now.'

They shuffle their feet uncomfortably before one turns and heads off towards his car. The other two follow a moment later.

I wait till they have driven off before getting out of the car.

'Thanks,' I say to Claire.

'No problem, all part of the service.'

I look over at the teenage lads still hanging about opposite.

'And I'd piss off too if I were you,' I call out, 'unless you want to get in trouble with the law for bunking off school.'

They mutter something under their breaths and slink off.

I catch Claire looking at me. 'No one messes with our family,' I say.

'No,' she replies. 'So I see.'

I knock on the door and it opens almost instantly although there is no sign of anyone inside. I step in and find Mum behind the door, her eyes red and puffy.

'Hey, come on,' I say, giving her a hug. 'There's no need for that. Claire's got rid of the photographers – they won't be bothering you again.'

'It's too late though, the damage has already been done. What are people going to think?'

'That the bastard paper is shit-stirring, that's what.'

'But everyone thinks he's got summat to do with Ella going missing now.'

'I don't think so. Beating up a guy in a pub is not exactly in the same league as abducting a kiddie, is it? Besides, there's plenty round here that have done worse than that.'

'We've put out a very strongly worded statement, Tina,' says Claire, stepping into the hall behind me. 'We've made it abundantly clear that no one in your family is a suspect.'

'Well, you'd better tell Vince that,' she says. 'If he'll calm down long enough to listen.'

We walk through to the living room. Dad is sitting in the armchair with torn-up pages of the *Sun* littering the carpet around him.

'This,' he says, 'is what I think of that bloody rag. I wouldn't wipe my arse with it, let alone wrap fish and chips in it.'

'I'm sorry,' says Claire. 'I had no idea what was going to happen. I should have been more careful.'

'So it weren't some sort of set-up?' asks Dad.

'Absolutely not. I wouldn't be party to anything like that. You're looking at the cleanest copper going here. It doesn't always make me popular with my colleagues but they know damn well I'd grass on them if I thought one of them had leaked information to the press.'

Dad looks at her for a moment as if sizing her up.

'What do we do about that, then?' he asks, pointing at the bits of paper on the floor.

'We've issued a statement to the media making it very clear that no one in your family is a suspect in this case. We've told the paper that if there's any repeat of that, its journalists will no longer be welcome at our press conferences.'

Dad nods. 'You going to let our Tony know that too? He rang me from the garage – a couple of lads had got the paper on their way in.'

'I'll go and speak to him next,' says Claire, 'and to his boss. I'll put the record straight, don't worry.'

'Right then,' he says. 'You'd better bugger off. And be sure to tell your lot that if they don't find my granddaughter soon they'll have me to answer to.'

Claire nods and steps out of the living room back into the hall.

'You going to be all right?' I ask Dad. 'Dealing with this lot round here, I mean.'

'Have you forgotten who your old man is?'

I smile and shake my head. 'No. We're doing another press conference this afternoon, so it's going to be everywhere again. Just so you know, like.'

'Good,' he says. You give 'em hell from me.'

I stay with Tony while Claire goes in to see his boss. The other lads are looking through the window into the little room we are in.

'I'm sorry,' I say.

'What have you got to be sorry for?'

'Well if I hadn't lost Ella, none of this crap would have happened, would it?'

'You didn't lose her, Sis; she was taken.'

'Still on my watch though, wasn't it?'

He wipes his hands on his overalls, and when he looks up his eyes are glistening. 'I don't know anyone who's done more for their kids than you have. All the things you gave up for Chloe, all the hours you worked when you were a single mum. You're bloody amazing, you are.'

I look at him. The brother who has never said anything like that to me before. The brother who, at some point when I wasn't paying attention, appears to have grown up.

'Thanks,' I say. 'I am sorry though – about you getting dragged into all this. Did your boss know about your previous?'

Tony shakes his head. 'He's sweet about it, though. Says he knows I'm a hard grafter and that's all that bothers him.'

I nod. 'Claire will put him right too. She's bloody good, you know.'

We're quiet again for a moment.

'Mum all right?'

'Just worrying, as usual. I thought we'd given her enough to worry about by now, me and you.'

Tony manages half a smile. 'We'll find her, Sis. We'll get her back.'

I nod and go and wait outside so he doesn't see me crying.

There is a strange familiarity about the second press conference. It doesn't make it any more pleasant but at least I know what to expect. Chloe sits on my right. I squeeze her hand under the table and stare out at the faces opposite. I have no idea whether they are the same ones who were here on Saturday and, if so, whether they have now changed their minds about our guilt or innocence. All I know is that I still need their help.

DS Johnston speaks first. He reads the police statement about Tony from this morning and makes it clear that nothing further will be said on the matter. He outlines the facts of the case again, goes through the timeline, the gap they want to fill in on the day she disappeared. He also gives an update on the investigation so far, everything the police have done and are still doing. I don't know whether to feel comforted by it or concerned that if they've been looking so hard they should have found her by now. And then Joanne, the press woman, asks if they have any questions for us. She chooses a short woman with blonde hair from the BBC first. Maybe she thinks it'll be an easy one, I don't know.

'Can you tell us how Ella's disappearance is impacting on your family?' she asks. I look at Alex, who nods to say he'll take it.

'It's hard for all of us,' he says. 'Ella's brother and sister, who is here today, are finding it really tough, but we're a strong family and we'll support each other. It's all we can do.'

Alex sounds remarkably composed. I'm not sure I'd even be able to form words, let alone coherent sentences. Chloe has her head down, her hair pretty much covering her face; I don't think she likes the flashes. Joanne points to someone else, a guy from Sky.

'I understand it should have been Ella's first day at school today. How difficult has that been for you, Mrs Dale?'

Everyone turns to look at me. The flashes are going off again. Alex opens his mouth to say something but I shake my head.

'It's been very hard. She was really looking forward to it. She tried on her uniform every night last week before bedtime.'

'What would you say to anyone who is holding her or has information?' he continues.

I hesitate, wanting to make sure my words don't come out squeakily. I am not going to do what they want me to. I am not going to break down in tears. I don't care what sort of mother that makes me. All I care about is getting Ella back.

'Just give her back,' I say. 'Let her come home to us, where she belongs. And if you know where she is or have any suspicions about someone you know, please call the police.'

I blink once and what feel like a million flashes go off. It will probably look like I was crying in the photos. I'm not though. I stare straight ahead, glad that I can't see the journalists' faces for a moment. Wondering whether they are pitying me or suspecting I may crack under the pressure at any moment.

A reporter from the *Daily Mail* is next. 'Do you think your daughter is still alive, Mrs Dale?'

'Yes,' I say, staring straight at him and answering without hesitating. 'Yes, I do.'

14

MURIEL

I am in the kitchen washing up the lunch things when the news comes on. I haven't really had the radio on since the child came here but she is in the lounge playing with Melody and I put it on without thinking.

I hear the name first, 'missing four-year-old Ella Dale'. Even then I do not immediately associate it with the child in the lounge. It is only when I hear 'from Halifax, West Yorkshire' that it slots into place. They are talking about her. They are talking about me, though they have no idea, of course. I drop the knife I am holding, cling to the side of the sink, my wet Marigolds squeaking on the stainless steel. They say the police have no new leads. I cannot help thinking it is laughable. All this fuss and she is less than a mile away from where she was last seen. It does not fill you with great confidence in our police force. It's a bit of luck for the child that she was taken for her own safety. If she had been abducted by a paedophile, what he would have done to her by now doesn't bear thinking about.

And then they mention that a press conference is about to be held. The police have issued a statement denying that any family members are suspects in the case, following revelations in a national newspaper.

The newsreader moves on to another item. I stand there, my mouth gaping open. They know. They know about the mother. It is only a matter of time now before it comes out. I need to hear the press conference. Hear what they are saying about the mother, about the child, about what has happened. I take off my Marigolds and fiddle with the dial until I find Radio 5 Live. They broadcast these press conferences live. It is why I never normally listen to the station. Everything live and urgent. No time to reflect before they are on to the next live and urgent thing.

The first voice I hear belongs to a man. It sounds like the detective, the one I saw at the last press conference. He is surprisingly softly spoken for a police officer. He starts by reading a statement out. 'Following reports in a national newspaper, West Yorkshire Police wish to make it clear that members of Ella Dale's family have been questioned purely as a routine matter. No family members are suspects in the case and therefore no further questions on the matter will be answered during today's press conference.'

They know about her. That much is clear. They are saying that because they clearly haven't got the evidence to do anything about it yet but I am reassured. It is why they are doing another press conference. The police do that sometimes, put the family up to see if they will crack under pressure. She must know too. Know that they are on to her. That soon her story will be exposed for the tissue of lies which it is.

The detective carries on speaking. He says Alex and Lisa Dale will be answering questions. And that the other person on the table next to them is Ella's older sister. Presumably, the one the child told me about, the half-sister. Unless she has other half-sisters. Who knows with a mother like that?

He details the police investigation so far. Talks about gathering material from CCTV. He doesn't say where the cameras are but I can't imagine there are any around the park. He mentions ports and airports. Interpol. Liaising with forces in other countries. Going through the sex offenders register. I don't understand why they are doing all this when they know about the mother. Maybe they aren't and this is just a smokescreen to lull her into a false sense of security. Or maybe they really don't get what has happened. No one is thinking about the child. About what might be best for her. No one is thinking like a mother.

When the detective has finished, the journalists start asking questions. The father answers the first one. He strikes me as being more rational, more organised than the mother. He did at least always pay the boy's lesson fees on time, I'll say that for him. Come to think of it, he was the only one who ever brought him for his lessons. Where was the mother on Saturday mornings? Having a lie-in? Playing on her phone? Conspicuous by her absence, I would say.

And then someone asks the mother about the fact that it should have been the child's first day at school. She says that the child was looking forward to it. That she had tried on her uniform every day. She has no idea of course that the child is in her uniform now. Her new uniform. The one she will be wearing for her home schooling.

Another journalist asks what message she has for anyone who is holding the child. There is a moment's hesitation. She is probably working out what to say, what people will be expecting. And then she comes out with, 'Let her come home to where she belongs.'

I shake my head and go over to turn off the radio, unable to listen to any more of this nonsense. The child belongs here with me. There is no question about that. I can give her everything she needs. Matthew might not need me any more but I still have so much to give as a mother. So much that she can benefit from. I realise for the first time that I do not want to give the child up, even when the police find out for certain about her mother. I couldn't hand her over to the authorities, not now I have built up a relationship with her. When she trusts me. I could not bear to lose her now. To have my life go back to what it was before.

I hurry to the front door and open it a little, suck the fresh air from outside into my lungs. It is not enough though. I need to go for a walk to get my brain working properly. To work out what I am going to do. I grab my keys from the ledge and stumble out onto the step, pulling the door shut behind me and locking it. I blink as the sunlight hits my face. It is as if I am emerging from a long hibernation. I feel disorientated. Unsure of where I am and where I need to go.

Fortunately I hear him calling to me, a sweet, excited 'Mummy!' A sound so welcome to my ears that my mouth immediately curls itself into a smile on their behalf. I am coming, I tell him. I will be right there. Mummy is coming for you. I straighten my back and set off down the garden path, the familiar sound of the gate clicking shut behind me providing some welcome reassurance in a world which feels rather alien after only a few days' absence. I should not have left Matthew for so long. It is not me they are looking for. I am not the one who is missing. And it is fine for me to revisit the scene because no crime took place there. Only an act of kindness.

When I reach the park I check to see if there are any police officers. There aren't. Clearly the search has moved on now. Wherever they have gone, this place is no longer of interest to them. It is quieter than the last time I was here of course, being a school day. And maybe some parents are keeping their younger children away because of what happened. The playground in the distance is like a toy which has been left behind after a party, waiting sadly for its owner to return. There are a few toddlers making the most of the space without the big boys. Matthew never liked the big boys either. Would immediately take my hand and ask to go home when they came. I take the narrow path through the park. It is not as hot as it was last week, thank goodness. Matthew would be wilting by now if it was. I look for him up in the canopies of the trees but there is no sign. I wonder for a moment if he has left, if he has given up waiting. But I know for certain that his voice came from this direction. Perhaps he is playing a game. Perhaps he is hiding. And then I see him squatting by the path at the exact spot where the child fell over. He is playing with something on the path, a stone of some kind. I walk closer and see that he is building a circle of stones. Each one slightly larger than the one which came before. Encircling, protecting, providing shelter. And then I realise what he is trying to show me. And I am so glad, so very glad that I have been given the chance to do this. To build a family of my own again. To take care of them. I do not believe in God. Life is far too cruel for me to entertain the thought that anyone intends it to be this way. But I do know it is a sign that I was right to take the child. A child chosen by Matthew. Not the sullen, defiant, easily led young man who he became but the child who called me to the park. The child who knew I would be able to save her. To take her home to the one place where he knew she would be safe. Away from the rest of the world.

He wants the child in his room, in his bed even. It is what he intended when he led me to her. He wants her to take his place. It has simply taken me a while to see it. He looks up at me, and I smile and nod, showing him I understand. And then I turn and walk away, back to where I am needed, where I built a home for him once. And where a child needs my protection and guidance now.

When I get home she is sitting on the floor in the hall, trying to scoop the soil from a fallen plant pot back into it.

She looks up, her eyes puffy with tears. 'It wasn't me. I didn't do it,' she says. 'Melody was chasing the string and she bumped into the little stand and it wobbled and the pot fell off and I am picking the dirt up and putting it back so the plant doesn't die.'

I nod. She doth protest too much. She looks as if she is expecting me to yell at her. Perhaps she is used to being yelled at. Her mother may well be a screamer. I smile so she knows that is not going to happen here.

'Where did you go, piano lady?'

'Just to get some fresh air.'

'Are the naughty boys still in the park?'

'Yes. Yes, I'm afraid they are.'

I take a breath and remind myself why I am doing this. What Matthew has asked of me. I smile at her and offer my hand. She hesitates before getting up bottom first, in the way only small children can, and taking my hand, her fingers lightly curling around mine. I lead her into the lounge, sit down on the sofa and pat the cushion next to me.

'I need to talk to you about your family,' I say.

'Can I go home now? Is Daddy coming to get me?'

'I'm afraid not. You see, I have been asked to look after you because I'm afraid your own family don't deserve to keep an animal, let alone a child.'

She frowns.

I go on: 'Remember I said your mother was poorly?' She nods. 'Well, she's been poorly for a long time and she's not going to get any better.'

'Has she got cancer? My great-grandma had cancer and she died and I got to watch *The Lego Movie* with Charlie Wilson while they buried her in a box.'

'No. She hasn't got cancer but she is poorly in the head, which means she isn't able to be your mummy any more.'

The child starts to cry. I stroke her hair. 'I will be your mummy from now on. I will ensure that you are brought up correctly. If you do as I tell you, you will be fine. I will protect you and keep you out of harm's way.'

'When's Daddy coming?'

'You're not listening, are you?'

'Will I do my piano lesson with Otis when he comes?'

'Otis will not be coming for piano lessons again. It is too late for him. It is you I have been asked to look after.'

'Just until Daddy comes?'

I look up at the ceiling. Perhaps it doesn't matter that she doesn't understand what I am saying. She doesn't need to comprehend it fully now. What is important is that the process starts. As each day passes this will become her reality. She will ask less and less about her family. In time she will forget them entirely. But there is no point in upsetting her any further by telling her that now.

'Let's play some piano, shall we?'

'Can Melody sit on top like last time?'

'I don't see why not.'

'What will they be doing at big school? Will they be playing in sand pit?'

'The sand pit,' I correct.

She frowns.

'This may be Yorkshire but we don't drop our "the" in this house, thank you very much. That way, people outside Yorkshire will still be able to understand what you are saying.'

She stares at me blankly. 'Never mind,' I say. 'It will come in time.'

In the park Matthew is humming to himself as he plays with his stones. It is a happy hum. He has done his job and he knows that I am doing mine. The child will be safe with me. I will mother the child because that is what it needs. The child never had a mother. Not one to speak of, anyway.

15

LISA

I sit at the kitchen table with Alex trying to remember what we talked about before this happened. Nothing major springs to mind, just the normal stuff, I guess: who was picking the kids up from school, whether Alex needed to get milk from the supermarket on his way home, how we could persuade Otis to practise his piano.

I wish we could have those conversations again now. Stupid, meaningless everyday conversations about stuff that doesn't matter. Instead of this massive ton weight of a conversation about whether or not our daughter is still alive.

'Did you mean it?' asks Alex. 'What you said at the press conference.'

'Yeah, I did. I do. I don't know if it's because I can't

bear to think about the alternative or whether it's some kind of intuition, but I still think I'd know if she wasn't with us.'

Alex nods and take a sip of his coffee, which he seems to have been drinking since four this morning, then says, 'You see, that's actually the thing I can't cope with. The thought of her being held by someone. About what he could be doing to her.'

'I know. I try not to think about that. I guess I hope there are some sickos who wouldn't actually do any-thing to her, would just get off on having taken her. I keep hoping we'll get a phone call demanding money. That would be all right, wouldn't it? If someone had just kidnapped her to get money. We'd get a loan, sell the house, whatever it took to get her back.'

Alex puts his head in his hands. 'It's ridiculous, isn't it? When your daughter being kidnapped would turn out to be a good scenario.'

My phone beeps. I pick it up. It's a message from Claire to say she's on her way. It's early, not even seven yet. She must have some news, something she wants to tell us in person. I do stomach crunches inside without actually physically moving and wish again that our family was having a row about breakfast cereals.

Claire shakes her head when I open the door. It isn't the worst, then. Although there are all sorts of degrees of bad that it might me.

'What's happened?' I ask.

'Let's go through to the kitchen,' she replies. I lead the way, wondering with every step what it is she is about to throw at us. I sit down next to Alex at the kitchen table. Claire sits opposite, her face set to neutral.

'I want to tell you a couple of things before you hear them elsewhere.'

I glance at Alex. He looks as worried as me.

'We've had a call from Sky. They're going to be running a story this morning about the fact that we've interviewed a man on the sex offenders register who lives near the park. They asked us for a comment.'

I stare at Claire, not wanting to believe what I am hearing.

'He has an alibi which we've checked out and is solid, which is why we haven't taken things any further.'

'Why didn't you tell us?' asks Alex.

'We've spoken to a lot of people. I would have told you if we'd had any evidence against him or reason to link him to what happened. To be honest, there are quite a few people on the sex offenders register in Halifax. One of the first things our detectives did was to speak to all of them. It's just that this one happens to live near the park.'

Claire looks at me, waiting for me to say something.

'What's his name?' I ask eventually.

'Taylor,' she says. 'Liam Taylor.'

'How old is he?'

'In his twenties.'

'What did he do?'

'It was an offence against a minor. I'm afraid I can't say more than that, Lisa.'

'He didn't kill her or abduct her, though?'

'No.'

'And you're quite sure his alibi stands up?'

'He lives with his mum. She says he was in all afternoon.'

'Well she would say that, wouldn't she?'

'We've got no reason to doubt her. We've checked his mobile phone records too. His phone was connected to the Wi-Fi at home all afternoon.'

'He could have left it there when he went out,' says Alex.

'We've interviewed them both at length. We're satisfied with what they have told us.'

I let out a sigh and look up at the ceiling.

'So what are Sky going to be saying about it?'

'We're not sure exactly. We've given them a statement and reminded them of the legal rules in terms of reporting restrictions.'

I groan and shake my head. 'Jesus, Dad's going to go ape shit.'

'What about the others?' asks Alex, turning back to Claire. 'You said there were other sex offenders in Halifax.'

'Yes, and we've spoken to all of them, taken statements and checked alibis. None of them are suspects, not at this stage of the enquiry anyway.'

'What's that supposed to mean?'

'Well you can never say never. Obviously if some new evidence came to light . . .'

My stomach clenches. She means if Ella's body is found. Or a murder weapon. That is what we are talking about here. I walk over to the kitchen sink and stare out of the window, wishing I could think of something positive, anything to cling on to.

'You said there were a couple of things,' says Alex.

'Yeah,' replies Claire. 'DS Johnston is going to make a further statement today. He's going to say that third-party involvement is now looking like the most likely scenario.'

I turn round in time to see Alex's face crash to the floor.

'You mean she was abducted,' I say.

'We mean that the longer it goes without any sightings, the more likely it is that somebody else was involved in her disappearance.'

'Like I said, she was abducted.'

'We still haven't ruled out the possibility that she wandered off, maybe in search of the balloon, but we're saying that as time goes on without any reported sightings, that scenario is becoming more unlikely.'

Alex puts his head down on the kitchen table. I walk over and wrap my arms around him, feeling his body shaking, hearing the sound of his first sobs.

'I'll be outside for a bit if you need me,' says Claire quietly.

We agree not to tell Otis. It's not a conversation either of us wants to have: 'Just so you know, the police have talked to a man who did a bad thing to another little girl and who lives near the park, but don't worry, he says he didn't take Ella.'

We try to do the normal family bit over breakfast. As normal as you can be when there is a child missing from the table and a policewoman making the tea. Otis is quiet. I think I preferred it more when he was asking endless questions.

'Spaghetti Bolognese for lunch today,' I say, glancing at the school newsletter on the table which I still haven't read properly.

Otis nods, his eyes almost hidden under his hair. I have no idea when we are going to be able to get it cut.

'Ella's coat peg is next to Charlie's,' he says. I put the piece of toast I am not really eating down on my plate.

'I had to take a message down to Miss Roberts' class and I saw Ella's coat peg on my way out. It hasn't got a sticker on it yet. You get to choose a sticker on your first day. There might not be any good ones left now.'

A huge swell of emotion rises up inside me, I look at Otis, sitting there worried that his sister has missed out on the best sticker. He has no idea, no bloody idea how this could all end. I feel my hands shaking, I put them under the table.

Alex stands up. 'Come on then, Otis,' he says. 'I'm going to take you this morning.'

'Can you tell Miss Roberts to save Ella a good sticker for when she comes back?'

'Course I will,' says Alex. 'Now let's go and get your teeth brushed.'

Claire waits until they have both left the kitchen before she comes over to me. At which point I empty myself into her arms.

'I hate him,' I say between sobs. 'The man who took her. I hate what he is doing to our family.'

Dad explodes into the kitchen an hour or so later, just as I had warned Claire he would.

'Why the fuck haven't you arrested the pervert?'

'Vince, don't,' says Mum, who has hurried in behind him. 'It's not Claire's fault, is it?'

'Well she's the only copper here so she's the one I'm asking.'

Claire walks over and fills the kettle before turning to face Dad.

'We haven't arrested the man you're referring to because we have no evidence to link him to this case and no reason to think he is involved in Ella's disappearance.'

'Other than the fact that he's a fucking paedophile, you mean?'

'He's on the sex offenders register, which doesn't mean he's guilty of every crime committed near his house. We've spoken to him and, as we told Sky, he is not a suspect in this case.'

'Who is then?' shouts Dad. 'Because she's been missing four days now and you don't seem to be any closer to finding her.'

'Dad, leave it,' I say. 'Mum's right – it's not Claire's fault. And keep your voice down. Chloe's not up yet.'

'Fine. Well, I'll go and see the copper in charge then.'

'No, you won't,' I reply. 'That's not going to help anyone, is it? I want him out there looking for Ella.'

'And you think this bloke's got nowt to do with it?'

'I don't know, but yesterday our Tony was on the front page of the *Sun* and he had nowt to do with it.'

He is silent for a moment. You can almost hear the air hissing out of the puncture.

'Tony says the same as me, reckons this guy should be arrested, put under pressure, see if he cracks. He says one of lads at the garage said on the first day it'd be some pervert who needs sorting out.'

Claire comes and stands directly in front of Dad. 'No one is going to sort anyone out, OK? That's not going to help the situation. What we need is for everyone to calm down a little. You're well aware of how easily the media will pounce on anything in the absence of definite leads.'

Dad sighs and looks up at the ceiling. I see him

swallow and turn his face slightly. At which point Chloe walks into the kitchen.

'What's going on?' she asks, looking from my face to Dad's.

'Your grandad's just leaving,' I say, 'and everyone's going to try to calm down a bit. And then I'll sit down and tell you what's going on.'

'They haven't found her, have they? They haven't found . . .'

'No,' I say, 'they haven't.'

I go to pick Otis up from school later. Everyone else offers but I don't want to hide away in our house. If Otis has to face dealing with everyone at school it's only fair that I should too.

The looks are completely different to last time, of course. I'm 'poor cow' material now. The same people who were pointing the finger at Tony have found someone else to point at. I know why they do it. They're scared. They don't want to believe that someone 'normal' could do a thing like this. They'd much rather pin it on some pervert.

I wouldn't though. I don't want to think Taylor's been anywhere near Ella, that his grubby little fingers have so much as touched her. I can't tell them that, though. And I don't want them all coming up and saying stupid stuff to me so I walk purposefully towards the school with my head held high, making eye contact with absolutely no one.

As soon as Otis comes out of the front entrance I know something's happened. He looks down as he sees me. His new teacher is standing behind him.

She gestures to me to come over. 'Hello, Mrs Dale,' she says. 'I'm very sorry to bother you but could you pop inside for a moment?'

I look at Otis but he still won't make eye contact. When we get into the classroom Mrs Griggs the head teacher is there too. Maybe she doesn't trust the new teacher; maybe they have brought in reinforcements because they think I will lose it.

'Hello, Mrs Dale,' she says. 'I'm so sorry to trouble you at this difficult time but I'm afraid there has been an incident at school today.'

'What sort of incident?'

'Otis punched another boy in the playground. A Year Six boy, actually. Fortunately he didn't retaliate.'

I shut my eyes and sigh. I should have known something like this was going to happen. I shouldn't have let him go to school. Otis has never punched anyone in his life. Never been in trouble.

I look at Otis.

He looks up to meet my gaze, tears gathering at the corners of his eyes. 'He said Ella was dead,' he blurts out. 'He said a man had murdered her, and that's why she's missing and that's why she's never coming back.'

I go over to Otis and wrap my arms around him, shield his teary face. I look up at the head.

'I'll leave you to deal with that then,' I say. 'And I think it's best that Otis doesn't come to school for the rest of the week.'

Otis is watching TV when the knock on the door comes that evening. We have given him the box set of *Doctor Who* we had put by for his birthday. That's what he needs right now, to escape to another world where the bad guys never win, to blot out everything in our world.

I run to answer it. Claire gives a little shake of her head before stepping inside.

'We've had a call,' she says when she reaches the kitchen. 'Someone who claims he saw Taylor with a girl fitting Ella's description on the afternoon she went missing.'

16

MURIEL

I open my eyes, annoyed as ever that I allowed them to close at some point during the night. The urgent need to relieve myself grips me. I am up and out of bed before my brain has had a chance to adjust to being vertical. I wobble slightly as I open the bedroom door. The first shafts of sunlight are clawing their way through the landing window, determined to hurl their brightness into my face. I squint as I grab the bathroom door handle. I push but nothing happens. I frown – it has never stuck before – and then I hear the tinkling noise from inside. It is the child. And she has locked the door.

'What have I told you about locking the bathroom door?' I call out.

'I'm doing a number one,' she replies.

'Well hurry up and open the door, please.'

'I've got to wash my hands first.'

'Just open the door.'

'You told me not to get germs on the handles.'

I roll my eyes. I try to clench harder but that is the trouble – it is as if the elastic has gone down below. I'm torn between running downstairs and waiting. Surely she can't be much longer.

'Leave your hands. Open the door now.'

A few seconds later I hear her struggling with the lock. I know instantly that it is going to be too late, but it is also too late to go downstairs. As she finally opens the door, the first trickle is running down my leg. By the time she looks up it has become a gush.

'You're doing a number one too,' she says. I push past her, trailing a stream of urine across the bathroom floor.

'Don't stand there gawping, girl,' I shout. 'Get out and shut the door.'

I make it to the toilet just before the stream ends. I sit there, my nightdress hitched up around my knees, my sodden knickers around my ankles and the bathroom floor swimming in my shame. This is what I have been reduced to. An elderly woman incapable of reaching the toilet in time. I don't suppose *she* does this. The woman Malcolm left me for. It's not the fact that she is younger that bothers me. I don't understand why that is a problem for anyone. Far better to be traded in for a newer model than simply swapped for something the same age because he dislikes you so much. No, it was the way he spoke about her when he told me he was leaving which bothered me. As if she was his equal. I never felt like his equal, not once in all those years. I was the wife, the mother, the school music teacher. I was not a fellow university lecturer like her, and I don't think he ever took me seriously because of that.

I knew, of course. Knew that he was seeing someone. I don't believe women who say otherwise. It is not a matter of men working late more frequently or even leaving some tell-tale receipt in their jacket pocket. It is simply how much more attentive they are when they are home. Guilt does that to a man.

I didn't say anything. I didn't even try to compete. It is pointless. They are like a child with a new toy. There is no point trying to distract them, you simply have to wait until their attention wavers. Until the novelty wears off and the other woman starts to make demands and they realise that they are bored with the new toy now. That they are better off with the old, familiar one. Only in Malcolm's case he didn't come to that conclusion. I pretended I had no idea, of course, when he told me. There is a limit to the degree of humiliation one can take.

I peel my knickers off over my feet. I should get something to help avoid these situations, I know. There are adverts in magazines aimed at 'women of a certain age' like me. Discretion is the key, it seems. But it is an admission of failure, and I am still, even now, not quite ready for that.

I turn to the trail of urine on the floor. I use a J-Cloth to soak it up, throwing it in the bathroom bin when it is saturated. I take another clean one, run some hot water into the sink and pour some Dettol in. I give the area a thorough cleaning then use an air freshener because I'm not convinced the smell has gone. I need to go back into the bedroom to change my wet nightdress and get my dressing gown before having a shower. I pray that the child will have got bored and gone to find Melody. She hasn't though. She is sitting cross-legged outside the bathroom door, still staring at the pool of urine on the landing. I look at her face. The scolding appears to have scorched her cheeks.

'Are you going to put me on the naughty step?' she asks.

'I'm sorry I shouted at you,' I say. 'We don't have a naughty step here. But in future you will do as you are told and not lock the bathroom door.'

'Mummy lets me lock it.'

'Yes, well, your mother did a lot of things that she shouldn't have done.'

'Why can't Daddy look after me?'

'Your daddy has to go to work.'

'Is Grandma looking after Otis?'

'I imagine so.'

'When can I see Grandma and Grandad?'

'You don't need to see them.'

'They give me sweeties and buy me ice creams.'

I sigh, then realise I can compete with that.

'Well you can have a little Magnum later today. I ordered some for us. The shopping man will be delivering them.'

She gets up and rushes forward to give my legs a hug. She steps back quickly and wrinkles her nose.

'Your nightie is all wet.'

I push her away. 'We shan't be speaking of this again, do you understand?' She nods solemnly. I hurry past her into the bedroom.

I am in the kitchen laying the table for lunch when I hear the knock on the door. My fingers grip the back of the chair. They have found out. I don't know how but they have. I realise I haven't thought any of this through. What I will do if they come knocking on the door again or ask to come in even. I haven't got anywhere to hide her, not really. Certainly nowhere with a lock. Maybe I could ask her to hide. Pretend it is all part of a game. Yes, she would like that. She may stay hidden for ages.

The knock at the door comes again, louder this time. Clearly they are not going to go away. I creep out into the hall. I can see the shadow of a figure through the panes at the top of the front door. It looks like a man. I suppose it would be for something like this. I don't suppose the police would send a woman, not if they thought it was something serious.

I haven't got time to get her to hide now, it will take too long explaining. I'll just have to hope that she stays where she is. That Melody will be able to distract her for long enough for me to deal with this.

I go to the door. My hand rests shakily on the handle. I haven't got a choice. The last thing I want is someone bashing my front door down. I would never hear the end of it from next door but one. I open the door a crack. The first thing I see is the red crate of Ocado carrier bags. I laugh. I actually laugh out loud. The delivery man probably thinks I am a bit simple. Though perhaps I am in a way. How else can I explain completely forgetting about the order I placed? Or the fact that I didn't think through this part of the process. That the child would be in the house when he came. And that he really mustn't see the child.

'Hello there,' he says, handing me the receipt. 'It's all here, no substitutions.'

'Thank you,' I say, taking the first carrier bag from him quickly. It is heavy or maybe it's simply that I'm feeling a bit light-headed with it all. I stagger back into the hall.

'Are you OK with that? Do you want me to bring them into the hall for you? Or the kitchen?'

'No, thank you,' I say, aware that the child is in the lounge, that she may run out at any moment and would certainly do so if someone came into the house.

'Are you sure? It's no trouble at all. Do you usually have them brought into the house?'

'No,' I snap. Followed, as I see the look on his face by a softer, 'No, thank you.'

I put the bag down just inside the door and hold my hand out for the next one. I need this to be over quickly. I need to get the door shut before she comes out to see who it is. He carries on talking though, far too loudly for my liking. Stupid things about how the items have been packed, the fact that it's a bit cooler today and that he's relieved as he doesn't like the heat.

I nod and mutter in agreement, trying to hurry things along. His voice is too loud though, too jolly. I know it is only a matter of time.

'Is it the shopping man?' comes a voice from the lounge. 'Has he got my Magnums?' I hear her footsteps racing across the wooden floor towards the hall. I have a split second to decide what to do. I shut the door in the delivery man's face and turn to the child.

'You're to stay in that room,' I hiss. 'You mustn't come out here.'

'Has he got my Magnums? Can I have one now?'

'Not unless you stay in the room and be quiet. Do you understand?' The child nods and trots back into the room. I breathe deeply and open the front door. The man is hovering on the step, looking at me uncertainly.

'I'm so sorry,' I say. 'I'm looking after my grandson

and I didn't want him running out into the road. You've left the gate open.'

He turns to check. 'Oh, sorry about that. I thought I'd shut it behind me.'

He still looks a little uncertain. Maybe he got a glimpse of her before I managed to shut the door. She might be at the window now, looking out at him. I wouldn't put it past her. I hold out my hand for the last bag.

'Thank you,' I say as he hands it to me.

'You're welcome. Bye now.'

I shut the door. Listen to the sound of his footsteps retreating, the van doors slamming. I walk into the lounge, my feet still unsteady. The child is sitting on the floor with Melody, looking up at me as she bites her lip.

'You're not to run out if someone comes to the door, do you understand?'

She nods.

'It's for your own good. Your own protection.'

'I want my Magnum. Can I have my Magnum now?'

'No, you can wait until you've remembered your manners.'

She starts to cry. I walk out of the room. Matthew never had to be reminded about his manners. Not when he was little. He never snivelled like that either.

I stop in the hall and take a few deep breaths. Clearly we can't go on like this. We can't live in hiding for ever. I need to make a plan. I need to think about what we are going to do.

I pick up two of the carrier bags and take them through to the kitchen. The date on the wall calendar catches my eye, daring me to look back at it. I turn away. I do not need to see it to know. I have a calendar in my head. Each day I tear off the number, screw it up and throw it into the corner of my mind. It doesn't change anything though. Doesn't dim the pain. Simply litters my head with reminders that time moves on. Whether you want it to or not.

I put the shopping away, each thing in its right place. Bur there are new things too. Things I have never had in the house before. I need to find new places for them. Need to create a new order.

Outside Matthew sighs. A sigh which threads its way upwards through the canopy of the trees. He finds it hard too, I know that. Perhaps he thought taking the child in would help all of us. Perhaps it is not just about saving her. Perhaps there is someone else who needs saving. I don't like seeing his young face so sad. I try to remember what we used to do, what used to put a smile on his face. And then it comes to me.

I put one of the small Magnums on a saucer and place it on the kitchen table. I walk briskly to the doorway of the lounge.

'You may come and have your ice cream now,' I say. The child looks at me warily then jumps up when she sees the expression on my face and follows me through to the kitchen.

I sit opposite her, watching the way she savours every mouthful, delighting in the way she licks the corners of her mouth at the end.

'You like those, don't you?'

She nods.

'When we go away on holiday you'll be able to have those every day.'

The child looks at me quizzically. 'Are we going on holiday?'

'Yes, to Whitby. You like it there.'

'Do I?'

'Of course you do. The beach and the chip shop by the harbour. Climbing the steps to the abbey. You can manage them all by yourself.'

The child continues to frown.

'And we'll go to Robin Hood's Bay. Remember how much you love it there? I think you spent the entire day in a rock pool the last time we went. We can even take your fishing net if you'd like to.'

'I haven't got a fishing net.'

I laugh, a cut-glass tinkle. 'Of course you have. It's in the shed. The net is green and there's some red tape on the end of the handle.' I look down. Two eyes peer back at me. Big and wide and trusting. I reach out and squeeze his hand.

'I'll go and get it if you don't remember. Stay here a moment, I'll be right back.'

I hurry to the front door, picking up the shed key

from the pot as I pass the hall table. I step outside, pulling the door to behind me. I jiggle the key in the padlock, it always was a bit stiff. I'll have to get Malcolm to put some WD40 on it. I reach for the far corner, where I can see the handle of the fishing net. It takes a bit of wriggling about to free it from the tools. As I go to shut the shed door I catch a glimpse of red in the corner and smile to myself. Of course. How could I have forgotten?

I hurry back through to the kitchen. The child is still sitting at the table.

'Here it is,' I say, holding up the handle of the net to him. 'And look what else I found – your bucket and spade.'

I see the child's face, a little uncertain.

I turn the bucket so he can see. 'There,' I say, pointing. 'It's even got your name still on it.'

The child looks closer. 'That's not my name.'

'Of course it is. It's just that the top of the M has rubbed off a little.'

There is a pause. 'When are we going?' he asks.

'Friday,' I reply. 'Straight after breakfast.

'Are Mummy and Daddy coming too?'

'Of course we are. We wouldn't let you go on your own, would we?'

MATTHEW

Sunday, 22 June 2014

I've had sex with Sparrow and Mum knows about it. That's like the best thing ever and the worst thing ever all rolled into one. Mum hasn't said that she knows, it's far worse than that. It happened on Monday. Sparrow came home with me and said she didn't want to wait any longer so we just did it, like right there and then. It was good, like really good. I mean I don't know what it's supposed to be like, only the stuff you see in films and it wasn't quite like that. It was messier than that and it took ages for me to put the condom on (she brought some with her, how cool is that?) and we didn't lie around naked for ages afterwards because we knew we had to get everything cleaned up before Mum came home. But the actual sex, her smiling at me as she opened her legs and me looking at her and feeling how wet she was and then being inside her for the first time and moving inside her and watching her face as she moaned before I just sort of exploded inside her, that was fucking awesome.

We had to get up pretty much straight afterwards. I'd put a towel down on the bed before we started and there was a bit of blood on it so I had to chuck it straight in the washing machine on a quick cycle with some other stuff of mine to sort of cover it up. And we had to remake the bed and smooth down the duvet and I checked about twenty times before we left that you couldn't tell and I really didn't think you could.

But when I came home from school Mum had changed the sheets on my bed. I'd forgotten that she always does that on a Monday, like we always have fish on Friday evening. Anyway, I put my earphones in and lay down on the bed and thought about what had happened earlier, and I still don't know how I saw it or anything but there was a strand of hair on my pillow, a very long strand of dark brown hair, Sparrow's hair, and it didn't hit me for a minute and then I just sat up and said, 'Shit. Shit, shit, shit, shit, shit.' Cos I realised it was Monday and Mum had changed the sheets. I double-checked just in case and they were white instead of the blue ones that were on before (and I know they were blue before cos Sparrow took the piss about the fact that Mum does them on a rota) and that was when I knew. Mum must have found Sparrow's hair on my pillow. She must have picked it up and put it somewhere and washed the sheets and put the new ones on and put the hair back on the pillow so that I would know. So now I know that she knows and she knows that I know she knows and I don't know if I'm supposed to apologise or say anything and if I do she'll probably turn round and say she doesn't know what I'm talking about and then I'll have really landed myself in it but if I don't say anything there's going to be this awful unspoken thing between us for ever. I mean, if she'd screamed and shouted at me I could have dealt with that, but this, this is just kind of weird. It's like she's left a calling card and she's watching me and I know what she wants me to do. She wants me to end it. And she's kind of saying that if I end it nothing more will ever be said on the subject. But there's no way on earth I am going to end it. So I don't know what happens now, whether we have some massive row or I just get the silent treatment for the rest of my life or if she's in her room sticking pins in a doll of Sparrow or something.

I texted Sparrow and told her. I didn't phone cos I had the feeling Mum would be listening outside my door. Sparrow reckons Mum is some kind of psycho. She said I should just ignore it, pretend it never happened and we carry on as before, but that's easy for her to say, she doesn't have to live with her. It feels like I've got to choose between them and I can't do that. Maybe Mum is a psycho but she's still my mum and I'm all she's got left and I can't just ignore her cos to do that would feel like I was stabbing her in the back.

And it's really crap timing cos our exams will have finished soon and then we're not going to be able to see each other in school any more and as soon as The Grange break up in a few weeks Mum won't have anything to do and she's gonna be watching me all the time. Every time I go out she's gonna want to know where I'm going, and I can't lie to her, not after this. Sparrow says I should front her up, tell her I'm eighteen and it's none of her fucking business where I am or who I'm with but I know if I do that she'll just do that whole 'not under my roof' thing and I will feel really bad for upsetting her.

So it's like I'm trapped in my bedroom now. I haven't even had the balls to go downstairs yet because she'll be sitting there in her favourite armchair doing that pursed-lips thing and I don't know what the fuck I'm supposed to say to her. The whole thing is a nightmare. I wish I could see Sparrow but she can't come round and I can't go there. So we're all texted out and I'm just lying here holding Sparrow's hair in my hand cos it's all I've got left of her right now. The whole thing is such a mess.

17

LISA

We watch it on TV, the police starting their search of Ogden Water. It is like driving past an awful pile-up on the motorway and knowing you shouldn't look but still sneaking a glimpse. Only in this case we are the grieving relatives on the hard shoulder, looking down on the carnage and wondering when they are going to bring out the body of our loved one.

Claire said it didn't mean anything, that we weren't to lose hope. It was simply something they had to do in the circumstances. The circumstances being that someone had reported seeing a man who looked like Taylor with a small girl who fitted the description of Ella in the car park at Ogden Water about an hour after she'd disappeared on Friday afternoon.

It was apparently only a fleeting glimpse; the man

and the girl were some distance from him and he couldn't remember exactly what she was wearing, although he thought there was some green in it. And it was only when he saw the photos of Taylor and Ella alongside each other on the TV screen that he came forward. And sometimes, as Claire had been at great pains to point out to us, people see what they want to see and make it fit when it doesn't because everyone likes putting the final piece in the jigsaw.

And that is why we are watching film taken from a helicopter of a police diver in Ogden Water. And why I am digging what is left of my nails into my palms and why Alex is physically shaking on the sofa next to me and why Otis has gone to Mum and Dad's for the day and Chloe is in her room refusing to come out.

We have muted the sound – the relentless speculation is more than we can bear – but neither of us seems capable of reaching over for the remote control and pressing the Off button. It is almost as though we feel we should be there for her when they find her. That having failed her so miserably in her short life, we should at least be there for her now in death. I am feeling it now, the sensation I thought I would feel if something had happened to her. It is a combination of acute morning sickness and apprehension. I do not like the feeling, I want to try to shake it off, chase it away. And there is only one way I know how to do that.

I get up. 'I'm going for a run,' I say. Alex looks up at me, his eyes big and hollow.

'What, now?'

'Yeah. I have to. I have to get away from this.'

He nods and shuts his eyes. I go upstairs to our bedroom and pull on my tracksuit bottoms. I even remember to put on my sports bra before my top. I hurry back downstairs, past the open door of the living room, where I can see Alex sitting with his head in his hands. I feel like such a cow, leaving him like this, but I can't stop here. If I stay here it will happen. I have to chase it away. I have to run as far as possible as fast as possible and I have to do it now. I grab my trainers, sit for a moment at the bottom of the stairs to do my laces, before opening the front door and stepping outside.

I start off walking, aware that I haven't done my usual stretches, and build my speed up slowly. I don't want to run in the streets anyway, it would only attract attention. Neighbours have probably seen me going out the front door as it is, no doubt wondering what the hell I am doing, just as Alex is. My pace quickens as I get to the recreation ground. I see the swings I have pushed Ella on more times than I care to remember, the slide she banged her head on once when she was little, the school that she should have started this week. I realise that I will not be able to stay in this village if she is dead. It would be like living on the set of her childhood, surrounded by her image at every turn. We will have to move, although I have no idea where to. That will be a massive hassle and Otis will hate it, which will make me feel really bad. And maybe it won't make any difference where we are anyway; maybe I will still see her face on every swing, in every playground.

I start running. My body feels stiff. I can't remember the last time I went five days without doing any exercise, probably not since Ella was tiny. I increase my stride and push harder. My heart quickens, my hair streaks back behind me. I run faster still. I like the way it is making me feel: pushing me, stretching me, forcing me to breathe hard. I run to the end of the rec, past the rugby club and out onto the lane. I am comforted by the sound of my trainers on the tarmac, pounding at a steady pace, relentless. I will keep on running, I will never stop. I simply will not let the events of this week catch up with me. If I run fast enough I might be able to make time go backwards, get the world to rewind, never take the call, never agree to let her hide again, never even go to the fucking park.

A Land Rover comes around the bend too fast. I catch the look on the driver's face as she sees me: shock, terror, guilt, all jostling for position. I throw myself against the drystone wall. She manages to brake in time, shakes her head and lifts her hand in acknowledgement at me for a second. It was her mistake but she got away with it. Some people are not that lucky.

Alex is still sitting on the sofa in front of the TV with his head in his hands when I get back. The BBC News Channel appears to have moved on to something else but Alex has not. I sit down next to him. My body is damp with sweat but it is the hurt seeping from Alex's pores which overwhelms me.

I stroke his hair. He looks up. For the first time I don't see any hope in his eyes.

'What's he done to her, Lis?'

I look at him, knowing it is my turn to be strong.

'He might not have done anything. He might not even be involved.'

'But if he's not, someone else is.'

'Whoever it is she'd fight,' I say. 'She'd put up such a fight.'

'I know. It wouldn't help her, though, would it? Not against a bloke. When I think of how tiny her hand used to look in mine ...'

I wrap my arms around him, feel his chest heaving.

'Don't push me away, will you, Lis? We're going to need each other to get through this.'

'I know. I just needed to get out. I feel like I'm suffocating in here sometimes.'

He nods. 'Did it help?'

'Only for a few minutes.'

I knock on Chloe's door at lunchtime. I want to get her out of her room. I want to sit down for lunch as a family. What little family I have left.

There is no reply but I go in anyway. I thought it would be different when she came home from uni, that our relationship would start to heal as she tried on adulthood for size and cast off the teenage 'I hate you' persona. It hasn't turned out that way though. Mainly because she still has a reason to hate me, and a bloody good one at that.

Her bedroom is white. Pure and sterile. You could perform surgery in there it is so clean. She lies on her bed reading John Green's *Looking for Alaska*. She got into him by reading *The Fault in Our Stars*. I didn't realise what it was about at the time. Afterwards, when I found her sobbing in a heap on the floor, I said I didn't think it was a good idea for her to go and see the film. She gave me a look of contempt and went anyway, of course, with Robyn. Her eyes were red raw when she came home. I didn't understand why she did that to herself but I knew far better than to say anything.

I sit on the corner of her bed. She looks up at me. I know what she is asking without her having to say a word and I shake my head. She closes her eyes for a second as if giving silent thanks.

'It might not have been her, you know,' I say.

'Always look on the bright side, eh?'

'It's true. Just because they're looking, doesn't mean to say it was her.'

She rolls her eyes.

'What's that supposed to mean?'

'I'm not a kid, you know. You don't have to try to protect me like you're doing with Otis.'

'We've got to keep hoping.'

'You're sounding like Alex now.'

'Well, he's right.'

'So why did you go for a run earlier?'

I sigh. 'I'm not saying it's easy, I'm just saying we've got to try.'

'Yeah, because everything might turn out OK. She might just have gone off with her fairy godmother to Disneyland.'

'Please don't, Chloe. Not now.'

'Why, because it hurts? Well, welcome to my world. What took you so long to get here?'

'Look, I know this is hard for y—.'

'No, you don't. You have no fucking idea at all.'

She picks up her book again and pretends to start reading. Her eyes are so moist I'm not sure she'll be able to make out any of the words. I want to say something, the right thing. But I don't have good form on that, especially not with Chloe. So I stand up and say, 'Lunch is downstairs if you want it,' instead.

*   *   *

We have barely finished lunch when Tony arrives, still in his overalls.

'What are you doing here?' I ask.

'Lunch hour. Boss says to take as much time as I want.'

'Can I get you a brew, Tony?' asks Claire.

'Nah, you're all right.'

Tony has never been known to refuse a cup of tea in his life. Claire gets the message and goes off to join Alex in front of the TV.

'Any news?' he asks.

I shake my head.

'Fucking pervert. Should never have been allowed out for whatever it was he did in the first place.'

'We don't know it's him.'

'Well there's not exactly a long list of suspects, is there?'

'He's got an alibi. His mother says he was at home.'

'And you buy that, do you? Look how many times Mum covered up for me when I was in trouble.'

'That's cos she's soft and for some reason she thought the sun shone out of your arse. But you know she wouldn't have covered up for something like this.'

Tony shakes his head and looks at me. 'You can't go on kidding yourself. I know it's hard but you've got to face up to what's happened, Lis, we all have.'

'So you think she's dead, is that what you're saying?'

Tony shuts his eyes and shuffles his feet. 'Well it's not

looking good, is it? She's been missing five days and not a single sighting until now.'

'Maybe someone's got her locked up somewhere.'

'Yeah, maybe. But I tell you this, if that bastard Taylor knows what's good for him he'd better spill the beans pretty sharpish.'

I have just got out of the shower the next morning when Claire rings.

'No news,' she says, knowing better than to start a phone conversation with me with anything else. 'We're still holding Taylor but we've got absolutely nothing on him. There's something I need to tell you, though.'

'Go on.'

'Someone put a brick through the window of Taylor's house in the early hours. His mum wasn't injured – she was asleep upstairs – but she's pretty shaken up. We've sent officers round there now to take a statement.'

'Oh Jesus.'

'I'm really sorry, Lisa, but you probably know what I'm going to say next.'

'You think it's one of us.'

'No, but it's going to be the first thing the investigating officers ask me when they get back. Do you think Tony might have . . . ?'

I sigh. 'I don't know, Claire. I don't know anything

any more. But just give me half an hour if you can and I'll find out.'

I park outside Mum and Dad's house and call Tony on his mobile. I feel bad doing it because I know what he is going to think the second he sees my name come up on the screen, but I don't want to knock and have to do this in front of Mum and Dad.

'It's OK. There's no news,' I say as soon as he answers, 'but I need to talk to you. I'm outside. Please come down quietly and let me in.'

I get out of the car and walk over to the front door wishing I didn't have to ask this and suspecting I already know the answer I am going to get.

A few moments later the door opens. Tony is standing there in his boxers and a T-shirt.

'What the fuck's going on?' he asks as I step inside.

'I was hoping you were going to tell me that.'

'What do you mean?'

'Someone put a brick through the window of Taylor's house early this morning.'

'Good for them.'

'Don't play games, Tony.'

'You think I fucking did it?'

I gesture to him to lower his voice. 'Last time I saw you, you were mouthing off about how he should never have been let out of prison.'

'Well, yeah, don't mean to say I'm going to go and brick his house, does it?'

'Are you saying you didn't do it? Only the cops are going to be turning up soon and I want to know before they do.'

'They think it's me?'

'Well you're a pretty obvious suspect.'

'I'm surprised it was just a brick, to be honest. Would have thought someone would have petrol-bombed it by now.'

'Don't piss me about, Tony.'

'You're the one who came round here accusing me of summat I didn't do.'

'I've only got your word for that, haven't I?'

'He didn't do it, Lis.'

I look up to see Dad standing at the top of the stairs in his dressing gown.

'How can you be so sure of that?' I ask.

Dad hesitates and walks a few steps down towards us.

'Because I did it,' he says.

I stare at Dad as he walks down the stairs, struggling to take in what he has just said.

'No, you didn't,' I say as he reaches the bottom and stands in front of me and Tony. 'You couldn't have. You don't even know where he lives.'

'I asked around,' says Dad. 'It weren't hard.' His face is serious. He's not mucking about. He actually bloody did it. I shake my head and turn to Tony.

'Did you know about this?'

'Course I didn't fucking know about it. I'd have gone with him if I had.'

'That's why I didn't tell you,' says Dad. 'It wouldn't have been fair on your mother.'

'Oh, so it's all right for you to get yourself banged up but not him, is it?' I say.

'Well someone had to do it, and I'd rather it was me than him who got done.'

I shake my head. 'You didn't have to do anything. You could have just left it alone.'

'How? How could I leave it alone when Ella is missing and this fucking pervert isn't telling us where she is?'

'We don't even know it was him.'

'Course it was him. And I am not having him sitting there, laughing at us, while the cops are diving in bloody lakes for my granddaughter.'

'Vince, what's going on?' I look up. Mum is standing at the top of the stairs in her nightie, her hair messy, her eyes wide with dread.

'It's OK,' I say. 'It's not Ella.'

'Well what's all the shouting about? Why are you here?'

'You'd better tell her,' I say, turning to Dad.

He looks down at his feet for a moment before looking at Mum. 'I put a brick through Taylor's window, that's all.'

Mum stares at him, a frown creasing her forehead.

'When?'

'Early hours of this morning.'

'But I didn't hear a thing.'

'I was hardly going to wake you before I went, was I? See if you'd make me a packed lunch for the journey.'

Mum sits down on the stairs. I can see her hands shaking. 'But why, Vince? Why would you go and do a thing like that?'

'Because it needed to be done.'

Mum shakes her head. 'I don't understand. Was anyone hurt?' She looks at me as she says it.

'No. His Mum was sleeping upstairs. She's pretty shaken up apparently.'

'I'm not surprised. You must have put the fear of God up her, Vince.'

'Good.'

'What do you mean, good?' I ask.

'I wanted to do that. That way she might stop lying to protect that fucking toe-rag of a son of hers.'

'Oh Jesus.' I roll my eyes. 'How could you do something so stupid?'

'I was doing it for you.'

'Me?'

'Yeah.'

'So how do you work that one out?'

I see Dad swallow, his face contorted. 'Because I can't bear to see you suffer like this. Because same way Ella's your little girl, you're still mine and I know that might sound soft or whatever but it's true. I'm supposed to protect you but I didn't, did I? I didn't protect Ella either. I'm supposed to be head of our family and I've let you all down. I lie in bed every night feeling so bloody useless and hating that there's nowt I can do and then this happened and I realised I could do summat to help. I just wanted to try to make it better, to make him say where she is, like. Put you out of your misery and get our little princess back, even if she's not even alive any more. I wanted to get her back for you.'

A solitary tear rolls down Dad's left cheek. He wipes it away but not before I see it through my own tears. I step towards him and he throws his arms tight around me, squeezes me harder than is comfortable as he sobs great, big Yorkshireman tears on my shoulder. And right now I hate this world. I hate God or whoever it is who's in charge, who could do this to a grown man. I hate the man who called my mobile in the park, the people writing horrible things about us on Twitter and Facebook and most of all the man who took Ella and took away our lives in the process.

I can hear Mum crying on the stairs behind me. I look up to gesture Tony to go to her but he is already there.

'She's gone, hasn't she?' asks Dad when he finally looks up at me.

'Yeah,' I whisper. 'I think she has.'

I am still there when the police come and arrest Dad on suspicion of causing criminal damage. I think Claire has had a word with them after my phone call because they knock very politely as if they are collecting for charity, not about to arrest someone.

And they have done what I asked and sent an unmarked car. The officers are still in uniform and no doubt some of the neighbours will talk anyway but it makes it a little easier for Mum.

I step forward and kiss Dad on the cheek before he goes. He clings on to my hand, his eyes looking like they have been punched into the back of his head.

'Sorry,' he says.

'Don't be a daft bugger,' I reply.

Mum sits on the stairs with Tony. I am not sure she has moved from that spot since she broke down, and for once she doesn't seem to care that she is in her nightie and hasn't done her hair. I think it is the first time in my life I've known her allow strangers to see her without make-up on. It doesn't matter any more. The same way the weather doesn't matter any more, or that someone forgot to get the milk, or what we are having for dinner later, or that the garden gate needs oiling. None of it matters or will ever matter again.

18

MURIEL

'No. It's a G. Come on, you know that. Where are you today, dreamland?'

The child looks down and swings her legs from the piano stool. Her fingers appear stubbier than I remembered. Certainly when compared to Matthew's. She is not concentrating. To be honest she seems incapable of concentrating. I start to wonder if she has that attention deficit disorder that so many children seem to have these days. I've always thought it was poppycock. Giving a medical name to what used to be known as downright disobedience. Maybe they have a point, though. Perhaps the genes have mutated and there is a generation of children who simply can't physically sit still for five minutes. I remember when I went on a school trip with The Grange last Christmas. Admittedly *Jack and the Beanstalk* in Halifax wouldn't have been my choice of theatre experience, especially not with a cast of talent-show and reality-TV people I had never heard of. But the fact was not one of the children was capable of sitting still for the duration of the performance. Umpteen toilet visits, complaining when their sweets and ice creams had been eaten, talking and fidgeting throughout the whole thing. And these were children from good homes. I dread to think what other children would be like. I told Mrs Cuthbertson straight afterwards that I wouldn't be accompanying them there again. As it happened, I left not long afterwards anyway. It wasn't my doing. I didn't see what the problem was, but Mrs Cuthbertson was always very touchy about parent complaints. One over-sensitive child says something to a parent and the next I knew, she was calling me into her office for 'a word'. I didn't give her the satisfaction, mind. Told her I was taking early retirement before she had the chance to say anything. She said she totally understood in the 'difficult circumstances', that she was surprised I hadn't taken the decision sooner. She even had the gall to try to pat me on the hand as I left her office. Not that I was having any of it. The fact is several of the children from The Grange still come to me for private lessons, so she didn't manage to turn all the parents against me. Not everyone believes the gossip you hear in the playground.

'I don't want to play any more,' the child whines.

'Well you won't get better if you don't practise.'

'When's Otis coming for his lesson?'

'He won't be coming any more.'

'Why not?'

'Because I'm too busy looking after you.'

'But I want him to come. I want to see Otis. And Daddy will bring him and he can take me home afterwards. I want to go home now.'

I sigh and shake my head. 'This is your new home, remember?'

'I don't want to live here.'

'That sounded rather ungrateful, you know. You're very lucky that I've taken you in when no one else could look after you. Often children get put in a home if their parents aren't fit to look after them.'

'Like Little Orphan Annie in the film?'

'Yes, just like that.'

Her face brightens for a second. 'Will I get a dog called Sandy?'

'No, of course not. That would hardly be fair on Melody, would it?'

She shakes her head.

'What I'm trying to make you understand is that you should count your blessings. I've given you a lovely home to live in, lots of toys to play with, and I'm taking you on holiday.'

She is quiet. Thinking for a moment.

'Will Grandma take Otis on holiday and get him new toys?'

'I don't know. She might not be able to afford it.'

She fixes me with a look. 'Do they have donkeys where we are going? Can I have a donkey ride?'

I stare down at the child looking up at me expectantly. Smell the salt in the air. Feel the unwelcome sensation of sand between my toes.

'Why of course they do. Don't you remember Ted?'

The child looks at me blankly.

'He's your favourite donkey. He's chocolate-brown and all the others are grey. You picked him out especially. You give him sugar lumps. The man lets you. Remember how you hold out your hand?'

She hesitates before slowly extending her arm.

'That's right. Hand flat, fingers straight. The opposite of what we do on a piano. And then he comes and takes it from you.'

'Does he bite?'

'No. Of course not. I wouldn't let you do it if he did. It tickles. You said it tickles and his muzzle feels all soft and velvety in your hand.'

The child smiles at last. A small uncertain smile but a smile none the less.

'Now,' I say, 'why don't I go and get you a drink and then we can go upstairs and start packing?'

The child nods. 'Ribena. Please can I have a Ribena?'

'Of course you can,' I say, smiling back. I go to the kitchen and get one of the little cartons which the shopping man delivered yesterday. I wonder again whether he glimpsed the child. Maybe he told someone back at the depot. Perhaps they check people's orders to see if they've bought anything unusual. It would all come up if they did. The Magnums, the SpongeBob Squarepants thing. The Ribena. Maybe we need to go away before Saturday. Friday, if I can find somewhere. The cottage brochure usually has quite a few places which start on a Friday, I will have a look later. I need to get away. I'm not sure I can face being in this house on Friday.

I go back in. The child is staring vacantly out of the window. I pierce the carton with the straw before handing it to her, reminding her not to squeeze too hard as she takes it.

'The shopping man brought some crumpets too.'

I wait for the shriek of delight but it does not come. She nods solemnly. Her mind appears to be somewhere else entirely.

I walk out into the hall. Matthew's photos line the walls. He tries so hard to keep me going, to spread joy when there is none. To fill the house with good memories when the floorboards creak under the weight of the bad.

I go to the bread bin, get out the crumpets and turn on the grill. The flame roars and then quietens as I adjust the knob. I turn towards the fridge to get the butter out and almost bump into her. She shuffles out of the way only to stand right in front of the cutlery drawer, where I am going next.

'Run along and play,' I say. 'Go and find Melody. I can't have you under my feet in the kitchen.'

She goes without a murmur. I don't know what has got into her. I thought she would be excited about the holiday. I sigh and busy myself with the crumpets, pour the child a glass of milk.

'Your snack is ready,' I call out once the butter has melted sufficiently. She doesn't come. I am reminded that six days ago she practically snapped my hand off. I call again. Nothing. I go out into the hall. She is sitting on the front doormat with a leaflet in her hand, silent tears streaming down her face. I see the West Yorkshire Police logo. I rush forward and snatch the leaflet out of her hands. MISSING is emblazoned across the top, along with her name and a large photo of her.

'Where did you get that from?'

'It came through letter box.'

'Yes, well you shouldn't have picked it up.'

'It's got my picture on it.'

'It was meant for me.'

'Why has it got my picture on it?'

'It doesn't matter. It's nothing to do with you.'

'It's got my name on it and it says I'm missing.'

I look up at the ceiling. I'd been hoping she didn't know the word. Wouldn't be able to read it.

'You said you didn't know your letters.'

'I see them on lamp posts with the doggy pictures.

Mummy said it's when doggies get lost and they're trying to find them.'

My mouth feels dry. I stare at the floor, unable to look her in the eye. It is all unravelling. Falling apart around me. I wish Matthew were here. He would help me find some way out of this mess.

'Your mother has told the police you are missing to cover up the fact that she has been a bad mother and lost you. They think someone naughty took you.'

She wipes her nose on the back of her hand.

'The naughty boys?' she asks. 'Do they think the naughty boys took me?'

'Yes. Yes, they probably do.'

'Are you going to take me back now?'

'Of course not. You know I can't do that. Your mummy isn't capable of looking after you. Anyway, we're going on holiday. We're going on Friday instead of Saturday.' We'll leave early, very early. She might even go back to sleep, which would be a blessing for the journey.

'I don't want to go on holiday. I want to go home.'

The silent tears become an audible sob.

'Enough of this nonsense,' I say, handing her a handkerchief from my pocket. 'You can't keep getting upset over this. You live here now. It's for your own good. You know it is.'

'Someone might find me. Someone found one of lost doggies when it went missing. A white one with a black patch over his eye. Mummy showed me a picture in paper.'

'No one's going to find you. And even if they do, you won't be able to go back to your mummy. They won't let you. Not when they find out what a bad mummy she is.'

She stares at me, tiny daggers stabbing at me from the corners of her eyes, then in an instant she leaps up off the mat and reaches up for the front-door handle. I lunge forward and grab her hand, pulling it away. She couldn't reach it anyway but I put the chain across just in case.

I bend down and look her in the face. 'Now, we'll have no more of that nonsense, thank you.'

She cowers back against the door. I mustn't lose her trust, I know that. I try to soften my face a little.

'Let's go and have that crumpet, shall we?'

She stares up at me, her eyes moist, and walks slowly through to the kitchen, her head hanging. I pick up the flyer, fold it in half and tuck it away in the magazine rack.

As I turn I catch sight of Matthew watching me. 'We're going away on Friday,' I say to him. 'All of us together. I'm going to start packing later. You can help me if you like.'

He smiles back at me and nods. He is a good boy, Matthew. Always such a good boy.

MATTHEW

Monday, 25 August 2014

Sparrow has dumped me. Dumped me for good, not like just a falling-out or something. She didn't get the grades to get into Leeds (which is probably my fault cos she was with me when she should have been swotting and I feel really bad because I got the grades to get in and she didn't) so she went through clearing and the only place she could get was at Lancaster Uni so she took it and told me we could still see each other at weekends and I told her we couldn't cos Mum will go ape if I go away when I haven't seen her all week, especially when she'll know who I'd be going to see. And Sparrow just lost it and said that I had to choose between her and my mum and if I couldn't stand up to my own mother then I obviously didn't love her as much as I said I did. I told her I couldn't do that. I told her I loved her more than anyone in the world but I couldn't hurt Mum, not after everything she's been through. Sparrow said she'd had enough of it, all the creeping around and secret meetings over the summer when Mum was off work (she hasn't been back to our house since the hair thing, she couldn't really). She said she's not going to spend the rest of her life living a lie and if I was so ashamed of her that I couldn't tell my own mother then it was over.

And the worst thing of all is that she's probably right. I mean it is pretty pathetic and it's not as if I've got anyone else to blame apart from myself. If I'd confronted Mum about the hair thing instead of buying into her control shit, then maybe none of this would have happened. I mean Sparrow still wouldn't have got into Leeds but it needn't have mattered – plenty of other people carry on seeing each other when they go to different unis. It's just that plenty of other people haven't got a mum like mine. It's like she doesn't want me to grow up, like she needs to control every aspect of my life. And I know she's had a crap year and all that stuff but it's not fair giving me this guilt trip. Neither of us have ever mentioned the hair but it's like it's hanging over us all the time. I know she's disappointed in me and she thinks I've let her down but I just don't get how she thinks I'm supposed to live the rest of my life just being the dutiful son and never going out with anyone or going anywhere outside a twenty-mile radius of the house.

She doesn't understand how much I love Sparrow and there's no point me telling her cos she'd just say it was teenage stuff and I should be concentrating on my degree course not throwing my life away for some girl. But she's not some girl. She means the world to me and I can't bear the thought of existing without her. I can't even think about going to Leeds now, I mean what's the point?

And the worst think about it is it's all my own fault and I wish I could just tell Mum to fuck off and let me live my life but I can't cos I'm not sure she could take it right now, not after everything that's happened.

She's still so fucking uptight all the time and we still never mention Dad and she doesn't even talk about Grandma much now she's gone. It's like her life's got smaller and smaller and it's just me and her and she's the puppeteer and she's pulling my strings. I think she gets off on it sometimes, I really do. Having this control over me, knowing that I can't say anything to her because if I do she'll bring up the whole hair thing and that will be the end of our relationship.

I have no idea what I'm going to do, no idea at all. I've lost the person I love most in the world and the only way I can get her back is to stick the boot into my own mother. What kind of choice is that? I mean it's no choice at all.

I keep texting Sparrow and telling her I love her but she isn't returning my texts and she won't take my calls and she probably hates me. Actually hates my guts and never wants to see me again. And I'm so weak and pathetic I can't do anything about it. I'm going to be trapped here for the rest of my life. I don't even want to go to Leeds now. I mean I know it gets me out of this place but all I'll be thinking the whole time is that Sparrow should be there with me and what's the point without her? There's no fucking point at all.

The only thing I do know is that I love Sparrow right now more than I have loved anyone in my entire life and that I will never love anyone else. And somehow I've got to find a way to make her see that.

19

LISA

I bring Mum back to our house when she is dressed. She had offered to look after Otis for us today but to be honest I think she is the one who needs looking after. Besides, I don't suppose it will be long before the press are back outside her house and I don't want her to have to face that on her own.

She did at least manage to put on a little bit of make-up, saying she didn't want to scare Otis. Alex takes her through into the living room and sits her down with a cup of tea.

'Why does Grandma look so old today?' asks Otis, coming through to the kitchen.

'She's tired, love,' I say. 'And worried, like we all are.'

'Where's Grandad?'

I sigh, unsure of what to tell him. It will be all over the

media soon and when Otis goes back to school he is going to hear about it, so it's probably better he hears it from me.

'Grandad's at the police station, love. He did something he shouldn't have done and he's gone to say sorry.'

'What did he do?'

'He smashed the window of a house where a man lives. He was angry at him because he thought he might know where Ella is.'

'Where is Ella?'

'We don't know, sweetie. That's why the police are talking to this man, to try to find out.'

'Why might he know – was he playing hide-and-seek with her?'

I hesitate. It is hard to know how to respond to that. Right now Otis's innocence strikes me as about the most beautiful thing in the world and I don't want to be the one to destroy it.

'He lives near the park, and he might have seen where she hid.'

Otis pauses, you can almost hear the cogs going round in his head.

'Is Grandad going to get in trouble for breaking the window?'

'Yeah, he is.'

'Will he go to prison?'

I shake my head.

'Why not? You always tell me people who do bad things have to go to prison.'

'He'll have to go to court, love. He'll probably get fined and have to pay for the window to be replaced.'

'He won't do that again then, will he?'

'No,' I say, managing a half-smile. 'He won't.'

Claire arrives shortly afterwards; even she looks drained now.

'Sorry,' I say as I let her in. 'We're not exactly making this easy for you, are we?'

'Not your fault,' she says. 'Anyway, I do need to talk to you both.'

I glance at Alex, unsure what she is going to throw at us now.

'Do we need to sit down?' he asks.

'It might be best.' We do as we are told and go through to the kitchen. Alex holds my hand under the table.

'We're about to release Taylor. A man came forward who was at Ogden Water last Friday with his daughter. To be fair she does look quite similar to Ella and the dad was the right sort of height and build as Taylor – a bit older mind.'

'So Taylor wasn't even there?'

'No.'

'And his mum wasn't lying about him being in all afternoon?'

'No, it seems not.'

'Fucking hell,' I say, putting my head down on the kitchen table. I don't know whether to feel relieved that they aren't going to find her at the bottom of Ogden Water or angry for being put through all of this. I realise I still have hold of Alex's hand, which is gripping mine tightly. I sit up and turn to him. His face is pale, and there are tears coursing down his cheeks.

'It's OK,' I say. 'She's not there. He hasn't touched her.' He pulls me towards him. I'm vaguely aware that Claire is leaving the kitchen.

A bit later, when we have had a chance to get ourselves together, she comes back in quietly and puts the kettle on before turning to us.

'We are going to have to charge your dad with criminal damage, I'm afraid. We've taken a full statement and we're going to drop him off home soon.'

'Does he know about Taylor?'

'Not yet. I thought you'd want to tell him yourself.'

Alex puts his arm around my shoulders. 'You didn't think it was Taylor, did you? Not even at the beginning.'

'I had my doubts.'

'Why?'

It is Claire's turn to sigh. 'I can't tell you the background but let's just say we had every reason to believe his mother.'

'Is she OK, his mum?' I ask.

'Yeah, just shaken up really. Very upset. She knows they're going to have to move, what with all the media attention. We've advised them to stay with friends out of the area tonight, for their own safety.'

'I'm sorry,' I say quietly. 'It's all a bit of a mess, isn't it?'

Claire nods.

'So where does this leave the investigation?' asks Alex.

'Pretty much back where we were before, I'm afraid. No positive sightings, nothing on CCTV, but we're still sifting through all the information that's come in. It's not like we haven't got other possible lines of enquiry.'

She is going into police-speak now. That is how bad it is.

'And the search of Ogden Water?' I ask.

'That's been called off. In the circumstances we think our resources would be better used elsewhere.'

Alex nods and squeezes my arm and I think that at least I won't have to watch any more men in wetsuits looking for my daughter on TV. Not for now, anyway.

Tony calls round later, after he's been home to see Dad. For the first time his face actually reminds me of our father, it is that haggard.

'How is he?' I ask.

'Quiet,' he says, which for Dad is about as bad as it gets.

'Are there lots of press still?'

'Yeah. Quite a few. I just kept my head down.'

'Claire says they'll probably be gone by tomorrow.'

Tony nods. 'I had a call, Lis. From a mate of mine called Big Don, after it was on the news and that. He used to live near Taylor, was in the same class as him, like.'

'Yeah,' I say, wondering where this is going.

'It was his sister. Taylor was found guilty of having sex with his own sister. That's why he was on sex offenders register. He didn't use force, like, but it was treated as rape because of her age. She was ten and he was thirteen. They'd both been sexually abused by their stepfather for years.'

'Oh Jeez,' I say.

'His sister told his mum what had happened and she turned him in, right after she kicked the stepfather out.'

I look up at the ceiling and shake my head. 'And now look what we've gone and done to her. Have you told Dad?'

'Nah. Not sure he can take it at the moment but I thought you should know.'

'Yeah. Thanks. Can I get you a brew?'

He shakes his head. 'No, ta. I'd better get back, make sure everything's OK.'

I text Claire after he has gone. Ask her to apologise to Taylor's mum on our behalf. But even as I do it I know it's too late for her family. In the same way it's probably too late for ours.

20

MURIEL

The child is quiet the following morning. It's like she is running on batteries and they are getting low. I hope the holiday will recharge her. I have booked a little cottage up on the cliffs. Very remote, somewhere we won't be disturbed. I have been given a key code. The lady said the key will be left in one of those little boxes. We won't even have to see anyone. They take pets too, so I can take Melody. I'll keep her in, of course. We will all need to stay in but we will be away from here, that is the important thing.

I have given the child one of Matthew's jigsaws which I dug out from the box room. I sit watching as she does it. It's a garden birds one, Matthew used to be a member of the Young Ornithologists Club. I don't imagine they have many members these days. Children don't seem capable of sitting still long enough to watch for birds. There are seventy-five pieces so it may be a bit old for her. Although I know for certain that Matthew could do it at her age. She doesn't appear to know about doing the edges first, just starts from a random point in the middle where she has found two pieces which fit.

'The corners,' I say. 'Haven't you been taught that you need to find the corners first?'

She turns to look at me, shaking her head. I go over and crouch down next to her on the floor, picking up a corner piece and handing it to her.

'There,' I say. 'Now you find the other corner pieces, then you can find the edge pieces which join them up. It's like a frame for the picture.'

'Did Matthew do this jigsaw?'

'Yes. It was one of his favourites. He always liked birds.'

'Did he have a pet bird?'

'No. We did ask but he never wanted one. Not even a budgie.'

'Why not?'

'He didn't like to see them caged, you see. Thought they should be free to fly off if they wanted to. Said no creature should be kept somewhere against their will. And that birds had wings because they were meant to fly, not be stuck in cages.'

I swallow and stare out of the window. Perhaps I should have known back then, the trouble it was all going to cause, these fancy ideas of his. Perhaps I should have gone against him. Bought him a budgie in a cage anyway so that he could see that it would be fine. Would be safe and protected. And that freedom was actually rather overrated.

'I like birds,' the child says.

'I know you do.'

'Have I got a favourite bird?'

'Of course you have. You've got that many things with them on.'

'What things?'

I laugh. 'All of your things. Do you want me to get them for you?'

The child nods.

I shake my head with a smile and go upstairs. There is a separate box with them all in. It made sense to keep them together. They were the only things Matthew actually asked me to keep. I put them away in the box for safe keeping. He has not asked me for them since, but he will one day. And when he is ready I will have them all here for him.

I lift the box with both hands, it will just about be manageable down the stairs. I take a break on the landing after the first flight. I glance at Matthew.

'I don't know what you're laughing at,' I say to him. 'You're the one who asked to see them.'

I pause again at the bottom of the stairs while I get my breath back. The child comes to the doorway.

'It's OK,' I say. 'You go back in; I'll bring it in to you.'

I put the box down on the rug in the lounge. The child is there immediately, opening the flaps, desperate to see inside. Melody rubs around the box too and sniffs at it.

'Now, let's see if you remember,' I say. I unwrap the tissue paper around the first object and hand him the black and white ceramic money box. He turns it over and shakes it, as if there might still be something inside. There isn't of course.

He looks up at me. 'Penguins,' he says in a little voice.

'Of course it's penguins. It's been penguins for as long as I can remember. Look how many penguin things you've got.' He looks in the box as I dig down and hand him other things. 'Here's your writing set,' I say. That had been hard to find. There were no Internet searches in those days, no eBay (thank goodness); just good old-fashioned leg-work. I'd found it in the indoor market in Todmorden, of all places. Never saw another one again, either.

'You liked it so much you didn't want to use the envelopes, see,' I say, opening up the set to show him them all still neatly inside, the penguin faces on the flaps. 'I had to use my own Basildon Bond ones to send your thank-you notes to Grandma.'

The child takes them and examines them more closely, touching the paper.

'And here's your snow globe,' I say, giving it a shake

and putting it down on the floor. He puts his nose to it and peers inside. He was the only one in the infants who knew that penguins lived in the Antarctic not the Arctic. I was very proud when Mrs Cuthbertson told me that.

'Oh, and your puppet,' I say, picking it up and placing my hand inside. 'We used to have such fun with this, didn't we? The shows you put on for me. You used to be so disappointed that I couldn't make real snow for you, though.'

The child takes the puppet and strokes it, his face serious, intense.

'And look, your door name plaque – I'd forgotten you even had that. We must have taken it off when we decorated and never put it back.'

The child takes the ceramic name plaque in his hand, his little fingers closing around it tightly, his face contorted.

'Why, what is it?' I ask. 'What's the matter?'

He turns and hurls it at the fireplace. It shatters on the tiles. Melody jumps in the air and yowls as she runs from the room.

'Matthew. What on earth has got into you?'

'I am not Matthew!' he shouts. 'I am Ella.'

'Don't be so silly. Go to your room at once.'

'It's not my room!' he shrieks. 'It's Matthew's. Matthew doesn't live here any more. He growed up and moved out like—'

'Upstairs,' I hiss, barely able to speak. 'Go upstairs right this minute and don't let me hear another word out of you.' He runs, his little feet stamping up the stairs, his bedroom door slamming shut.

It is happening again. He is turning against me. Somehow she has infiltrated my house. Whispering into his ear. Dripping poison.

In the park Matthew starts singing. That loud sort of singing people do when they don't want to hear what is going on. 'La la la, la la la.' He is covering his ears with his hands too. He doesn't like it. Never did like it when people cry, when they get cross.

There is no sound from Matthew's bedroom. It has been quiet for a long time now. I wonder if the child has cried herself out and fallen asleep. I'm aware that she hasn't eaten since breakfast. I check the clock. Six thirty. She would normally have had her tea by now. I would too. I'm a great believer in meals taken at the same time by all those in the household. I always used to insist on it with Malcolm and Matthew, and afterwards with Matthew. Not that I am at all hungry. My stomach has started to churn. Muscle is memory and I am sure it is remembering. Bubbling and turning over, aware of the rough ride to come. Every part of my body remembers. My palms are sweating. It is not something I ever suffered from, either before or since. But clearly they are remembering too. It is as if it is a disease, one which will reoccur every year, lying dormant in between. Shingles is like that. It lies dormant at the base of your spine after you have chicken pox as a child. Waiting in silence, ready to pounce when you are at your weakest. It preys on loss, on trauma. It really is the lowest of the low. If it was a criminal, the judge would lock it up and throw away the key. It doesn't really matter to the shingles though. It has done what it needed to do. It has got under your skin.

It took ages for mine to clear. A wretched itching and prickling in my lower back. The doctor warned it might prevent me sleeping. Which was almost laughable in the circumstances.

It went in the end, slunk away in the dead of night. Although I actually thought I felt a tingle in my lower back when I finally came face-to-face with her months afterwards. As if she was capable of bringing it back from the dead. They always say it's the quiet ones you have to watch out for. I never believed them – I mean Matthew was always very quiet. I should have, though, because then I could have drummed it into Matthew and he would have known to stay away from her. Once she had her claws into him it was too late. She poisoned him from the inside. The female of the species can be deadly like that.

I start to climb the stairs. My limbs feel heavy. They don't want to go there. They are remembering too. I wonder if my whole body might seize up on the stroke of midnight. Rendered incapable of functioning by the memory of past events. It is a powerful thing, memory. There have been times in the past year when I forgot where I put my keys and seriously hoped it might be the onset of something. Dementia would be a friend to me if it came visiting, one I would welcome in and tell to make itself at home.

I pause at the top of the stairs. Matthew is there on the landing. He is always there. Smiling at me from beneath a fringe which is a little too short, pleading with me not to make him wear that itchy jumper again, sitting awkwardly in his first school tie and blazer.

I keep him on the landing and in the hall because those are the areas I am always passing through, so I can glimpse him on my travels, wave to him as I pass, feel he is close by. I understand that he cannot be here all the time, though.

The rest of the time he is busy playing in the park. He never did like to stray too far from home. It is good that he is close by, where I can visit. Some people's children move a long way away. I would not have liked that. It is a comfort to know that he did not want to leave me either. Not really, he didn't.

As I round the corner, my hand on the balustrade, I see the child's photo. It jars now, whereas just a few days ago it seemed the right thing to do. I took her in, I made her my own. But she is not mine and she never will be. I reach up and take the photo frame down from the wall, push back the metal pins, remove the backing and take out her photograph. Matthew smiles back at me from underneath. I stroke his face. I was so wrong to think I was being sent another Matthew. Matthew was kind enough to send her to me in the hope that she would help, but he knows now. Knows that I do not need another Matthew. I just need the old one back.

I toss the child's photo onto the floor and turn to face Matthew's door. I have never shut it since. Always left it slightly ajar. But the child slammed it shut so I must prise it open, even if it means I avert my eyes as I do so.

I touch the door with the back of my hand. The fire brigade tell you to do that before entering a room. If the back of your hand feels the heat you will pull it away instinctively. Whereas if you touch it with your fingertips they will stick to the heat, melt with it, perhaps. I used to stroke Matthew's head with my fingertips when he was a baby. I was never afraid, you see, of the love I felt. If the heat melted me, then so be it.

I grasp the door handle and open it a fraction. There is no noise from within and it is that which causes the tightening in my stomach. The clenching of my fists. The prickling sensation along my spine.

I open my eyes little by little. Like a blind being rolled up slowly by someone anxious not to let too much light in. My brain sees the shadow but knows instantly that it is just a memory. The room is empty. I am relieved and

I stay that way for several seconds until it dawns on me that it should not be empty. There should be a child in here. The child I am looking after. My first thought is that my mind must be playing tricks on me. Perhaps I am indeed ceasing to function, unable to see what is in front of me. I pull back the sheets on the bed in case she has somehow slithered down inside. The bed is empty. She must have fallen out. I walk around to the other side of the bed and bend down to peer underneath but she is not there. And then it dawns on me. She must have heard me coming up the stairs. She will be playing hide-and-seek. She will be waiting for me to find her.

'You win. I give up,' I call out. 'Come out now, wherever you are.'

Nothing. I swallow and go to the window, check that she hasn't opened it. The catch on the sash window is firmly in place. I let out the lungful of breath I hadn't realised I was holding and turn back to the room, trying to think logically, rationally. There is only one possible hiding place, even for a child of her size. I go to the wardrobe and open the door. It is her eyes I see first, peering sleepily at me through the gloom at the bottom of the wardrobe.

'What on earth do you think you're doing in here?'

'I went to sleep. I made a bed and went to sleep.' I look down and see a pile of cardigans and sweaters at the bottom of the wardrobe.

'Well you've got a perfectly good bed out here – what's wrong with that?'

'I don't want to be in Matthew's bed, I want my own bed.'

I open the door wide, grab hold of her hand and pull her up and out of the wardrobe.

'I've never heard anything so ridiculous.' I stop as I notice the book she is clutching in her hand.

'What's that?'

'I found it in wardrobe.'

'What is it?'

She shrugs. 'It's got lots of writing in it.'

I snatch the book from her grasp. It is A5 size, black with a hard cover. I think I smell him first. It has the unmistakable scent of Matthew. There is nothing on the front. I open it and flick through a couple of pages. Matthew's small, sloping handwriting stares back at me. The ink has long dried but I see his pen flowing across the pages, his fingers gripping tightly. I always told him he needed to relax his hand more when he wrote. He never seemed to find it an easy process though, certainly not as easy as playing the piano.

There are dates written in it in Matthew's hand. It is not an actual diary but he clearly used it as such. I carry on flicking through until I get to August. My hand slows then as I turn the pages one by one. The last entry is on Thursday, 4 September. One year ago today.

'Where did you get this?' I ask again.

'In wardrobe.'

'Show me where.' I can't believe it has been there all this time and I have never seen it. She opens the door and crawls in, pointing at the part where the two panels meet at the back.

'In there. I saw the gold bit glittering. I pulled it out to look at it and then I fell asleep on my bed.'

I stare at her, struggling to take it all in. But I do not see her; I see an older girl standing there avoiding eye contact with me. Her lies buffeting my ears. Her voice getting louder all the time. And me sitting there shaking my head. Mouthing, 'You're lying,' over and over again.

'Get out,' I scream at her. The child clambers out of the wardrobe, her eyes bulging.

'You have no right to be in here. No right at all.'

Tears stream down the child's face. She doesn't understand what she has done.

'Get out. Get out of Matthew's room. Now.'

She runs to the door, pulling it shut behind her. A few seconds later I hear her feet running downstairs. Immediately I put the diary down on the bed and go to the other side to drag the bedside cabinet across in front of the door. It is a heavy one, made of solid wood. None of this MDF rubbish. She will not be able to move it. I turn back to the bed. To the diary lying on top of it. I shouldn't read it, I know that. Diaries are private things. But I am his mother; there should be no secrets between a son and his mother. I move slowly around the bed, my eyes fixed on the diary, as if deciding which angle is best to approach my prey. I perch on one side of the bed, pick up one corner and drag it towards me. I stroke the cover with my fingertips. He won't mind. I know he won't. I can hear him humming. He wouldn't be humming if he minded, I am sure of it. I turn to the last entry. His handwriting is not as neat as normal. Perhaps his hands were shaking as he wrote it. Or maybe it is just my hands shaking now as I read it that makes the letters appear so uneven.

The first words drip into me like antiseptic. They sting, yes, because the wounds are still raw, but I accept this because I know they are healing me, soothing the pain of her lies. But as I read on his words sharpen and pick at the wounds, pick until they are opened up, exposed. At which point the hurt pours in, searing into me, its jagged edges tearing me apart, contaminating the wound. His boots stamp over me, as if trying to extinguish a fire. He doesn't stop until every last spark has been put out and only the glowing embers remain. And then the words which smother even that: 'she's suffocating me'. They are her words, I am sure of it. But they come from his lips, or from his pen at least.

I sit, winded and wounded on the bed, for a moment before I am able to summon the strength to move. When I do so, it is to lift the diary, pick it up and hurl it across the room.

'No!' I cry. 'No, no, no, no no.'

I collapse onto the bed, my body shaking, my tears unable to replenish themselves quickly enough. I want to take it back, the moment when I decided to read the diary. Actually, I want to rewind further – to when the child found it, the moment I decided to bring her home to tend her wounds. Further and further still, rewinding through history until when Matthew is a child. A little boy oblivious to everything apart from the daisy chain he is making. Humming to himself in the park while I watch over him.

'Piano lady, did you fall over?'

I hadn't even heard her footsteps on the stairs. Or if I did, I thought I was imagining them.

'I heard a big thump. Did you fall over? Is that why you're crying?'

I don't reply. I am not capable of speech.

'Piano lady, I'm hungry.'

My tears come faster, scouring their way down my cheeks. I hear her try to open the door.

'I can't open it,' she calls out. 'Why can't I open it?'

I clench my body tighter into a ball, like a hedgehog. I am aware of the oncoming traffic but can do little about it. It will have to avoid me. I am wounded. This is as much protection as I can muster.

She tries for some time to open the door before I finally hear her footsteps going downstairs. I am relieved. I want to be left in peace. Outwardly, at least. Inner peace is not possible. Has not been for some time. I tell myself that he didn't mean it – the words he said, the arrows he slung. She had poisoned his mind, as I had always expected. We do not speak rationally when we have been poisoned. We spew words out in an effort to cleanse ourselves. That is what he was doing. Cleansing himself of her bile. He meant no harm. No malice was intended. I tell myself this time and time again as I lie, curled in a foetal position on the bed. He does not hate you. He hated only the situation he found himself in. And yet there must be a tiny chink in my armour. The armour which has protected me for so long. Because one of his arrows has got through. Has pierced my skin and in doing so allowed the doubt in. Doubt is my enemy. I know and understand its power. And yet once it is in, it is very hard to get rid of.

I lie rocking and sobbing on the bed. My skin feels dry, my hair coarse, as I wrap my arms around myself. I sucked the life out of him. And in doing so I drained myself as well. Withered and died inside, became dry and brittle on the outside. The humming has stopped. Matthew doesn't hum any more. He hasn't hummed for a long time. I am aware of the light starting to fade outside. He will be cold. He will need to do up his cardigan. I feel the need to be near him, to hold him close to me. Slowly I uncurl, one aching limb after another. I raise my head. I can see the diary on the floor in the corner. I need to smell it again. To stroke the pages which Matthew touched.

I get rather unsteadily to my feet and shuffle towards the corner of the room. It will hurt, I know that. But sometimes you have to face the things which hurt you most. I stoop and pick it up, feeling the crackle of electricity as my fingers make contact with him.

'It's only me,' I say. 'I'm not going to hurt you. Not any more.'

I pick it up, move back to the bed. Like someone dragging a wounded animal from the roadside. There is no hope for it, of course. No chance of being revived. I will hold it close though. It is the least I can do.

I curl up on the bed again, the diary pressed against my chest. I keep it there for some time, letting his smell seep into me, his presence in the room warm me. And finally, as the light fades from the room, I draw it out, give a cursory glance at the cover before turning to the beginning. Because sometimes you need to start at the beginning in order to make sense of the end.

I do not sleep and I do not wake. The poison has left me drowsy so I slip between states of consciousness, flick between pages in history. Intermittently I am aware that there are noises from downstairs but I don't let them interrupt me. I am cocooned here. No one from outside can get in. I am alone with my son. Which is how it should be.

The art of reading is to know and understand the things which go unsaid. There is as much to be learned from the spaces between, the empty lines, as there is from the words on the page. I know that and I cling to it, my life raft through the rough seas. It keeps me afloat but no more than that. It does not offer me any real protection against all that is being thrown at me. I am buffeted and blasted from all directions. I lie there and take it. There is no longer any fight left in me. It is not a case of the wind having been taken from my sails, more a case of not having a sail left at all. I lie quietly until the storm has subsided and the last wave has washed over me, leaving its debris behind. And then, from this prostrate position, I survey the wreckage. Me, my withered and weathered body lying alone and desolate.

I brought this upon myself. However much I know she was to blame, I still let her get to him. I did not protect my own flesh and blood. I was not there for him when he needed me and the one thing I know now is that he needed me, more than I ever realised at the time. I have been found wanting. It is not something any mother ever wants to hear. Particularly not from her own son. All those promises I made. To myself and to him. All the hope, the joy. It is hard to remember either now. But remember I must.

I hear him first. The giggle is unmistakable. A lot of parents say their baby giggles but most of them do not. What they are referring to is more of a gurgle. Matthew giggles though. Giggles in the way that a boy does, rather than a baby. A boy in a blue romper suit in a baby bouncer, suspended from the door frame, his toes just able to touch the floor. He uses them wisely, pointed and outstretched, and pushes into the floor at the last possible moment, sending himself soaring up, at which point the giggle can be heard, filling the house with joy. He knows, you see. Knows that the future is all his. That already he is brighter than others his own age, who merely sit and stare straight in front of them. Matthew has never been one for sitting. Not when he can be doing this. He likes the feeling of being propelled through the air. He never appears frightened. I have heard others say their babies are not sure about bouncers. It is because they don't understand. They haven't grasped that they are both safe and free at the same time. It is too complex for them. Matthew knows though. He understands that this is the time to push into the floor and send himself soaring. There is no danger of being catapulted away from safety. He knows that it is not merely the harness which is suspending him, it is my love. He understands that I will let no harm come to him. I will give him boundaries, top and bottom. Allow him to dip his toe into the sea and feel the breeze blowing through his hair. But all the time I will have hold of the piece of elastic, so that if he steps or flies towards danger I will haul him back in. He giggles because he knows that. Even so young, he knows that I only have his best interests at heart. Other parents will unhook their child too early, allow them to fly and so fall, to come crashing down to earth. Far better to continue bouncing. Safe in the knowledge that no harm can come to you.

He giggles again and I smile back at him. My beautiful bouncing boy, face beaming, eyes fixed on me. I hold his gaze as he moves up and down. He never tires of this and nor do I. Sometimes he spins wildly and twists, but always he trusts in me. Knows that in a moment he will come back to me and that I will always be here.

The pages turn; the clock ticks relentlessly. I try but fail to halt its progress. I know what is coming, know that trying to stop it is futile, but still I strain every muscle in my body. Muscle has memory and I do not have to remind it what is on the other side. I can fight off sleep, I can refuse to close my eyes but, as much as I try, I cannot prevent the passing of time.

'Piano lady, I'm hungry.' The whisper comes from the other side of the door. It is wrong of her to intrude. It was wrong of me to let her. I should not have allowed myself to become distracted. You only need to take your eye off for one moment.

I stay silent, knowing that if I do so she will think I am asleep.

'And it's dark outside. You've forgotten to put me to bed. Piano lady?'

There is a shuffling sound and a slight whimpering for a few minutes, but I stay very still and eventually the whimpering fades into the distance.

I turn back to the doorway. I only took my eye off him for a second but that is all it needs.

His toes are not touching the floor. That is the first thing I notice. They hang, loose and limp. There is no upward momentum. No spring in his step. The boy is not bouncing any more. He hangs.

He hangs from a position to one side of the doorway. The same doorway he used to bounce from. But his body is still now. There are no giggles, only silence. My gaze crawls slowly up his body. But inside I am fighting this: my eyes refusing to see, my ears refusing to hear, my brain refusing to take in.

It has not happened. It has not come to this. It is the shadows playing tricks on me. In a moment he will start giggling, will push down with his toes and soar into the air. I am holding the other end of the piece of elastic. I have not let go at any point. It is simply impossible that he could have done this while I was holding on. I gather up the piece of elastic, faster and faster, desperately trying to find the end. Only to discover when I get there that he is missing. He has somehow uncoupled himself. I was holding on to thin air and I didn't even notice.

My gaze reaches his face at exactly the same moment that a piercing scream shatters the silence. It is my scream, although I don't recognise it as such. His hair is flopping down over his eyes. I am grateful for that, for once relieved that he was overdue a haircut.

It is his school tie which is around his neck. I suppose he had no other. I remember tightening it for him on his first day and telling him to do it up properly on countless other days when he was older. It is tight now. It is attached to the hook in the ceiling. The one we had put in especially so we could hang his bubble chair from it. He'd wanted one for ages. Wanted to be off the ground, the sensation of being in flight. We gave it to him for his thirteenth birthday. A handyman my mother knew had to come round to fix the hook into the ceiling because Malcolm was never any good at that sort of thing. Matthew loved that chair. He would sit in it for hours on end reading a book or listening to music. Just hang there, suspended in mid-air. It was like watching him as a baby again, his toes dangling, his face beaming.

His toes are dangling again now. I step forward, sink to my knees and touch them, my baby's tiny feet. He giggles and turns to face me, his eyes sparkling with aliveness. He is mine for life. I will never let him come to harm. Will never take my eyes off him.

I am vaguely aware in the stillness of the knocking on the front door. Of Judith, my neighbour, calling out to see if I am OK. A few minutes later the phone rings. It continues until the answering machine cuts in. I hear my own voice from the landing, bright and breezy and businesslike. The phone rings a few times after that. On every occasion I answer on the machine in the same voice. And still I kneel there on the floor, holding my baby's feet, tickling him, trying to make him giggle.

At some point later I hear the garden gate clink open, a key in the door, a key I had forgotten he still had. Footsteps, unfamiliar and yet familiar at the same time, coming up the stairs. Malcolm on the landing shouting, 'Oh no. Dear God, no.' He takes hold of me, tries to pull me away, drag me almost. But I am not having it. I am not leaving Matthew. I will not take my eye off him. My little boy whose feet are not long enough to touch the ground.

'Let me go!' I scream. 'Can't you see he's enjoying this? Look at his face. Listen to him giggle. He doesn't want this to end.'

MATTHEW

Thursday, 4 September 2014

It's no use, I know that now. My life may as well be over. Not being with Sparrow is like torture. All I've done for weeks is lie in my room listening to music and bawling my eyes out. I couldn't hurt Mum and by not doing that I've lost Sparrow, the most amazing girl I've ever met in my life and the only one who's slept with me and probably the only one who ever will. I mean what kind of fucking idiot would do that?

And even though Mum won and I chose not to hurt her, I hurt her anyway. I've seen the look in her eye when she thinks I'm not looking. It's like she's been betrayed. She can barely bring herself to look at me let alone touch me. It's like I'm soiled and dirty. I've ruined all her memories of her precious little Matthew and she's never going to forgive me for that. She's still got all my stuff, you know. All my toys and clothes and that, all stored away. She used to say she was keeping them for her grandchildren but I don't know how that's going to happen as she made the only woman who I would ever want to marry dump me. Nice move, that one.

And the truth is I didn't mean to hurt either of them but I've ended up hurting both of them, which shows how totally crap I am. And what makes it worse is that although they've never met, they hate each other. Sparrow hates Mum because she says she broke us up and she's too controlling and all that stuff. And Mum hates Sparrow, I see it every time I look in her eyes (which is why I try to avoid doing that). I used to think that maybe one day if I introduced them Mum would like Sparrow and kind of accept her (cos she is really lovely) but ever since Mum found the hair in my bed it was like she hated it. Like she absolutely loathed one single strand of hair. Can you imagine what she'd be like if she ever actually met her? All of that hatred multiplied by however many hairs there are on Sparrow's head. I want to be brave and tell Sparrow I don't give a toss about what Mum thinks but the trouble is I do. And it's not like I can talk to Mum about any of this – I've never been able to talk to her about stuff. And now when I look at her I don't see Mum at all, I see some kind of Dementor-like figure because I just go sort of cold and it's like she's sucked the life out of me. Sucked all the warmth and love and just left me with the emptiness and the guilt inside. All I want to do is get back together with Sparrow but I can't because to do that I'd have to hurt Mum. It's like she's suffocating me with her love. She doesn't mean to, I know that, but she is too much. She won't let me breathe for myself, and I don't want to live my life on some kind of artificial respirator with her taking all the breaths for me.

Though to be honest I don't think I can live without Sparrow anyway. She is my entire world and there is no point, no fucking point at all, without her. She was right. I am lame and pathetic. I'm no better than Dad, letting down the people I love, failing so badly.

And what have I got to look forward to? Going away to university and spending the entire time wishing Sparrow was there with me and hating every minute of every day without her. And coming back here at week-ends to be given the evil eye by Mum because I haven't got the balls to stand up to her.

I've lost her. Lost my ticket out of this life. I know that I will never love anyone else in my entire life the way I love Sparrow. And every time she refuses to take my calls and every time I text her and she ignores it, it just like kills me inside all over again.

I need to find a way of showing her how much I love her and that I do have the balls to stand up to Mum. I know it's too late for us but at least she might finally understand how much I love her. The thing I want more than anything else in the world is for her to know that.

21

LISA

'You OK, Sparrow?' Mum asks as Chloe comes into the room. I haven't heard her called that for years. When she was younger she used to get called nothing else. It was something she said once to me when she was three, not long after she had started nursery and met Robyn, who even then she had decided was going to be her best friend for life. We were looking out of the window when I pointed out a robin on the garden fence and she looked at me rather dolefully and asked, 'Is there a Chloe bird too?'

I told her that if we kept looking we might just see one. And when the sparrow landed on the fence a moment later she looked up at me so hopefully that I said, 'There you are, see. That's a Chloe bird.'

We kept it up for a couple of years afterwards, until they were learning about birds in Year Two and I thought

I ought to tell her so she didn't embarrass herself. She was upset at first, of course. Although I told her she could still go on calling them Chloe birds if she wanted to.

It was Mum who came up with the idea of calling her Sparrow. Told her that she might not have a bird named after her like Robyn did but that didn't mean she couldn't have a bird's name instead. She liked it at first. For a long while we weren't allowed to call her anything else. And by the time she was a teenager and didn't seem so keen we were all so used to calling her Sparrow that it was hard to stop. I always thought it rather suited her, to be honest: her long brown hair, her stick-thin legs, the way she wasn't flashy or anything but you still knew the world would be a much lesser place without her.

I look at her now, her eyes dark and achy, and wonder whether she will turn her nose up or make some comment to Mum about it. She doesn't though. She sits down next to her on the sofa, buries her face in her shoulder and starts to cry. I wonder if I should say something, sit down next to them. But I do not want to intrude, do not want to stop her when she is finally letting it out, so I shut the door quietly behind them and leave the room. I need to get out again. I need to try and clear my head.

It is my fault, bad timing as ever. I am running past the school at the exact moment the coach returns with the reception children, who have been on a school trip to Eureka.

The lane is narrow and there is no room to get past safely. I have no choice but to stand there and watch as they burst down the steps, full of chatter and laughter and bubbling over with excitement.

Charlie Wilson is brandishing a piece of green paper with some splats of colour on in his hand. He holds it up to me as he goes past.

'That's nice,' I say. 'Did you do that?'

'Yes,' says Charlie. 'All by myself.'

And I have to turn away so he won't see me crying because I know that when he gets home his dad will do one of those looks of mock awe and say it is amazing and not even ask what it is because it doesn't matter and he does not want Charlie to know it is not obvious, and later that night, when Charlie has gone to bed, he will put it on the fridge door with a magnet and it will stay there for years, even when he has done far better drawings, because it was the first one he did at school. And usually I hate all that stuff and I am the one who instigated the night-time recycling of art from school in an effort to save our house from disappearing under the weight of the stuff, but right now I want that first picture of Ella's more than anything in the world. I want to take it home and stick it on my fridge and look at it and smile every time I get the milk out. And it is not fair, so bloody not fair, that all the other parents will do that tonight but I can't and I want to come back at home time and tell them that. Tell them to guard that picture of whatever it is with their lives because you don't get a warning, you never know when all of this is going to be taken away from you and I would do anything right now to have that fucking stupid piece of green paper stuck on my fridge.

I walk away, aware that the last thing any of these children need to see is my tear-stained face, and start running again as soon as I get past the coach. I had actually been on my way home but I know I can't go back now. I have to keep on running until the tears have dried, until I can get myself together enough to face Otis and Chloe. Because my children, the two I have left, need me to be strong. They need to know that the whole world around them may crumble but I am not going to crumble with it. I am going to be strong for them and somehow, although I have no idea how at the moment, we are going to have to find a way through this.

Alex is sitting at the kitchen table with a gas bill in his hand when I get back. He looks up as I walk in the door. If anything, his face looks worse than mine.

'What?' I ask.

'I checked the bank today. Things are getting a bit tight.'

'Oh,' I say. That's the trouble when you're both self-employed. No monthly salary coming in. When we stop working the money stops.

'I think I need to go back to work on Monday.'

I stare at him. Not quite sure I am hearing this right.

'But you can't. That's like giving up on her.'

'Please don't make this harder than it is, Lis. One of us needs to be earning. We can't afford to go on like this much longer.'

'But how can you even think of going back with Ella missing?'

'Because we have to pay our bills. The last thing we need right now is to be getting into debt on top of all of this.'

'I don't care about the bills. The bank can bloody wait a bit, can't they?'

'Come on, love. We've got to try to keep on top of this.'

'And what if they find her body later, are you still going back to work then?'

'Lis, please, don't.'

'Well what am I supposed to say?'

'I don't know. I don't know how this is supposed to work. I'm just trying to muddle through the best I can. To do something to try to look after my family.'

He walks out of the room. I sit down at the table and cry. I don't even look to see how much the gas bill is.

I am getting used to Claire's serious faces now. Serious but not doom-laden. I would rate this as somewhere around a five. It is not what we are dreading but nor is it good news either. It is simply something she has to tell us. Mum is with Otis. Chloe is upstairs in her room. I figure it's as good a time as any.

'Go on,' I say.

'They want to do a reconstruction,' she says. 'Tomorrow afternoon, in the park.'

It makes sense, of course. It will be a week. The longest week of my life but still only technically seven days.

'Will I have to—'

'No,' interrupts Claire. 'We've got a policewoman to do it. She's about the same size as you, does a lot of running.'

I nod. 'What about Ella?'

'One of the desk sergeants at Halifax has a granddaughter the same age, very similar hair. I've been asked to bring a photo of her to show you. You don't have to see it, of course. It's only if you want to. And if you don't think the girl is right please say so and we'll find someone else.'

I glance at Alex, who shrugs.

'OK,' I say. 'We'll look.'

Claire takes the photo out and puts it down on the kitchen table. The first thing I notice is her eyes – she has the exact same colour eyes as Ella, which is weird as they are quite unusual. Her hair is a touch longer but a very similar colour. She doesn't have the dimples but other than that she is very convincing. Almost too convincing to be comfortable.

Alex looks at me; I can see he thinks so too.

'Are you happy with using her?' Claire asks. I nod, still unable to formulate any words.

'Great, thanks. I should let you know that we've got hold of a dress the same as the one Ella was wearing, from Boden. So she's going to be wearing that.'

I nod again. It will be on television and there will be pictures in the newspapers. It will look like Ella, she'll be wearing the same dress even, but I'll know it isn't her.

'Can I have the dress?' I ask. 'Afterwards, when you've finished the filming, can I have the dress to keep?'

Claire nods and looks down. 'Yes,' she says. 'Yes, of course. Obviously you're both very welcome to watch the reconstruction but I completely understand if you don't want to. There's going be a brief rehearsal this evening, without any media, if you're interested in going to that . . .'

'I don't know,' I say. 'I'm not sure if I can go to the park yet.'

'I'll go,' says Alex. 'I'll film it on my mobile. I can show you when I come back, so you can check they've got everything right.'

'Thanks,' I say, aching at how much I know I've hurt him and still he comes back at me with nothing but love.

'Can I go too?'

I turn. I hadn't even realised Chloe was standing in the doorway.

'Oh, um . . . I don't know. I'm not sure that's a good idea.'

'Not to the rehearsal, to the real thing. I want to see what happened. I want to watch it with my own eyes. I want to try to understand.'

I hesitate. It feels like she doubts my version of events. That she somehow thinks I have missed out some vital piece of information. But then she doesn't trust me, I know that. And I understand why too.

'OK,' I say, 'if you're sure.'

She nods. Her eyes have an empty, haunted quality to them. Although to be honest, they have looked like that for quite a long time now.

Dad warned me that the press were still outside their house. He said I shouldn't come. That he'd got himself into this mess and I had enough on my plate.

As I pull up outside and see the lenses pointing in my direction I wish I hadn't argued with him.

I get out and slam the car door. There is a shouted question about how I feel about what Dad has done. A lens is poked very near my face. I hate them right now. Hate the way they are gathering like vultures as our family disintegrates. But I also know that I can't make things any worse than they already are because they are still our best bet and we need to get them back on our side. I keep my head down, stride briskly up to the front door and ring the bell.

Tony answers straight away. We used to have a running joke about him being Anthony from *The Royle Family* when he was a teenager because Dad always made him answer the door. He shuts it behind me quickly.

'Fucking arseholes,' he says.

'How is he?'

Tony shrugs. 'Think he's feeling a bit sheepish, to be honest. Hardly said a word on the way home after I told him about Taylor.'

I nod. 'And how about you?' I ask.

'Me?'

'Yeah. You, Tony, Ella's favourite uncle.'

'Only cos she's only got one.'

'No, probably more because you spend a fortune on her at Christmas.'

Tony looks at his feet. 'You want the truth?'

'Yeah.'

'Then I feel like I've been winded and kneed in the balls at the same time and I don't think I'm ever going to stop feeling like that.'

'I know what you mean.'

'Except you haven't got any balls. Actually, no, that's not true. You got more balls than most blokes I know.'

I manage a little smile and walk into the living room. Mum and Dad are sitting on the sofa with the front curtains drawn, which looks pretty weird in the daytime, it has to be said. They both look suddenly old and small – I swear they've shrunk in the past week.

'Sorry,' says Dad, catching my eye before looking down again. 'That's about the last thing you need – those little shits sticking their lenses up your nose.'

'I take it they got you too?'

'Yeah. Front page we'll be tomorrow. You can rely on your old dad to screw things up for you.'

'You've got to stop saying that.'

'Why? It's true.'

'Well even if it were I wouldn't care. I don't give a toss what people think any more. Not sure I ever did, to be honest.'

'Your father's been told he's got to appear in court on Monday.' Mum says this like she is distancing herself from him, pretending he's not in the same room even.

'Fine, we'll all go then.'

'Don't be daft,' says Dad. 'I'm not having any of you there. I got myself into this mess; I should be the one who has to deal with it.'

'Except no one's on their own in this family, are they? That's what you both used to tell me when I was grow-ing up. And you didn't chuck me out on the streets when I got myself in trouble, did you?'

'That was different,' says Dad. 'You were only a kid.'

'Well, there's no age limit on screwing up, is there? So if you're going to be in court I'm going to be with you, OK?'

Dad nods. Mum starts to cry again.

'And we'll have none of them tears on Monday,' I say.

'We hold our heads up high in front of the cameras; you plead guilty; Claire's going to put a statement out saying how sorry we all are and then we can get back to looking for Ella, all right?'

They nod. And for first time ever I feel like their parent instead of their child.

It is late when Alex comes back with Claire. Otis has gone to bed and Chloe is in her room, though the chink of light underneath her door suggests that she is not even trying to get to sleep.

Alex's face is pale and drained. I wonder if he wishes he hadn't gone. Going back to work on Monday will probably be a welcome break from this. Claire puts the kettle on. Alex sits down at the kitchen table and takes out his phone.

'You sure?' he asks.

'Yeah, I'm sure.'

He fiddles with the phone for a second before handing it to me. I press Play. I see a girl in a green and white striped dress. One with a big pink flower on its side. She has green leggings on too and green Crocs, which are a slightly different shade of green to Ella's but I don't think it matters. And I see a woman in running vest and shorts. A woman holding a red balloon and a mobile phone. A woman who, unlike me, looks like she hasn't got a care in the world.

It is shot from some distance away. Maybe Alex didn't

want to get too close, maybe he wasn't allowed to. I watch the girl run over to the climbing frame.

'She couldn't get up to the big slide on her own,' says Alex, 'so she just went a little way up.'

I nod and think how proud Ella would be that we couldn't find a girl her age who could do what she could do. The woman playing me looks at her watch and the girl mouths, 'Please.' The woman walks over to the tree – they've even got the right tree – while the girl runs away. She pretends to fall over. I can hear Ella saying that it is not a very good pretend, that she could do it much better. She can't though. She can't play herself in this because she is not here.

And I run over to her, not me but the woman playing me. The girl screws her face up a bit and pretends to cry. I brush off her hands and knees and she points at the tree again. I turn and walk over to it, and although I know what is going to happen and know it is not real, I still will myself not to answer the phone when it rings. I do though, and as I do I let go of the red balloon. The last shot is of it drifting off into the sky. I have an overwhelming desire to stick a pin in it and burst that bloody red balloon.

22

MURIEL

At some point the shadows lift and the sun has the audacity to show its face through the window. The world went on. That was the thing I never understood. How everything and everyone else continued as if nothing had happened. How I was the only one for whom time stopped that day. And who even now, a year on, has never been able to get the clocks right.

There is a sudden rush of consciousness. Images, sounds, events, flicking through my mind in quick succession. I am unsure if they are in the right order. I do not know what the right order is any more.

I do know there is a child. A child who looks like Matthew. Not outside, in the park, but inside my house. I put my hand out to push myself up and realise that the sheet is sodden. The smell fills my nostrils. It is guilt and sadness and shame. It is my smell. It is what I have become.

I get up slowly and drag the bedside cabinet from in front of the door. The child is not outside when I open it. I go to the bathroom, not that it is really worth it now but I must retain some degree of normal functioning. I remove my blouse and my wet skirt and knickers and wash my hands before taking my dressing gown from behind the door and folding it around me. My mouth is papery, my breath musty. I brush my teeth, aware suddenly of my rumbling stomach. Of my need for a cup of tea.

I go through to my bedroom, the silence closing in around me, take a fresh blouse and skirt off their hangers in the wardrobe and dress slowly before returning to the landing. Matthew smiles at me. Matthew always smiles. Matthew has never stopped smiling.

I descend the stairs, holding on tightly to the rail as I do not feel at all steady on my feet. The silence in the hall is oppressive. I have a crushing sense that there should be noise although I am not really sure why. And then I reach the kitchen and see the child lying there on the floor. For a moment my heart stills and I look to see if there is any blood, if she is hurt at all. But her little chest rises and falls as it should do. Her head is inside Melody's basket, Melody herself curled tight against her shoulder. The biscuit bowl beside them is empty. The water bowl is too. Melody senses me first and gets to her feet and stretches, miaowing loudly as she does so. The child opens her eyes. She looks at me, at Melody standing above her and then back to me.

'I asked Melody if I could share her bed. She said I could.'

I nod and swallow.

The child sits up, glances at the empty biscuit bowl and looks down again. 'Sorry,' she says. 'I was hungry. I only had what Melody left. I didn't really like them.'

I stare at the child. Hear the noises in the park. Touch her bloody knee. Smell the Germolene.

'Crumpets,' I say. 'We'll have crumpets for breakfast.'

She nods and yawns at the same time. I go to the cooker and turn the grill on. The flame roars at me. It takes a long time for the heat to filter through.

Afterwards, when she has finished every last crumb of her second crumpet and slurped her milk thirstily, she looks up at me.

'Why were you crying?' she asks. 'Why wouldn't you let me in? Were you poorly?'

'Yes,' I reply.

'And are you better now?'

I shake my head. 'It's not a poorly that gets better. Not ever.'

'Are we still going on holiday?'

'Yes. Of course. We'll go upstairs to pack in a minute.'

'Is Matthew coming? Are you going to pack for him too?'

'No. He's not coming. Not this time.'

'Because he's all growed-up now?'

I nod. Unable to form any words.

'Why have you still got all his old things?'

'Because I don't like throwing perfectly good things away.'

'Mummy puts our old things on eBay. She says there wouldn't be room for us if we kept stuff.'

I raise my eyebrows but say nothing. I can't bear the thought of it, to be honest. Selling your memories to strangers like that. Everything seems to have a price nowadays.

'Is that why you haven't got any other children?' she asks. 'Because there wasn't room for them with all Matthew's stuff?'

I look down at her. She is oblivious as to how her words scour my skin, revealing traces of the flesh underneath. Flesh that is still smarting from the years of trying for a child.

'Sometimes, when you have a special child, a child so perfect in every way, you don't need another one.'

She thinks for a moment. 'Chloe must have been very naughty then because Mummy still had Otis and me.'

The name, *her* name, shatters the stillness around us. I see long dark hair and dark eyes beneath when she flicks the hair back off her face.

I stare at the child. 'Your sister's name is Chloe?'

'Yes, she wasn't named after a big black singing lady.

Mummy said she wasn't named after anyone. She just liked the name.'

I should leave it there, I know that. But I feel the need to pick at the scab.

'How old is she? Your big sister.'

'Nineteen. She's a big girl. She's all growed-up like Matthew.'

My fingers tense. Inside my stomach tightens. It is ridiculous to even think it, of course. What would the odds be? Besides, it is not that unusual a name. Not really.

'What's her last name?' I hear myself asking. 'Does she have the same surname as you?'

The child shakes her head. 'No, she has Mummy's old name because she didn't have a daddy.'

'And what is it? Her name?'

'Benson,' she says. 'Chloe Benson.'

I nod slowly and close my eyes. Something agitates inside me. As if someone has put their hand in, swished everything around and brought some debris to the surface. Things I don't want to see or think about. Snapshot images. A strand of hair. A stab of anguish. I should have realised. It is obvious now. Obvious why Matthew picked the child.

Something rises from deep within me. Surges up, rushing through my veins. I think for a few moments that I can hold it in, keep a lid on it. But when I open my eyes I do not see the child any more; I see her sister standing in the courtroom at the inquest. Standing knee-deep in a puddle of conceit. The girl who does not think she is to blame. I can see where she gets it from now, of course. She is her mother's daughter. Both of them so damn sure that they haven't done anything wrong.

I put my face closer to the child's. The words, when they come, practically spit at her. 'She is worse than naughty. She destroys lives. She doesn't think about anyone apart from herself. It's what comes from having a mother like yours.'

The child recoils in her chair, her eyes wide and staring. 'I want to go home. I want my mummy.'

'She's not a good enough mummy to look after you. That's why I've been asked to take care of you.'

'Who asked you?'

I take a moment before replying.

'Matthew asked me. He knew you were in danger.'

'How did Matthew know?'

'Matthew sees a lot of things that other people don't.'

'How did he see me?'

'He saw you fall in the park.'

'I didn't see him. I didn't see any big boys.'

'Well he saw you.'

'Was he playing hide-and-seek?'

'Yes,' I say. 'I suppose he was.'

I take her hand before she has a chance to protest and lead her upstairs to Matthew's room. She wrinkles her nose as soon as she enters.

'Did you have an accident? Is it because you're poorly? Otis had an accident once when he was poorly and he's a big boy.'

I start stripping the bed, yanking off the sheets and freeing the pillows from their cases. I will not have *her* contaminating my home. I will not allow it.

'What are you doing, piano lady?'

'Stripping the bed,' I shout, 'to get rid of the smell.'

'Why does your wee smell?'

'It's not my smell I'm getting rid of,' I say, lowering my face to hers. 'It's your sister's.' She stares at me, her eyes wide, her frown deepening. But all I see is her sister staring back at me. Dark, little button eyes. Turned-up nose. A mouth that spouts nothing but lies.

'How did Chloe do a smell in Matthew's bedroom?'

'She came here,' I say. 'Came here uninvited. And she took Matthew away from me.'

She frowns again. 'Chloe's on holiday. She went with her friend. Her friend is called Robyn not Matthew. Robyn is a big girl she used to go to school with.'

So the tears were crocodile ones. Put on at the inquest to try to make people feel sorry for her. Her life clearly didn't stop that day. She's off gallivanting with her friend. That is how much she cared about Matthew.

'She's a bad girl, your sister. That is what comes of having a bad mother like yours.'

I push past her and hurry downstairs. I need to get the smell out of my nostrils. Get the images from my head.

Simply looking at the child now fills me with repulsion. I need to get away from here but going on holiday with the child is now clearly out of the question.

The sound of crying drifts down from upstairs. I brought her here but now I don't know what to do with her. I wonder if I should call the police. Tell them about the mistake I made. But it comes to me then, the realisation of what they will think. That I did this on purpose. They will have me down as some kind of stalker. Think I planned all this out as a way of getting back at the family. Because it makes perfect sense, if you think about it. I have a motive, and revenge is a very powerful thing. They will think I tracked the mother down, followed her in the park, waited until her back was turned and then pounced. They wouldn't believe me for a moment if I said I didn't know who the child was when I took her. I mean you wouldn't, would you? It all sounds like such a perfect plan. Such a carefully thought-out way to hurt the person whose own daughter hurt you so much. An eye for an eye. They will laugh at me if I try to tell them otherwise. Tell me my story borders on the absurd. And I can't say I would blame them. Imagine what a jury would make of my defence that it was a coincidence. That I had never met the mother, had no idea who she was, when her husband, both daughters and son had all been in my house. It is almost as if the mother laid a trap. Lured me to the park. Behaved so badly knowing that I would not be able to stand by and watch. Made me take the girl because she knew that once I had her, they had me. There would be no way I could give her back without landing myself in trouble. And so here we are. I am stuck with her child. I can either be a prisoner in my own home or give myself up and probably go to prison for the rest of my days. It is not much of a choice to make.

I sit down heavily at the foot of the stairs. Fool that I am, I have walked into this with my eyes open. Too ready to give of myself. To put the welfare of others first. This is why people walk on by nowadays. Because it is always the good people who end up on the wrong side of the law. The police won't listen if I tell them about the child's mother. They won't be interested in her neglect. They haven't got the intelligence necessary to work out what has happened here. They will simply want to close this case and get back to whatever it is they do on quiet days in Halifax. Play cards, probably. Or do they play games on their computers these days?

It comes to me suddenly, the only thing left to do. I will not give her back and I will not stay here waiting to be found. There is another way out. For both of us.

I hurry back upstairs and go to the wardrobe in the guest room, take out the clothes she was wearing on the day I found her and carry them through to Matthew's room, where I lay them on the dry side of the bed.

She stops crying and her face looks up at me expectantly.

'Are you taking me back to the park? Have the big boys gone now? Will Mummy be waiting for me?'

I do not reply, simply start dressing her, making sure she looks presentable. I don't want people to think I didn't look after her well. When she is ready I turn her to face the mirror.

'I don't look like Matthew any more,' she says. And she is right. She doesn't.

She follows me downstairs asking constant questions which I do not answer as I fill Melody's bowl with biscuits and top up her water. I pick up my bag, take my keys from the pot on the occasional table in the hall and turn to the shoe rack, where her lime-green Crocs lurk ominously on the bottom rack.

'You'd better put those on,' I say, pointing. She sits down on the floor in one swift movement, in the way small children can, and a few seconds later is back on her feet again.

'Right, let's go,' I say.

'Where are we going? Are we going to the park?'

'No.'

'Are we going on holiday?'

'No.'

I reach for the door handle, see my shaking, bony hand before me. I turn back and take Matthew's waterproof from the peg.

'Is it raining?' she asks. 'I haven't got my wellies.

Grandma says Crocs are no good when it's raining because of the holes.'

I slip her arms into the sleeves and pull the waterproof around her.

'It's too big,' she says. 'My arms are all flappy.'

It's only until we get to the car.'

'Have you got a car? I didn't know you had a car. Why haven't we been out in it? Why didn't you drive me back home?'

I open the door.

'It isn't raining,' she says.

'I never said it was,' I reply, pulling the hood up over her head. 'But you still need to wear it.'

I take her hand and hurry towards the car. It is a red Nissan Micra. It is reliable. At least it was the last time I drove it. My fingers fumble with the key fob. I open the rear passenger door.

'Where's your car seat?' she says. 'I have a blue car seat in Mummy's car and a red one in Daddy's. And a booster seat for when I go to Grandma's.'

'I haven't got a car seat.'

'You'll get into trouble. The policeman will get cross. And Mummy won't let me go in a car without a proper seat.'

'Just get into the car, please,' I say.

'Are you taking me home? Is Mummy well again?'

'No,' I say. 'That's not going to happen. Not now. We're going somewhere else. Somewhere very beautiful.'

I pull the seat belt across her and clip it in. She is craning her neck, struggling to see out of the window.

I slam the passenger door and walk round to the driver's side. When I get in she is still complaining about not being able to see out. I start the engine. Classic FM comes on the radio. I squint in the bright sunlight, pull down my visor and check my mirrors before flicking down the indicator. Malcolm always used to say I drove the way people do when they take their driving test. That is the thing with shoddiness though. Once you give in to it, it's a downward spiral.

I pull away from the kerb, wondering if anyone saw us leave the house. If they recognised her or maybe thought how odd it was that a child should be wearing a waterproof jacket six sizes too big for them on such a sunny day. I am not very good at this. It would be laughable really if it wasn't such a serious matter.

We drive past the park and down through King Cross, past Tesco. The child's chatter is constant but I tune it out, relegating it to the status of white noise. Like the white noise which used to get Matthew to sleep when he was a baby. I put him in front of the washing machine in his baby bouncer when he was at that over-tired stage. He would be asleep long before the spin cycle.

Hebden Bridge is busy with tourists, the type who think mooching about from one tea shop to the next is a good way to spend one's morning. There is no shortage of them, it seems. People with nothing better to do.

I wait to turn left at the traffic lights. The white noise breaks up and becomes words again.

'Where are we? Why aren't you taking me home? Is Daddy going to collect me?'

I drive up the hill and bear right, out into open countryside. The trees of Hardcastle Crags shield the sun. I still remember where the car park is although it is a long time since I was here. Matthew used to know the landmarks to look out for. He was always very good at that sort of thing. I turn in, pull into a space in the far corner and pull on the handbrake.

'Are we here?' asks the child.

'Yes, we are.'

She cranes her neck again. 'Where is it? Where's Daddy's car?'

I get out and walk round to open the passenger door and unclip her. She scrambles out in a tangle of hot nylon and flailing limbs and starts to undo the zip on the waterproof.

'Keep it on, please.'

'Why?'

'You might need it later.'

'How long are we staying? Have you got a picnic? Mummy always has a picnic. I like strawberries best.'

I take her hand and lead her towards the footpath, worried already that the steps further down will be too steep for her to manage.

'Mind your legs with the nettles,' I say.

'Are they stinging ones?'

'Well, I don't know of any other kind.'

'Daddy says you need to find a duck leaf if they sting you.'

'Dock leaf,' I correct.

'Do they make it better too?'

We walk on. It is further than I remember and she is a slower walker than Matthew used to be. We have to keep stopping when she gets stones in her Crocs. At last I see the ridge. A huge chasm opens up in front of us, a river snaking through far below. On the other side a massive bank of trees stretches into the distance. I stand near the edge of the ridge. I have the child's hand in mine. I think, if he could have, Matthew would have chosen to come here. It was simply that he didn't have the transport.

'I don't like it,' says the child. 'I don't like looking down.'

'Then close your eyes,' I reply.

23

LISA

I come round suddenly, thinking I heard a noise but unsure what it was. I seem to have discovered a mode, like the standby button on the TV, where I'm not awake but not truly sleeping either, just able to switch on instantly. I check the alarm clock. It's half past seven. I look at Alex still fast asleep and feel a little like you do as a new mum when you wake up to find it's morning and your baby has unexpectedly slept through the night. Although I also remember as a new mum being mad as hell at Alex for being able to sleep through Otis and then Ella waking at night. He was always apologetic in the morning, always said I should have dug him in the ribs to wake him up, but I was never quite enough of a cow to do it.

I get up straight away, pull my dressing gown on and

leave the room, closing the bedroom door behind me. The house is quiet, too quiet somehow, even allowing for Ella's absence. I go to Ella's room first. It has become a ritual, checking in on her like this while the rest of the house is sleeping. I don't know whether there is a deluded part of me which actually expects to find her in there one morning or whether it is simply that it makes me feel close to her, but I can no longer imagine starting the day without doing this. I lie on her bed as usual, breathe her in, stroke her pillow, see her in my head smiling back at me. And then, as usual, reality kicks me in the teeth and all I hear is the silence of the room, all I see is the empty bed and all I smell is my own grief.

I get up again, tired of the relentlessness of it all, and go back to the landing. My next stop is Otis's room. Even in a week I have learned how to feel my way around his bed in the dark more expertly. I find his foot – for some reason I always seem to find his right one first – and follow his body upwards, as if making sure he is all there. Satisfied, I leave the room.

I pause outside Chloe's room and think for a second about going in to check on her but decide against it, knowing I would get my head bitten off if she did happen to be awake. I go to the toilet then head downstairs. I don't know why I look at the front door as I reach the bottom but I do. Something is making me uncomfortable; something is different. And then I see it – the top and bottom bolts are undone. Alex fitted them a couple of days ago. Said he thought they may help me sleep. I opened my mouth to say something about shutting the stable door but thought better of it. He was trying his best. I understood that. I know he slid them across last night. I watched him do it. Did he go outside in the night and forget to shoot them across again? Or has somebody come in? Could they be in the house now? I freeze and listen for any sounds but all is silent. I go to each room downstairs and check the windows but nothing is broken or forced. I would have heard it anyway if someone had smashed something. What I heard when I woke didn't sound like glass breaking, it was more like a door shutting. I hurry back to the hall and look at the shoe rack. Chloe's Converses have gone. She has other shoes but she never wears them. Her jacket has gone from the peg too. I run upstairs and into her room. The bed is empty. She has put the duvet back as if she has never slept in it. She has gone. I am losing all my fucking children one by one. I check on the chest of drawers. Her mobile isn't there so she does at least have that with her. I creep back into our bedroom, grab my phone, take it back to Chloe's room and call her. It goes straight to voicemail.

'Chloe, it's Mum. Ring me. Or text me. Please let me know where you are and that you're OK.'

Perhaps she's gone to Robyn's. I'd ring her but I don't have her mobile. I sit down on the bed, trying to calm myself. She's nineteen years old. She's entitled to go off on her own, she's just been to bloody France. But that was different, that was a holiday, I knew where she was going. I drove her to the fucking station. This is different. She doesn't just take off like this. Maybe it's the reconstruction this afternoon; maybe she's worried about it. Perhaps she's changed her mind and doesn't want to go.

I stare at the calendar on the wall opposite. Seven days since I saw Ella. The seven longest days of my life. I count off the days, my mind replaying the events of each in my head on fast forward until I get to today. Friday, 5 September. There is an uneasy feeling in my stomach. And something is agitating inside my head. Knocking softly at first but, when I fail to listen, soon hammering at my skull. I see the scrunched-up tissues on Chloe's bedside cabinet and look, for the first time in ages, at the small photograph in a frame she keeps on it.

'Fuck,' I say out loud. 'Fuck, fuck, fuck.'

I run through to our bedroom and wake Alex up. 'Chloe's gone,' I say, watching as his eyes struggle to focus. 'It's Matthew's anniversary. I completely forgot.'

'Oh shit,' he says, sitting up.

'I'm going to go after her; you hold the fort here.'

'Where are you going?'

'To his grave,' I say. 'She'll have gone to his grave.'

I work it all out as I drive into town. It was the front door I heard when I woke. There's a bus at half past seven. She'll have been on it. I should have remembered. Even with everything that has gone on this past week I should have fucking remembered. She's my firstborn, possibly the only daughter I have left, and I've let her down. Again.

I shake my head. I don't blame her for hating me. I don't blame her one little bit. It's hard to imagine any mother screwing up quite so spectacularly as I did. But it's also hard to work out how you can unintentionally hurt someone so badly when you love them so much.

The roads are starting to get busy. I tap my fingers on the steering wheel as I wait at the traffic lights on the main road. When they finally go green, I turn right and take the first left. I only realise as I do so that I will be driving past the park. A coldness runs through me. I haven't been back since. It is too painful, even watching the video on Alex's phone last night felt too close. My hands start to shake on the steering wheel. I keep my eyes firmly fixed on the road ahead but even so I can see it out of the corner of my eye. The wall, the trees, the roof of the butterfly house. The sights and sounds and smells of the day rush back to me. I drive on, gripping the wheel tightly. I still see the green in my rear-view mirror, the big lush tops of the trees. I want to stop the car and go and shake them, demand that they reveal their secrets, tell me what they witnessed. Because nobody else seems to fucking know.

It is half past eight by the time I pull up in the

cemetery car park. There are only two other cars there. According to the sign it only opened at eight. I wonder if Chloe got here earlier than that, if she was waiting outside when the gates opened.

I only realise when I walk through the gates that I do not know where Matthew's grave is. I didn't go to the funeral, which was fair enough as I didn't know the boy. But Chloe didn't go either. She wanted to but the funeral was private, strictly family only. It was like a second bereavement to Chloe, not being able to say goodbye to him. I told her to go, that she had every right to be there. She didn't though. Said she didn't want to cause any more upset than she already had.

She's come since, of course. With Robyn the first time and after that on her own. She even allowed me to drop her off once and wait because it was cold and wet and she didn't have enough money for the bus fare. I asked if she wanted me to go in with her but she just gave me one of her looks. When she got back to the car she didn't say a word, just nodded and we drove home in silence.

I know I should have tried harder, taken all the knock-backs and kept trying, but I think I was scared, scared that I was pushing her further and further away and maybe what she needed was space to try to come to terms with this in her own way. Turned out to be a load of bollocks, but that's what I thought.

I look around me. The trees are still in full leaf and it's hard to see past them to the far side of the cemetery.

I look at the gravestones at the end of each line as I walk. Most of them are old, very old, from a time when it seemed you were lucky if one of your children made it into adulthood. But then I get to an area where there are some newer graves, children's ones. One has a photo of a baby in the headstone, another has a collection of soft toys around it. The carving in the stone is new and easy to read as I pass. The boy was four years old when he died.

I hurry on, trying not to think, trying to block it all out. I am here for Chloe. She is the one I am looking for today. And then I turn a corner and see her, standing by a headstone underneath a huge tree fifty yards in front of me. She has her head bowed and her back to me. I wonder if I should say something as I approach but the truth is I am scared to do so in case she runs away. I have had enough of seeking and I do not want to give her the opportunity to hide.

I walk up to her and take hold of her left hand. She turns to face me, her eyes red and puffy, a frown on her face. It seems to take her a second or two to realise that I should not be here. I wonder if she is going to pull her hand away and run but she doesn't.

'I'm sorry,' I say quietly. 'I'm so, so sorry.'

She screws up her eyes and collapses into my arms, crying like a little girl again. I pull her in tight to me like I used to do. I stroke her hair, pull a soggy strand of it back from her face and stroke her cheek.

'I miss him so much,' she says.

'I know. I know you do. And I've been so crap because I should have been there for you, but I knew it was all my fault and I knew you blamed me and I think I was scared that if I kept trying to reach you you'd push me further away.'

'I don't blame you.'

'Well you should,' I say, wiping another of her tears away. 'Telling you to dump him when I didn't know him from Adam. I thought all teenage lads were like your father, that they just needed a kick up the arse sometimes to show some commitment. I didn't know he was such a sensitive lad.'

'Yeah, but I did. I should have realised how he'd react. I shouldn't have pushed him that far.'

'Yeah, but he was messing you about – all that crap about keeping things secret. I knew it was doing you in, that's why I said summat. I didn't want you to let him walk all over you.'

I look up at the sky, wipe the tears from my own eyes.

'I didn't even want to break up with him,' says Chloe. 'I just wanted him to stand up to his mum It was like she owned him, like she didn't want anyone else to have a piece of him. She was such a fucking control freak.'

'She was probably just being overprotective,' I say. 'It's hard letting go, you know, when your little girl or boy grows up.'

She looks at me and I wish so much that I could reach

inside and remove the ache in her heart, take all the hurt away with a cuddle and a kiss and the promise of an ice cream later. I can't though because this is proper, grown-up hurt. Love and death and grief and loss, and it all came to her so, so early.

'The thing is, Chloe, I know it hurts and I know it always will, but what I'm so scared of is that you're going to beat yourself up over this for rest of your life.'

'But I can't stop thinking about him.'

'I know, but at some point in the future I want you to give someone else the chance to find out what an amazing person you are. I want you to give yourself permission to be happy again.'

She shrugs and turns back to his gravestone.

'They're beautiful,' I say, looking at the red roses she has left there. 'May I?' She nods. I crouch down and read the card attached to them.

'I'm so sorry. Love you and miss you for ever. Sparrow x'

I stand up and wipe my eyes.

'It's what he always called me,' she says. 'I told him about the Chloe bird thing. He said it made him smile, said he wished we lived in a world where everyone had a bird named after them.'

I smile and take hold of her hand.

'You know, all I ever wanted was to be like you,' she says. 'The way you brought me up on your own when you were only the same age as I am now.'

I shake my head.

'What?' she says.

'All I ever wanted was for you not to be like me. That's why I gave you all those bloody lectures about not getting yourself in trouble.'

She is silent for a moment.

'I did sleep with him,' she says. 'Just the once, though. She found out, his mum. Went mental. I think she had a screw loose, to be honest.'

'She hasn't left any flowers,' I say, looking down.

'No, she never has. None that I've ever seen, anyway. Robyn heard from someone that she'd cracked up a bit, lost her teaching job at The Grange. She does piano lessons from home now.'

The blood inside me comes screeching to a halt against the wall of my chest. I feel myself thrown forward. My head hurts with the sudden impact. Chloe grabs hold of my arm as my legs buckle beneath me.

'What?' she says. 'What is it? Are you OK?'

'He lived near the park, didn't he? Matthew lived near the park.'

She nods.

'That's where Otis goes,' I say. 'That's where he goes for his piano lessons. And Alex takes Ella to the park until it's time for them to pick him up. What's her name? What's Matthew's mum's name?'

'Muriel,' she says. 'Her name is Muriel.'

24

MURIEL

'I don't want to close my eyes. I don't like it here. I want to go home.' The child tightens her grip on my hand. I feel my body sway slightly in the breeze. I am teetering on the edge, in every sense of the phrase.

'Matthew always liked it here. It was one of his favourite places.'

'Is he coming today? Is he bringing the picnic?'

'No. He's not.'

'Why not?'

I glance at the child. She is trying very hard not to look down. It is a moment or two before I can get the words out.

'Because he's dead.'

She looks up at me, a frown creasing her brow. I am aware of a tear running down my cheek. I try very hard to ensure it isn't followed by another one. It is though, shortly after the point when I realise she is squeezing my hand.

'When did he die?'

'A year ago today.' I inch forward, aware that my big toe is now sticking out over the edge.

'Did he have cancer? Lots of people die from cancer but you can't catch it from someone.'

'No. No, he didn't.'

'What did he die from? Was it something Chloe did?'

I close my eyes for a second. I could do it now. I could step out from the edge. I have her hand. She would fall with me. There is nothing she would be able to do about it. And all things would be equal then. An eye for an eye and all that. Her mother would understand, truly understand what I went through, am still going through every second of every day. Her life would be blighted for ever like mine. The child grips my hand tighter. I wonder if she knows on some subconscious level what I am going to do. I don't think she does. I glance down and see her looking up at me with enquiring eyes. And I realise that I do not want her to die thinking that about her sister. I do not want her to have that shard of guilt in her heart.

'No,' I say. 'It wasn't her fault. It was mine, actually.'

She gives a little laugh, like I have just said something ridiculous.

'No,' she says. 'You're his mummy.'

I look down at her. We stand there for a while in silence, the breeze playing with the bottom of my skirt and gently flapping the sleeve of her waterproof jacket.

'Ah, but I loved him too much, you see.'

'You can't die from that. You can die from being run over by a car or from being shot by a man with a gun – or from melting but only if you're a snowman like Olaf in *Frozen*.'

I find myself smiling unexpectedly.

'Did your mummy take you to see that film?'

'Yes, and Otis came too but he said he didn't want to because it was a girls' film, but I saw him crying when Olaf nearly melted. He said he didn't afterwards but I saw him. And I said I didn't want an Elsa dress last Christmas, but I do now and Mummy says I might get one for my birthday if I'm good.'

I nod, unable to stop another couple of tears squeezing themselves out of my eyes, and ask, 'When's your birthday?'

'Next month. September the 29th.'

'It's this month actually. It's September already.'

'Is it? How many sleeps?'

I bite my lip and look down. I deserve to be down there, lying in a heap on the rocks. I know that only too well. But she doesn't.

'Twenty-four,' I say as I step back from the edge.

'I'll be a big girl then, won't I?'

'Yes,' I reply. 'Yes, you will.'

I take another step back. Something rushes into the void inside me. Fills it until it is in danger of overflowing. It is soft and warm and comforting. 'Come on,' I say. 'It's time to go.'

'Where are we going?'

'There's somewhere I need to go. Somewhere I should have gone a long time ago.'

'OK,' she says before turning with me and leading me back up the path.

I haven't been since the funeral. To visit would have been to acknowledge it had happened. To put Matthew firmly in the past tense. That's why I visit him in the park instead. Where he is very much in the present.

The first thought I have when I arrive at the cemetery is that I won't be able to find Matthew's grave. The funeral was all very much a blur. I have a vague recollection of being guided to the graveside, possibly by Malcolm, or even the vicar, I can't be sure.

And then I see the tree and it comes back to me, the sense of wonder that they should have chosen this plot for him. 'Underneath the Spreading Chestnut Tree', I used to sing to him at the park when he was a toddler. We used to do the actions to it. It always made him smile.

That they had chosen for him to lie here is the closest thing I have felt to comfort. It almost makes me believe there is a god. Almost but not quite.

The tree is in full leaf, as it was on this day last year. I sometimes wish I had asked Malcolm to take a photograph of it. I didn't, of course, because that is not the done thing at funerals. But I wish now that I hadn't cared so much about that.

As I walk towards the tree, the child's hand still firmly in mine, all I can think about is what it must look like in autumn when the colours are rich and golden. And in spring, when the buds bring promise of what is to come.

'He's there,' I say. 'Underneath that chestnut tree.'

'Does everyone get a tree when they die?'

'No. Not everyone.'

'Is it because Matthew was special?'

'Yes,' I say. 'Yes, I think it is.'

She is quiet for a moment, seemingly deep in thought. As we draw closer I can see flowers on the grave. Fresh ones, presumably left this morning. Red roses. About two dozen of them.

'Who are they from?' the child asks.

'I don't know.'

The child lets go of my hand and walks closer. She has taken the waterproof off now. I said she could. There doesn't seem to be any point in keeping it on any more.

'Look,' she says, picking up a card and and running back to me with it before I can tell her not to. I hold it in my hand. I think I know before I look at it. I think that is why my hand is shaking.

I read the words and swallow hard, conscious that my vision has blurred. She did not come to the funeral. I put a notice in the *Courier*, a death announcement. I got them to put 'Private Funeral, Family Only' in bold letters. It was my way of letting her know she was not welcome. It must have been hard for her, not coming. Not having the opportunity to say goodbye. I didn't really think about that at the time, I was so consumed by my own grief. And then later, when I saw her at the inquest, when she read out her statement, said that he hadn't told me about her because he knew I wouldn't be able to bear it if someone took him away from me, I was glad I hadn't allowed her to come. Glad she hadn't been able to take him away from me in death as she had done in life.

I look down again at the card, step forward and put it back among the flowers. Back where it belongs.

'Who are they from?' the child asks.

'A friend. Someone who loved him very much. Who misses him almost as much as I do.'

She comes and holds my hand without being asked to.

'I'm glad Matthew had a friend like that,' she says.

'Yes.' I nod, wiping my eyes. 'So am I.'

25

LISA

Alex's phone only rings once before he answers.

'I'm with Chloe,' I say. 'She's OK. What's the name of Otis's piano teacher?'

'Why do you—'

'Just tell me, please.'

'Miss Norgate,' he says. 'I don't know her first name but I write the cheques to Miss M. Norgate.'

'Muriel,' I say. 'I think she's called Muriel. I think she's Matthew's mother. She lost her job teaching at The Grange. Chloe says she teaches piano lessons from home.'

'I don't understand.'

'She hates us, Alex. She blames Chloe – me as well, probably. She's got a grudge against our family.'

'Fucking hell. Are you sure?'

'I don't know. Let me put Chloe on. She's been there, Matthew's house. Tell her what it looks like, where you go for Otis's lessons.'

I pass the phone to Chloe. I see her nod repeatedly, watch as what little colour she has left slides from her cheeks.

I take the phone back. 'It's her,' I say. 'It's the same person.'

'Oh Jesus.' There is a slight pause before Alex continues. 'She cancelled, didn't she? She texted to cancel his lesson. On Saturday. The day after Ella disappeared. And she's got a cat. Ella always strokes her cat.'

'Is Claire there?'

'No, not yet.'

'Phone her now. Get her to tell Johnston straight away. Get them to go to her house and see if Ella's there. We're going there now.'

'Lisa, don't do anything stupid.'

'What, like get my own fucking daughter back?'

'You know what I mean. Don't knock on the door or let her see either of you. You don't know what state she's in.'

'I do. I know exactly what state she's in. Call Claire now. Tell her everything. Get her to send someone straight away.'

We run back to the car, past the grave of the four-year-old, further and further away from it. She could still be alive. Ella could still be alive. She's been taken, kidnapped, except she would have gone quietly. Because Ella knew her. She probably chatted all the way to her house.

My mobile rings as we get to my car. It's Claire.

'Lisa, we're on our way there now. Plain-clothes officers in an unmarked car. You're not to approach the house before we get there, do you understand?'

'Yeah, whatever. I have to be there though.'

'I know, but park around the corner or something, somewhere out of sight. Have you got your go bag with you?'

'Yeah, it's in the boot, like you told me.'

'Good. Well stay in your car when you get there, OK? I'll call you when I'm there.'

I end the call.

Chloe looks at me. Her face is ripped with guilt. 'This is all my fault,' she says.

'No, it's not. I should have worked it out earlier. I can't believe I didn't think of her.'

'You never met her?'

'No. Alex always takes him. I've never even spoken to her on the phone. I couldn't have told you her name. She's just the piano lady.'

'She's doing this to get back at me,' says Chloe. 'She holds me responsible. I could see it in her eyes at Matthew's inquest.'

I curse myself for not going. Chloe didn't want me there though. She went with Robyn. I bet Matthew's mother couldn't believe her luck when Otis came for his lessons. I wonder when she realised. Whether Otis said something. She could have been stalking us for months, waiting for the right moment.

'Come on,' I say. 'We need to get there. We need to get Ella back.'

'Her car's not there,' says Chloe as we drive past the house. 'She's got a red Nissan Micra. Well, she used to, at any rate.'

She might not have come back to the house afterwards. She might have taken Ella somewhere else.

I park on the other side of the road but further along. I am not hiding round the corner. She doesn't even know what car I have. She has never seen my car, not unless she has been following me. It doesn't matter if she has, though. I have to see what is going on. I have to see her the second she comes out of that house.

I undo my belt and call Claire. My hands are shaking as I do so.

'We're here,' I say. 'Chloe says Muriel's car's missing.'

'OK, I'll let them know. They'll be there any minute. Don't leave the car.'

We sit in silence, my heart battering against my ribcage.

Chloe is the first to speak. 'At least Ella won't have been—'

'I know,' I say. 'That's what I keep thinking. That's

what I was most scared of. What a man might be doing to her.'

Chloe grabs hold of my arm. We sit there clutching each other's shaking bodies. I see the police car drive past and pull up outside her house, and two plain-clothes officers get out. I lower the window so I can hear what's going on. I need to know if she is screaming because if she is I am going to go in there and no one is going to stop me.

One of them knocks at the front door. This strikes me as being ridiculously polite, like saying, 'Please can I have my child back.' There is no answer. He knocks again. A minute later I see him call something through the letter box before going to look through the front window. He signals to another copper who I hadn't noticed in the back of the car. He gets out and goes up to the house next door, then when there is no reply, to the house next door but one. An elderly woman comes to the door. I see her shaking her head and gesturing as she talks to him. A few moments later he speaks to the other officers and disappears around the back of the house. One of the remaining officers gets something out of his pocket.

'They're going to force the door,' says Chloe.

'Ella will hate that,' I say. 'She won't understand what's happening.'

We cling to each other as they do it. Seconds later and with a minimum of fuss they are in.

My phone rings. It is Claire.

'I'm just pulling up,' she says. 'I can see you.'

'They've gone in.' I say. 'They've just forced the door.'

'I know. Stay there. I can see you.'

Seconds later she is next to us. She puts her arm through the open car window and holds my hand. Chloe is still clinging on to my other arm.

'She's going to be dead, isn't she?' sobs Chloe. 'Both of them are going to be dead.'

'Come on,' says Claire. 'You've got to keep positive. She could walk out of that house any moment. You need to keep strong for her.'

I can hear muffled noises on Claire's radio, doors banging and voices shouting, 'Clear!'

'What's happening?' I ask. 'I need to know what's happening.'

'They're going through each room in turn. They haven't found her yet. They haven't found anyone. But they're saying that a child's been living there.'

I screw up my eyes and start crying. Ella was here. All this time we were looking for her and she was so fucking near. If we've lost her, if she's gone, I will never forgive myself.

We wait for what seems like for ever. Claire walks away. I wonder what it is they are saying that she doesn't want us to hear. I see her talking into the radio, nodding. Her face remains neutral. She walks slowly back over to the car and leans in.

'It's clear,' she says. 'There's no one in there. There's

no blood or any sign of violence. There are children's toys and books around, signs that she has been fed and watered. Some bedding is damp, possibly urine, but apart from that, nothing to cause concern.'

I nod, swallow hard. 'I need to call Alex,' I say. I hold the phone in my hand, picturing him at the other end, dreading the call.

'The house is empty,' I say as soon as he answers. 'But they think she's been held there – a child has been living there. There's no blood, nothing like that. There are some toys.'

I hear Alex crying on the other end of the phone. Relief and dread all rolled into one.

'Where's Otis?' I ask.

'He's here.'

'Tell him it's OK. Tell him the piano lady's been looking after Ella. Tell him the police are going to go and find her now.'

I end the call and look up at Claire. 'Where are they?' I ask.

'We're going to find out. We'll get her car reg out to all forces, get checks on the cameras on the roads. We're going to have everyone looking for them.'

'Can I go in? I want to see where she's been kept.'

'Sorry,' says Claire. 'It's a crime scene now. They can't let anyone in. Forensics are on their way. We need to get you home. Are you going to be OK to drive or do you want to come with me?'

'I'm fine,' I say, even though I am far from it.

'OK, if you're sure. I'll follow you just in case.'

She goes back to her car and gets in. Part of me doesn't want to go; I want to be close to Ella and this is the closest I can get at the moment. The closest I have been for the past week.

I turn to Chloe. 'Do you think Muriel would—'

'I don't know,' says Chloe, saving me from having to ask. 'I don't know what she's capable of any more.'

Alex opens the door and I collapse sobbing into his arms.

'She was there all the time,' I say. 'So close. I can't believe we didn't realise.'

'It's my fault,' he says. 'They kept asking about anyone we knew who lived near the park and I didn't once think of her.'

'We weren't thinking it would be someone like that though, were we?'

'Yeah, but I took her Lis, I took Ella to that bloody house every Saturday.'

I look up, aware that Chloe is standing awkwardly behind us. I put my arm around her.

'I'm sorry,' she says. 'This is all my fault. It's because of me and Matthew.'

'It's her fault,' I say. 'She's the one with a screw loose. You haven't done anything wrong.'

'I made her hate me,' she says. 'That's what I did wrong.'

'Yeah, and look what Matthew did to be free of her. Jesus, the woman's a psycho.'

A car door bangs behind us. 'Let's all go and sit down,' Claire says as she gets to the front door. 'I'm going to put the kettle on.'

'Where's Otis?' I ask, turning to Alex as we follow Claire into the kitchen.

'I asked your mum to take him.'

'How was he?'

'A bit shell-shocked really. He doesn't understand what's going on.'

'I'm not surprised. I don't bloody understand what's going on.'

Claire puts her hands on my shoulders and gently sits me down at the kitchen table.

'OK,' she says. 'I'll tell you what we know. We have reason to believe a child has been living at that address. Forensics are sweeping the place now to see what they can pick up.

'What we haven't been able to do so far is to confirm that it's Ella. We haven't found her dress, or leggings or Crocs. It may be that they've been disposed of, it may be that she's still wearing them. We're going through the bins and doing a thorough search.'

'What about the wet bed?'

Claire nods. 'There are damp patches on some bedding which indicate that she was there very recently, possibly as recently as this morning. There's food in the fridge and things in the bin which support that. Also the cat appears to have been fed.'

'Jesus,' says Alex, shaking his head. 'She kidnaps our daughter but doesn't let the cat go hungry.'

'We've spoken to some neighbours, although there isn't anyone living next door. None of them has so far reported seeing or hearing a child but one of them did say that they hadn't seen her all week, which was unusual as she usually went for a walk in the park every day. There's nothing at the property which suggests the child has been locked in a cupboard or a confined place. She appears to have been sleeping in a bedroom at the back of the house.'

Chloe looks up at the ceiling and whimpers.

'Matthew's bedroom?' I ask. She nods. I squeeze her hand.

'There are some children's clothes in that bedroom, although they are not girls' clothes.'

'They'll be Matthew's,' says Chloe before I can say anything. 'She kept all of his old clothes. He showed me once.'

I look at Alex. I have no idea what we are dealing with here.

'Thanks, Chloe,' says Claire. 'We'll want to speak to you in more detail. You and Alex. As soon as possible if that's OK with you both?'

They nod.

'What about me?' I ask.

'Did you ever meet her?'

'No.'

'Speak to her on the phone?'

'No. Alex always took them while I was working. I don't even know what she looks like.'

Claire takes out her mobile and calls up a picture. 'We've copied this from a photograph at the house,' she says. 'Do you recognise her from the park at all?' She holds it out to me. A photograph of a woman with wavy silver hair in a neat lilac blouse. She is smiling at the camera without showing her teeth. Her nose is slightly on the large size. She is the most unremarkable-looking woman you could ever see.

'No,' I say. 'I don't.'

'OK. Well, we just need to speak to Alex and Chloe for now then. We're putting this photo out to the media and we've got officers going through all the CCTV stuff. Everyone is looking for her. She's not going to get far.'

Alex clutches my hand. 'They'll find her,' he says.

I think they will too. But I am worried that it is going to be too late.

Claire's phone rings. She goes into the hall to answer it. She comes back a few minutes later, a serious look on her face.

'They've found some fair hair in the bathroom bin, quite a bit of it. They've taken it away for DNA tests.'

'She's cut it,' I say. 'She's cut Ella's hair.'

'They've also asked me to show you this for identification purposes. It was found on the landing.'

She hands me her phone again. I stare at the picture on the screen. A photo of a child with short fair hair wearing a boy's school blazer and tie.

'Jesus Christ,' I say, 'it's Ella.'

26

MURIEL

We get back in the car. I clip the child's seat belt in. She tells me off again for not having a car seat.

I get in the front and pull my own belt across.

'Why have you still got all his things?'

'I'm sorry?'

'Matthew's things. Why have you still got them all if he's dead?'

I swallow, adjusting the rear-view mirror slightly as I do so.

'Because I can't bear to part with them. They're all I have left of him.'

'You've got lots of photos.'

'Yes. Yes, I have.'

'And you're still his mummy. Grandma says you never

stop being a mummy, not even when you're old like her. She says you never stop worrying too.'

'Where do you live?' I ask after a moment.

'Next door to Charlie.'

I manage a slight smile into the mirror.

'Anything else you can tell me about it?'

'The other next door has a little dog who always sits in the window.'

I nod. Clearly this is not going to be easy.

'Do you know your street name?'

'It's not a street, it's a drive.'

'But you don't know the name of it?'

She shakes her head again. 'No, but it begins with a H.'

'What part of Halifax do you live in?'

'Grandma says it's the nice part. Nicer than her part.'

I nod, aware we are at least narrowing down the options. There are not that many nice parts of Halifax.

'What about the name of your school – do you know that?'

'Maypole Lane Academy.'

'Thank you,' I reply as I check the mirrors and pull away.

There seems to be a hold-up on Free School Lane so I go the other way, away from my house, up past the far side of the park.

'Have the naughty boys gone now?' she asks.

'Yes,' I reply. 'Yes, they have.'

*   *   *

Her grandma is right: it is a nice part of Halifax. Malcolm and I used to come to the pub here when we were first married. They did a very nice Sunday lunch. The Maypole, it is called, after the one they used to have in the centre of the village. I remember Malcolm telling me all about it. He was always interested in his local history. They replaced it with an old-fashioned lamp post. It is nice enough – they've taken the trouble of putting hanging baskets on it, at least. But it's not as nice as the maypole would have been.

The child is sitting up straight, craning her neck to see out of the window.

'Can you see?' I ask. 'Do you know which way it is?'

'That way,' she says, pointing right as we go past the turning. I turn round in the village car park and go back to where she said.

'And now where?'

'Down there,' she replies as I drive past a left-hand turn. I pull up immediately afterwards. I am aware that my palms are sticking to the steering wheel although it is not as warm as it has been. Perhaps there will be a policeman outside their house. You see that on the news sometimes when something serious happens. I haven't really thought this through. Not any of it. The child is jumping up and down on the back seat and I don't know what to do now. I suppose I should just let her out here. She will make her way back home or someone will find her. She has the dress on, the one she was wearing when I took her. Someone will recognise the dress.

She starts to whimper like a dog as she scrambles for the door handle, desperate to be let out. I unclip my belt and walk round to her side. I open the door and she tumbles out onto the pavement. She stops to put her left Croc back on properly and looks up. For a moment I don't know whether I should bend and kiss her on the cheek but somehow I don't feel that would be appropriate.

'Right you are then,' I say.

'Aren't you going to come with me?'

'No, you'll be fine on your own. Big girl like you.'

'Where are you going to go?'

It is a good question. I am not altogether sure yet.

'Back home to Melody,' I say.

She nods.

'Can I come and see her again when Otis does his piano lessons?'

I smile at her. A sad smile. 'Let's see, shall we?' I say.

She nods and skips off round the corner. I get back in the car, blinking hard. I glance in the mirror and see a car coming, one of those ridiculous four-by-four things they have these days. I watch as it turns left sharply behind me without even indicating. I have a lurching sensation in my stomach. I jump out of the car and run round the corner to see the child just about to cross the road in front of it.

'Ella!' I shout.

She stops immediately, one foot in the road. The car drives on without even slowing down as I hurry up to her.

'I'm sorry,' I say. 'I shouldn't have left you on your own. Not at your age.'

'But I'm a big girl now. I'm nearly five.'

'I know but I'm still going to come with you.'

I take her hand and we walk across the road together. She is chattering away, talking about seeing Iggle Piggle again, about playing with her red balloon and eating Charlie Wilson's birthday cake. She pulls on my hand as we round a bend.

'It's that one,' she says, pointing to a house some distance away. 'That's my house. Look, there's the doggy in the window next door.'

She is right. There is a dog in the window. Small and white and looking more like an ornament until he moves when he sees us. The house itself is very ordinary-looking. There is no policeman standing outside. Not that it really matters now. I know that. I am just wondering what I should do if no one is in when the door opens and a woman steps outside with car keys in her hand. Her hair is pulled back in a scruffy pony tail, her face pale, her mouth turned down at the sides.

'Mummy!'

The child pulls away from my hand and runs full pelt down the road towards her. The woman stares, her mouth falling open, before she hurls herself at the child, clutching it to her, their arms clamped around each other in a tight embrace.

The woman picks up the child and stares across at me, tears streaming down her face. I do not know exactly what she is feeling because it is something I have not experienced and never will now, of course. Nothing is going to bring Matthew back to me. But I am pleased for her, I know that much. Pleased that for her, at least, the suffering is over.

Your body realises you have lost your child before your brain does. Every morning it registers the emptiness, the hopelessness, the ache, and sends a signal to your brain before you are even awake. You never recover from losing a child, you see. It is the first thing you think about when you wake up and the last thing you think about before you go to sleep. If you sleep, that is. Many of us do not manage anything approaching real sleep. Even shutting your eyes is hard. Because you lose control when you do so. You lose the right to say, 'I had my eye on them.' You didn't, you see. You weren't watching, you weren't paying attention. And whether that was the case for a matter of seconds or for a lifetime, it doesn't really matter. You can never shut your eyes again. Because the insides of your eyelids will constantly replay what happened, the images projected large, the sound turned up loud. And if you do somehow manage to drop off, even with your eyes open, when you wake suddenly in the night there is a flickering white screen in front of you as if you have lost the signal, and a sea of white noise crashes down across your head.

That is why we have a haunted look about us. We are haunted by our lost children – and deservedly so. We cling to the past because that is all we have to hold on to. There is no present and no future. Not for the mothers of the dead.

ACKNOWLEDGEMENTS

Special thanks to the following people: My editor Kathryn Taussig for believing in this book and letting me write something a bit different; the whole team at Quercus for getting behind it; my agent Anthony Goff for his ongoing wisdom and support, and being one of those lovely, and all too rare, people who still make proper phone calls on the landline; everyone at David Higham Associates for all the important bits; David Earl, for invaluable police research (all mistakes are my own – or artistic licence); Mary Cuthbert, Clare Townley and Millie for braving the camera for the book trailer and Kathy Kim for voicing it much better than I did; Lance Little for the fantastic website (www.linda-green.com); Samir Mehanovic, whose powerful documentary provided the quote at the beginning of this book (please go to srebrenica.org.uk to help); amazing authors Isabelle Grey, Dorothy Koomson, Barbara Nadel, Amanda Prowse and Emily Barr for their quotes and all those authors, book bloggers, readers and reviewers who have helped to spread the word (and kept me entertained on Twitter); brilliant libraries everywhere for stocking it; wonderful independent book shops for still being there to do the same; my family and friends for their ongoing support; my wonderful son Rohan for all his ideas, quotes and enthusiasm (and always offering to turn my books into shows when he's a director!); my husband Ian, without whom I'd have to get a proper job, for his unstinting support and belief; and you, my readers, for being there at the end of it to make the whole thing worthwhile. Please do get in touch via Twitter @lindagreenisms or Facebook Fans of Author Linda Green. It's always so lovely to hear from you.

And finally, apologies to readers in Yorkshire (which makes this sound like a Victoria Wood sketch). As an adopted Yorkshirewoman, I do know that people in Halifax say 'were' instead of 'was' and drop 'the' rather a lot etc, but out of consideration for the rest of the country – and as compensation for not living anywhere half as nice – an editorial decision was taken to write it without the dialect so they can understand what my characters are saying. Please forgive me and feel free to re-Yorkshirefy it in your heads. Thank you.

What if the only way to save
your child's life . . .

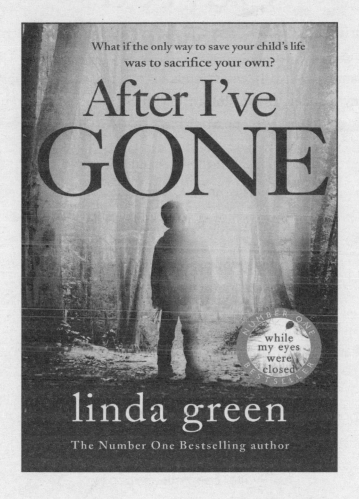

. . . was to sacrifice your own?